For
my

Cheers,
Amy R Reade

THE WORST NOEL

The Juniper Junction Holiday Mystery Series: Book One

AMY M. READE

Pau Hana Publishing

BOOKS BY AMY M. READE

STANDALONE BOOKS

Secrets of Hallstead House
The Ghosts of Peppernell Manor
House of the Hanging Jade

THE MALICE SERIES

The House on Candlewick Lane
Highland Peril
Murder in Thistlecross

PRAISE FOR AMY M. READE

Secrets of Hallstead House: "Thank you, Amy, for taking me to a new place and allowing me to imagine." From Phyllis H. Moore, reviewer

The Ghosts of Peppernell Manor: "If you're a fan of ... novels by Phyllis A. Whitney, Victoria Holt, and Barbara Michaels, you're going to love *The Ghosts of Peppernell Manor* by Amy M. Reade." From Jane Reads.

House of the Hanging Jade: "House of the Hanging Jade is a suspenseful tale of murder and obsession, all taking place against a beautiful Hawaiian backdrop. Lush descriptions of both the scenery and the food prepared by the protagonist leave you wanting more." From The Book's the Thing
House of the Hanging Jade: "I definitely see more Reade books in my future." From Back Porchervations.

The House on Candlewick Lane: "As in most gothic novels, the actual house on Candlewick Lane is creepy and filled with dark passages and rooms. You feel the evil emanate from the structure and from the people who live there ... I loved the rich descriptions of Edinburgh. You definitely feel like you are walking the streets next to Greer, searching for Ellie. You can feel the rain and the cold, and a couple times, I swear I could smell the scents of the local cuisine." From Colleen Chesebro, reviewer

Highland Peril: "This is escapism at its best, as it is a compelling mystery that whisks readers away to a land as beautiful as it is rich with intrigue." From Cynthia Chow, Kings River Life

Murder in Thistlecross: "Amy Reade's series has a touch of gothic suspense, always fun, and this particular entry has the extra added attraction of the old Clue board game (later a movie that was equally delightful) wherein the various suspects move around the castle and the sleuth has to figure out who killed who, how and where." From Buried Under Books

Pau Hana Publishing

Print ISBN: 978-1-7326907-0-7

Ebook ISBN: 978-1-7326907-1-4

Printed in the United States of America

For Nana, who loved Christmas

CHAPTER 1

L illy awoke hours before dawn to the sound of her alarm clock going off. She flung her hand in the general direction of the nightstand to find the snooze button and stop the incessant ringing, but only succeeded in knocking the clock to the floor.

"Ugh," she groaned. She leaned over the side of the bed and clawed the floor, trying to reach the clock. When she found it, she turned it off and sat up groggily, wiping sleep from her eyes and yawning. Barney, the family's Soft-Coated Wheaten Terrier, lifted his shaggy, brindle-hued head and stretched across the foot of the bed.

"I hate Black Friday," she said to Barney. The biggest shopping day of the year brought a level of anxiety that gave her nightmares the other three hundred sixty-four days. She peered into the bathroom mirror before heading downstairs. Her brown hair was tangled from sleep and her eyes, normally bright hazel, were hooded and sported bags.

She needed coffee and lots of it. She went downstairs to find that the kids had left the kitchen light on all night again. "Good," she muttered to herself. "I was hoping to give the electric company a nice fat check for Christmas." She switched off all the lights but one and started the coffeemaker. Before long the kitchen was filled with the aroma of ground Arabica beans and Lilly's senses started coming alive.

After showering, dressing, and grabbing a quick breakfast, Lilly poured herself a travel mug of coffee and slipped out the side door without making a sound. Normally Barney followed her downstairs for breakfast, but it was too early for him.

The car didn't even have time to warm up during the short drive to Juniper Junction Jewels. Lilly drove along Main Street, smiling at the Christmas lights that hung from the shop fronts and the street lamps. She loved this festive time of year. And since this was Colorado, there were several inches of freshly-fallen snow on the ground to make the lights seem even prettier. At the end of the block, she swung her car around the back of the row of shops and pulled into one of the parking spots allocated for her jewelry store. Each store got two parking spots so employees wouldn't have to go searching for spots when Main Street got really busy, as was often the case in the upscale Rocky Mountain resort town.

It was so early the plows hadn't even been out yet, so Lilly stepped carefully when she got out of the car. Shifting her shoulder bag from one arm to the other and holding her coffee, she reached for the doorknob at the back of the shop.

It was unlocked.

Lilly's stomach lurched; her body stiffened. This was a shop owner's worst nightmare, made even more horrible when the shop sold precious stones, expensive gems, and custom jewelry. Lilly turned the knob slowly and pushed the door open, peering around it to make sure there was no one waiting for her in the back room.

She didn't see anyone, so she closed the door softly behind her and set her bag and coffee down on her desk. She had been the last one to leave Wednesday afternoon and the shop had been closed for Thanksgiving Day; she shuddered to think that the shop had been unlocked for thirty-six hours. She wracked her brain trying to remember locking the door behind her on Wednesday, but she couldn't. She couldn't remember setting the alarm, either, but that obviously hadn't gone off because the alarm company had her home number and her cell number.

Quickly walking over to the vault where she kept her inventory when the store was closed, she stopped short when she saw that the door to the vault was slightly ajar. She put out one finger to push the door open a bit farther; wave after wave of nausea swept over her when she saw that one of the sliding shelves that held the jewelry had been moved. She stepped into the tiny vault and pulled the shelf out a bit further—there was a necklace missing. A pearl necklace. She frantically pulled out all the other shelves in turn, not daring to breath until she satisfied herself that nothing else had been taken. She backed out of the vault and strode to her desk, where she leafed quickly through the papers littering the top. Nothing else seemed to be missing.

She pushed open the sliding barn door that led to the interior of the shop.

Lilly prided herself on making Juniper Junction Jewels a homey, rustic place that looked like someone's living room. As such, the lighting inside the store was provided mostly by lamps set strategically around the shop rather than cold, sterile fluorescent lights.

She turned on the lamp closest to the office. She didn't notice the body lying on the floor behind one of the glass cases until she tripped over it.

CHAPTER 2

L illy recoiled in terror. She fled to the back room where she called the police with fingers trembling so that she could barely push the numbers. At the dispatcher's urging, she went out and sat in her car while she waited for the police to arrive.

They were there in just a few minutes, this being a day when most murderers stayed home. The Black Friday pickpockets and petty thieves didn't get started until a bit later in the morning.

Lilly got out of the car and stood shivering in the cold, dark alley when she heard the police came roaring down Main Street, sirens blaring and lights flashing. She wondered what good the lights and sirens did now that the person in the shop was already dead.

The police cars pulled to a stop in the alley, blocking the entrance on each end. The first officer at Lilly's side was her brother, Bill. He ran up and put his hand on her shoulder. "You all right?" he asked. Bill was just a few years older than Lilly and looked just like her—brown hair, though his was in a buzz cut, and hazel eyes. He wore glasses, while Lilly preferred contacts.

She nodded grimly. "I don't know who's in there," she said.

"We should know soon." As he spoke other officers, guns

drawn, fanned out along the length of the alley and around the corner onto Main Street. At the signal from the officer closest to the shop door, they all moved forward. Bill joined them, following the lead officer into the back of the shop.

Lilly waited, her body tense and cold, for the all-clear from the police before going back into the shop. The signal came within just a minute or two; it was a small shop and there was nowhere to hide except the vault. Besides, she had already told them there was no one else inside the shop—no one living, that is. She shuddered, wondering what had possessed her to go inside alone once she realized the back door was unlocked.

Lilly went in and found an officer there waiting to talk to her. She wondered where Bill was. "The deceased is Eden Barclay. You know her, don't you?"

Eden Barclay. Just hearing the name gave Lilly the jitters. She was a troublemaker who owned JJ's General Store, the shop kitty-corner from hers.

"I know her, yes," Lilly answered, sitting down hard on the edge of her desk. "What happened? Why is she in here?"

"That's what we need to find out. Interestingly, her husband reported her missing just yesterday."

"Has she been in here since then? How did she die?"

The officer fixed Lilly with a hard stare. "We've got a call out to the medical examiner. She should be here soon. But it looks like Ms. Barclay was strangled with a strand of pearls."

"What?!" she exclaimed. "How do you know that?"

"There's a string of pearls lying on the floor under her."

Lilly was speechless. The missing pearl necklace.

What had Eden been doing inside the jewelry store?

"I don't believe this." A murder in her store on Black Friday was going to put a damper on the day's sales, to say the least. She shook her head as if to dislodge such a heinous thought— Eden Barclay's dead body was lying on the floor of her shop and all she could think about was how much money she was going to lose that day. Thank God the police officer couldn't read her mind.

Eden Barclay. Lilly couldn't honestly say she'd miss the woman, though she didn't think Eden deserved to die for all the chaos she enjoyed creating.

"Lilly?" Bill broke into her thoughts. "The medical examiner is going to be here soon and Officer Vasquez is going to take you down to the station."

"For what?"

"To get a statement from you."

"Can't we do that here? I'm opening in a little while." Bill gave her a look that said *Are you really that dumb?* "Don't look at me like that," she said. "What's the matter?"

"You can't open the store. We'll be in here all day."

"You have got to be kidding me. You know this is the biggest shopping day of the year, right? I can't afford to lose my Black Friday profits."

Bill was shaking his head as she spoke. "Sorry, Lil. This takes precedence."

"One more reason to hate Eden Barclay," Lilly said with a loud sigh, then clamped her hand over her mouth when Bill shot her a dark look.

"Why do you hate Eden Barclay?" asked an officer, walking into the back room at just that moment. Lilly closed her eyes, not believing she had said something so stupid. Bill just shook his head.

"She is a thorn in the side of every shopkeeper on Main Street," Lilly answered. "She's vindictive, she hates everyone, and she's done nothing but complain to the city council about the other store owners since she came to town." Out of the corner of her eye Lilly could tell Bill was cringing as she spoke. She could practically read his mind. It was screaming, *Call your lawyer!* But the truth would come out sooner or later—might as well get it out in the open now so she could get back to work.

The police officer held up a plastic bag he was holding.

There was a string of pearls inside. "Does this look familiar?" he asked.

Lilly looked closely at the bag for a moment, then said, "I assume that's the one missing from the vault, but I can't tell for sure without looking at it under the light and feeling it."

"That's not gonna happen," he said. "Not here, at least." He turned to Bill. "I'm taking her down now."

"But—" Lilly began.

"Come on," he said, putting his hand on her elbow.

Does that guy even know Bill is my brother? Lilly wondered. If so, he was being awfully rude. And if not, someone needed to tell him.

It was still dark as the police car made its way up Main Street and toward the police station. As they passed Juniper Junction Jewels Lilly craned her neck to see if she could tell what was going on inside. Several police officers stood conferring near the front window. Another was taking pictures. No one else was about on Main Street, though some shop lights had been turned on. She noticed a few shopkeepers staring out their front windows in the direction of her store, no doubt wondering what on earth was going on.

CHAPTER 3

When Lilly arrived at the police station Officer Vasquez led her inside and to a room furnished with only a table and a few chairs. The walls were painted an industrial mint green and the room smelled of stale coffee and bad breath.

Officer Vasquez sat down across from her at the table and pulled out a notebook. Lilly looked at the table with distaste. It had an ancient wooden top and graffiti from years of witnesses being left alone in the room criss-crossed the grain. She was careful to keep her hands to herself. God only knew what disease a person might catch from the germs living in the crud on the table.

"So tell me again what you know about Eden Barclay," Officer Vasquez began.

"She owns JJ's General Store," Lilly said. "She bought it from the old owner when he retired a few years ago." Her eyes strayed toward one of the lines of graffiti that read *Born to lose*.

"And?"

"And what?"

"You mentioned that no one liked her. Why is that?"

"She was always complaining about something, whether it

was because someone parked in her parking spot behind the store or she didn't like the color of the flowers the town planted along the sidewalk in the summertime or someone in the Memorial Day parade threw candy from a float and it landed in front of her store. I mean, she was always unhappy. I don't think she was happy unless there was something to complain about."

"Did she ever complain to you?"

"Sure. She would bitch to anyone who would listen. Not that I wanted to listen—sometimes she didn't give you a choice."

"Did she ever complain about you?"

"Not to my face. I don't know if she complained about me to any of the other shop owners. It seems like I would have found out about it if she had."

"Do you get along with the other shopkeepers in town?"

"Yes, very well. You probably know I'm the president of the Chamber of Commerce and I know a lot about what goes on along Main Street. I suppose that's part of the reason Eden zeroed in on me when she was up in arms about something."

"She figured you could do something about it?"

Lilly shrugged. "I guess so."

"You mentioned that she complained about someone parking in her parking spot. Did she complain about that directly to you?"

"Yes. She wanted me to ask the City Council for money to have special parking signs made for each store owner. She wanted people's names on the signs and everything."

"And did you do it?"

"Of course not. That's a ridiculous request. Besides, there are already signs posted in the back of all the stores saying that the parking spots back there are for store employees only. For the most part people heed what the signs say and don't park there."

"And her other complaints? Did she approach you directly about them?"

"She approached me directly when she didn't like the color

of the flowers that the City Council had planted last summer. They planted purple and yellow. She wanted red."

"And did you do anything about that?"

"Yes. I told Eden that I had absolutely nothing to do with the color of flowers the city wanted and I thought purple and yellow were very pretty." A tiny smile played across Officer Vasquez's face.

"Did you like Eden Barclay?"

"No. No one likes Eden. She's a bully. Was a bully," Lilly corrected herself.

Officer Vasquez proceeded to ask Lilly about Juniper Junction Jewels, her finances, her inventory, and her security precautions. Lilly answered all the questions quickly and efficiently and was allowed to leave after about an hour of questioning. Officer Vasquez drove her back to her shop, which was still abuzz with activity. The body had been removed and a few police officers were moving around the store, gathering evidence, taking notes, and talking to each other. Bill was nowhere to be seen. Lilly went in through the back door and found one of the officers sitting in her desk chair. He got up quickly when he saw her.

"Is this investigation really going to take all day?" Lilly asked him.

"Yup," he answered, "and probably a good portion of the weekend. I'm sorry about that. I know how much all the business owners in Juniper Junction look forward to Black Friday."

Lilly grimaced. "'Look forward' is a strong way to put it, but yes, it's an important day for us. The profits give us a boost through the rest of the holiday season."

"Maybe you can have a Black Monday sale when the store reopens," he joked.

Lilly wasn't in the mood for jokes. "You should probably lay off the stand-up comedy," she said. He looked away and said nothing else.

She thought about going home and fixing a proper breakfast for her kids while the police were working in the store, but she decided against it. She wanted to make sure she was around in case there were any questions. She also wanted to make sure the police didn't make too much of a mess in their evidence-gathering, plus the masochistic side of her wanted to keep an eye on the number of people who tried to come into Juniper Junction Jewels and were turned away.

And she wasn't disappointed. Time after time would-be customers tried the front door only to find it locked. To a person, they would peer in the front windows and their eyes would widen when they saw the police gathered around. They would whisper to their companions, if there were any, and move back so their friends could look inside, too. Some people stood back on the sidewalk and snapped a photo of the shop front with their camera phone and then hit buttons furiously. Lilly imagined they were texting their friends or posting something online.

She couldn't have dreamed up a better publicity stunt.

Too bad it wasn't a stunt.

CHAPTER 4

I t wasn't long before Laurel, Lilly's sixteen-year-old daughter,
called. "Mom, what's going on over there? The store is all
over the internet."

Lilly pressed her lips together, wishing she could keep this
information away from her kids. "You know Eden Barclay, the
owner of the general store? Someone killed her in here."

Laurel gasped. "You're kidding. Who did it? And why in
your store?"

"Haven't figured out either of those things yet. But the
police are working on it. Are you going out shopping today?"

"Nah. I'm too smart for that. Too many people."

"Good. Can you make dinner? You and your brother eat
whenever you want. I'll probably be home late, but I'll warm up
whatever you make."

"Sure. Does Tighe have to help?" Tighe was a year older
than his sister and she was always keen to make sure he did his
fair share of the work around the house.

"Don't start, Laurel. He has his own list of chores
for today."

"Aren't you afraid to be in the store?"

"Not at all. The police are still here. There's nothing to be afraid of. Eden and I look nothing alike, so it's not as if someone was targeting me and got her by mistake. Whoever killed her intended to kill her."

"Yeah, but it was in your store."

"Laurel, don't worry about me. I'm totally fine and I intend to stay that way."

"All right. See you when you get home."

"Okay, honey. And have Tighe call me when he gets up, will you?" Lilly looked at her watch. It amazed her how much her two teens could sleep. Tighe would sleep all day if Laurel didn't make enough noise to wake the dead.

It wasn't long before Tighe called. "Hi, bud. What's up today?" Lilly asked.

"I've got homework, but I don't think that's fair."

"It doesn't matter whether you think it's fair or not. Just get it done. Hopefully you won't get any homework over Christmas break." Tighe scoffed.

"Are you going out today?" Lilly asked.

"Yeah, probably. I have to get dressed and eat first. Laur said something about the cops at the store?"

"It's true. Someone was killed in here."

"No way."

"Remember Eden Barclay? The owner of JJ's General Store? Someone killed her."

"That's terrible. Her son is in our school." Lilly hadn't known Eden had any children.

"That's so sad. To lose his mother, especially at this time of year."

"You don't like her, do you?"

"She wasn't my favorite person, that's for sure. But I didn't want to see her die, either."

"Better not tell the police you didn't like her."

"Too late."

"Uh-oh."

"Don't worry. I explained that she wasn't a very nice person. Anyone would vouch for that."

By noontime Main Street was teeming with people. Shop owners on their lunch break came to the back door of Lilly's store to gossip and find out what had happened. Lilly didn't have much information other than what was already available on the street, so most of her colleagues went away disappointed. There seemed to be a general consensus, though, that Eden Barclay would not be missed.

Doing paperwork by herself at her desk was not the way Lilly had envisioned her Black Friday unfolding, but she had to admit that she was able to get a lot done without much interruption from the police. By late afternoon the officers who had been there most of the day were going off duty. They told Lilly she would have to leave and followed her out the door after sealing both the front and back doors with special tape. They had also called for an officer to remain on duty overnight to make sure no one tampered with the crime scene.

When Lilly got home she found Laurel making spaghetti for dinner. She paused in the doorway for just a moment, marveling not for the first time how much Laurel looked like her father—sandy blond hair, long limbs, skin the color of honey. She kissed Laurel's cheek. "How was your day?" she asked.

"Better than yours," Laurel answered.

"Where's Tighe?"

"He went to Gran's house. She called and said she lost her puppy so he went to help."

Lilly looked heavenward and blew out a long breath. Her mother didn't have a puppy. When Lilly was working and her mom was having one of her bad days, Laurel and Tighe took turns going to their grandmother's house and humoring her through whatever imagined crisis had taken place.

"I'm glad he went over. Poor Gran," Lilly said sadly. Her mother was only in her early seventies, but she had been increasingly forgetful and lately she had been confused, too.

Lilly and Bill had talked about it a little, but neither wanted to be the one to broach the subject of moving Mom out of her house. As long as the kids were around to help when Lilly and Bill were working, it would be all right.

"Let's eat," Laurel said. "Tighe can eat when he gets home."

"No, I should go over to Gran's house first," Lilly answered. "Make sure she's okay. You keep dinner warm and when Tighe and I come home the three of us can eat together." Laurel shrugged.

Lilly got back into her car and drove the short distance to her mother's house. Before he had left her and disappeared, her ex-husband, Beau, had been furious that Lilly and her mother spent so much time together. It had been one of the things they fought about the most. But Lilly had always loved having her mother nearby and was especially grateful for the two-short-block distance between them now that her mother's mental health was failing.

Every light in her mother's house was on when Lilly pulled into the driveway. She got out and went inside through the front door.

"Hello? Anybody home?" she called from the foyer.

"We're in here, Mom," came the answer.

Lilly pulled off her boots and set them by the front door then went through to the kitchen. Tighe and her mother sat at the table playing cards. She smiled when she saw them, and wondered how Tighe, fair-skinned with darker brown hair, could look so unlike his father.

Lilly leaned down and kissed her mother's soft cheek. "Did you find the puppy?" she asked.

Her mother fixed her with a confused look. "What puppy?"

Lilly caught Tighe's eye and he shook his head at her almost imperceptibly. She cringed inwardly. She should have known better than to ask about the puppy. Her mother was probably lucid again and wondering what in the world Lilly was talking about.

"My friend Mike lost his puppy, Gran," Tighe answered. "Yeah, Mom, we found him." Lilly smiled at him in thanks and sat down.

"How were things at the store today, Lilly?" her mother asked. Her dark green eyes, which had once been full of light and spunk, were now, more often than not, clouded by confusion. Her soft white hair curled around her ears.

"Fine, very busy," Lilly replied. She had spoken to her mother's doctor at an appointment recently and he had pulled her aside to say that her mom needed to minimize stress. Lilly did her best to keep stressful conversations to a minimum.

"Black Friday is always a busy day. I was watching the television earlier and I saw that three people were trampled to death in Denver at some store. Ridiculous," she said, shaking her head and making a *tsk, tsk* sound.

"We don't need to worry about that in Juniper Junction," Lilly said. "No big box stores, no chain stores, as long as the very vocal minority of business owners doesn't get its way. It's busy on Black Friday, but not crazy."

"That's good, dear. Have you spoken to Billy?" Lilly and Billy. Her parents had bestowed rhyming names on their children in a fit of what Lilly could only assume was misguided humor.

"Yes. I saw him today, as a matter of fact."

"He works too hard, poor boy." Lilly glanced at Tighe, who was smiling. He knew Beverly had a tendency to believe Bill worked harder than Lilly.

"He's fine, Mom. Don't worry about him. Do you want to come over and have pasta with us tonight?"

"No, thank you. I have plenty of those wonderful Thanksgiving leftovers. I'll have those." As much as Lilly loved the Thanksgiving feast, she couldn't bring herself to have it two nights in a row. As long as she had lived away from home, she had always avoided Thanksgiving leftovers on Black Friday. She would start digging into those Saturday for lunch.

"Suit yourself. Tighe and I should get going so our dinner doesn't get cold," Lilly said.

"All right. Thank you for coming over to keep me company, dear," Beverly said to Tighe.

"It was fun, Gran. See you later."

Tighe had walked to Gran's house, so Lilly drove him home. "What happened with the puppy?"

"By the time I got there she wasn't confused anymore, so I let it drop," he said. "We just played cards the whole time. She cheats."

Lilly laughed. "I know."

CHAPTER 5

L illy was at the store before the police got there the next morning. She didn't see the officer who was supposed to be watching the place. She parked the car and decided to walk around to the front while she waited for the police to arrive so she could go inside. She wandered around the end of the alley and onto Main Street, where the white lights twinkled, as they would day and night until the first of the year. As she stood looking up at the sign for Juniper Junction Jewels, an officer emerged from the bakery across the street.

Can I help you?" he called.

"I'm Lilly Carlsen. I own the jewelry shop."

"Oh. I was watching the store from the big front window inside the bakery. I haven't seen a single movement all night long."

"That's good to hear, I guess. Can you let me inside? I have keys, of course, but I don't
want to go in if I'm not allowed."

"You're not allowed, as a matter of fact," the officer said. "It's still a crime scene, so no one can go in without an investigator accompanying them."

"Any idea when they'll release the store back to me?" Lilly asked.

"Nope. Hopefully sometime today, though."

"I hope so. I'm losing a lot of business."

"I'm sorry about that, Ms. Carlsen. I know how hard it is for business owners. My wife owns a restaurant supply store, so she feels the pinch when she can't open for some reason. Usually it's the weather."

"It's not easy, that's for sure."

"Why don't you go home until the police are ready to let you back in?"

Lilly said she would, then went back to the alley for her car. At least she could make breakfast for the kids. Before she started the car she made a quick phone call to her best friend, Noley Appleton.

"Noley? Hi. How would you like to have breakfast at my house this morning? No, the shop's closed today. I'll explain when you get there."

When she pulled into the driveway Barney bounded through the snow to greet her.

"Barn! What are you doing out front?" she asked, looking around and expecting to see one of the kids. No one appeared. Even in the snow, Lilly could feel her insides grow colder. "Come here, you," she said to the dog, grabbing Barney by the collar as he dashed by Lilly.

She walked around to the backyard through the gate, which was unlatched.

"One of these days I'm going to lose my temper with those two," she told Barney. She stomped up the back steps and was surprised to see the back door open.

"Laurel! Tighe! You left the door open and the dog got out!" Lilly yelled from the doorway. "Come get him. He's covered in snow and I don't want it tracked through the house." She listened for the kids to respond. No answer. "Honestly," fumed to the dog. "I'll just do it myself. Thank goodness I came home when I did or God knows where you could have gone." She always kept a big bin of towels next to the door; she grabbed the oldest, rattiest one and rubbed Barney's coat with it, then wiped off each of his paws.

After she took off her coat and boots she went into the kitchen. She filled the kettle and set it on the burner to heat and turned around to see what still needed to be cleaned up in the kitchen.

That's when she saw the note on the table. *Mom, I'm going to Mike's house. Laurel went out to breakfast with some friend. T*

The kids weren't home. Lilly could feel her heart start to beat a bit faster as a small trickle of anxiety wound its way through her body. She reached for her cell phone and dialed Tighe.

"Hello?"

"Hi, honey. It's Mom."

"I know that." Lilly could practically see him rolling his eyes.

"Oh. Did you know you left the back door unlocked when you left earlier?"

"No I didn't. I remember locking it because I dropped my keys in the snow after I locked the door. I said something inappropriate and Mrs. Laforge from next door yelled at me."

"You must have said it pretty loudly if Mrs. Laforge could hear you."

"You didn't call just to tell me not to swear, did you?"

"Of course not. I called to ask about the door. But as long as we're on the topic, please don't swear."

"Maybe Laurel forgot something and went home. Did you check to see if she's there?"

"I yelled, but there was no answer. Maybe she's in the bathroom. I'll go check."

"Bye, Mom."

Lilly hung up and looked down at Barney, who was sitting on the floor next to her. She would have sworn Barney was smiling because he had enjoyed an unsanctioned romp in the snow.

"Come on, Barney. Let's find Laurel."

Barney led the way up the stairs. Lilly called her daughter and knocked on her bedroom door and the bathroom door, but Laurel wasn't home. Lilly swallowed hard and her breath started coming faster. Someone had let the dog out and left the door open. Who could have done that?

She went downstairs and straight to the back door to look at the handle. It was then she noticed for the first time that the handle was broken. It tilted to one side and was loose when Lilly jiggled it. It had been in perfect condition when she left for work.

Now she was afraid. Someone had broken into the house. She reached for her cell phone and called Bill.

CHAPTER 6

"Bill, someone's been in my house. They left the back door open and Barney got out."

"Is he lost?"

"No, he's fine. I just happened to come home from the shop and found him in the front yard."

"Are you in the house now?"

"Yes, but there's nothing missing and no sign that anyone was in here except the broken door handle."

"Where are the kids?"

"Tighe is over at a friend's house and I think Laurel is out to breakfast."

"Call her just to make sure that's where she is."

Lilly's insides twisted and tightened. "Do you think she's all right?"

"Yes. I just want you to make sure, that's all."

Lilly hung up without another word and dialed Laurel's cell. "Laurel? Are you all right?" she said in a rush when her daughter answered.

"Yeah, I'm fine. I'm having breakfast with Nick."

"Nick who?"

"Nick from school. Is that all you wanted, Mom?"

"Yes. Just checking on you, that's all."

"Why wouldn't I be all right?"

"No reason. I'm just a little jumpy, that's all. Who's this Nick?"

"Not now, Mom." Nick must have been sitting nearby where he could hear the conversation.

"All right. I'll see you later. Be careful and don't do anything stupid."

"Mom." Laurel was getting frustrated.

"Bye."

Lilly hung up and dialed Bill again. "Laurel's fine," she said as soon as he answered. "What do you think happened? This is the last thing I need after Eden's murder." Lilly had a sudden thought. "Bill, you don't think these two things are related, do you?"

"I doubt it. It's probably just *really* bad luck. Besides, you didn't kill Eden, so why would anyone break into the house because of that?"

"I don't know. I'm scared to death."

"I'll be right over."

Lilly was too spooked to wait in the house. Instead, she and Barney went out to her car and waited for Bill and Noley there. Barney seemed to sense that something was amiss and he sat whimpering in the passenger seat. Lilly reached over to rub his fluffy head. She pulled out her phone and did a search for nearby locksmiths. She chose the one at the top of the list and called him to make an appointment to have the doorknob replaced and the lock changed, just in case.

"Don't worry, Barn. We'll get to the bottom of this." Barney snuffled happily in return. Lilly leaned her head back, yearning to close her eyes but too afraid to let them close for even a moment.

Noley pulled her car into the driveway behind Lilly several minutes later. The sound of Noley's tires crunching on the snow sent Barney into a frenzy of barking. Lilly opened her door and cringed while Barney bounded across her lap and over to Noley's car. When Lilly got out, she scanned the street in front of the house to make sure no one else was around.

"What's going on? Why are you out in the car?" Noley asked. She was carrying a large shopping bag.

"It's been a horrible couple of days," Lilly began, leading the way into the house. Barney jumped around Noley's legs the whole way. Noley laughed.

"Barney, leave me alone and I'll give you a treat." She had said the magic word and Barney bounded back and forth across the kitchen floor, his nails sliding on the smooth tile.

"He is the greatest dog," Noley said, reaching into the shopping bag. "Here, Barney. Come get it." She held out a bone-shaped treat that Lilly could smell from where she stood.

"What is that? It smells terrible," she said, wrinkling her nose.

"It's a liver treat. I made them this morning."

"What's wrong with peanut butter?"

"Nothing. I just thought my good friend Barney might like to try liver." And indeed, Barney was gobbling the treat at an astonishing pace. Noley laughed again. "See? I knew he would love it." Barney came to her side and looked up at Noley, clearly expecting more. Noley obliged and held out another one. Barney pranced happily to his little corner of the kitchen and munched away happily while Lilly poured tea for herself and Noley.

"So what's been happening?" Noley asked, sitting down at the table. Her long dark hair, normally in a ponytail, fell down around her shoulders, making her look even prettier than usual.

"Did you read the paper this morning?" Lilly asked.

"No. I got in from my parents' house late last night and I haven't turned on the news or looked at a paper or anything. It's been quite nice, actually."

"Then you haven't heard about Eden Barclay."

"No. What happened?" Noley knew Eden Barclay through past business dealings.

"Eden was strangled with a strand of pearls in my store. I found her when I went in early yesterday morning."

Noley gasped and her hand flew to her mouth. "I don't believe it. Who did it? And why in your store?"

"I don't have any answers. The police are still over there. I couldn't open yesterday and I've been told they're still going to be working in there today."

There was a knock at the front door and it creaked open. Lilly gave a start but heard her brother's voice almost immediately.

"Lilly? It's me."

"We're out here, Bill," she called.

"Hi. Hey, Noley. How've you been?" He didn't meet Noley's eyes, but looked away quickly.

"Good, Bill." She smiled, even though he wasn't looking at her.

"I'll be right back. I'm just going to make sure there's no one in the house," Bill said. Lilly could feel her heart constrict. Why hadn't she thought to do that? It didn't take him long to search the house; Lilly could hear him opening closet doors upstairs, so she knew he was doing a thorough job.

"Doesn't look like anyone's been in the house," he said when he came back to the kitchen. "Are you sure the doorknob isn't just broken?"

Lilly shook her head. "I don't think so. It worked fine when I left earlier this morning."

"Maybe it broke when one of the kids closed it." Lilly doubted that. Bill pulled on a pair of gloves and went straight to the back door. He bent down to examine the broken doorknob, gently turning it this way and that. He took out his cell phone and snapped some pictures, then opened the door and looked down at the landing and the back steps.

"Did you notice any unusual footprints in the snow when you came in?" he asked Lilly.

"No, but I wasn't looking. I had the dog and I was mad because I thought one of the kids had left the door open."

"It doesn't matter. Whatever footprints may have been there are obliterated now," he said with a sigh. "I'm going to call someone who can bring a fingerprint kit over. We'll see if the person who was in here left any prints. Have you touched anything?"

Lilly looked sheepish. "I've touched a bunch of things in the kitchen, plus the bathroom doorknob upstairs and the doorknob to Laurel's room. Probably the railing going upstairs, too, but I don't remember for sure."

"Lilly, how long do you have to be the sister of a cop before you learn not to touch anything when someone has broken into your house?"

"How long do you have to be a cop before you learn that I didn't realize the second I came inside that someone may have broken in?" she retorted.

"All right, all right. There's no sense arguing about it. Please don't touch anything else until the fingerprint guys get here. I've got to go over to the station, but I'll make sure someone gets here soon."

He kissed her on the cheek, said goodbye to Noley, and left through the front door.

"What do we do now?" Lilly wondered. "We can't touch anything, so we can't cook anything. We can't leave because I want to be here when they come to look for fingerprints. All I want to do is get out of here."

Noley smiled and pointed to the bag on the floor. "You're lucky we're friends. I brought biscuits and jam. And winter fruit salad with a honey lime dressing. I knew you were planning to make breakfast, but I figured you wouldn't mind."

Lilly grinned. "I should have known you'd bring goodies. I'm starved."

Noley hauled her creations out of the bag and placed them on the table. "I'm testing out some new recipes for the magazine. These biscuits have orange zest in them and I'd like your opinion on whether I should use more or less zest or keep it just the way it is. I also want to know how they taste with the jam, which has pears and cranberries."

Noley was a recipe developer for a national cooking magazine and Lilly was the happy guinea pig for many of Noley's innovations. As far as Lilly was concerned, Noley never had an unsuccessful attempt at cooking, though Noley found plenty to criticize about her own abilities. Her palate was very discerning and for something to impress her it had to be utterly spectacular.

"I don't think the police will mind if we get a couple plates from the cupboard," Lilly said. "I'm sure whoever was in here wasn't looking for crockery."

Noley smiled. "Maybe you should use a towel or something around your hand to open the cupboard, just in case."

"You're probably right." Lilly grabbed a kitchen towel from where it hung next to the sink and wrapped it around her hand. She opened the cupboard and took two plates down. She took the butter plate down, too. "Want butter on your biscuit?"

"I don't know yet. We'll try them without butter first, then with butter. I need to know if they're good enough without butter."

The biscuits were still warm and they practically melted in Lilly's mouth. "These are so good," she told her friend.

Noley was looking at her biscuit with a critical eye. "I don't know. Maybe a little more zest?"

"No way. They're perfect. I can taste the zest."

"All right. Try it with butter and see what you think."

Lilly was happy to oblige. "Even better."

"That's the problem," Noley answered, slowly chewing her unbuttered biscuit. "They should taste just as good without butter."

"Not true. Everything tastes better with butter," Lilly said between bites. "Can I try some of the jam now?"

"You don't take enough time to enjoy the experience," Noley scolded her.

"Bah. I'm starving. All I want is breakfast and this is delicious."

Noley smiled and passed the jam. They were just taking the first bites of the fruit salad when there was another knock at the front door. Lilly froze, but then recovered herself and went to answer the door. There were two police officers standing on the front porch; one was carrying a silver case.

CHAPTER 7

"Have you come to get fingerprints?" Lilly asked.

"Yes, ma'am. Bill sent us over. May we come in?" Lilly stood aside so both officers could enter. Lilly pointed toward the kitchen, but the officer with the case set it down on the floor and opened it. The two men busied themselves getting equipment out of the case and then went to work immediately. One stayed at the front door and the other went through the kitchen to the back door. Lilly and Noley watched him work as they sat at the kitchen table in silence.

The officers went through the house methodically and efficiently, gathering fingerprint impressions from surfaces such as doorknobs, railings, light switches, and drawer handles. By the time they left Lilly and Noley had polished off the fruit salad and the biscuits, along with half the jam in the small jar. They limited their conversation to small talk while the officers were there.

When the officers left Lilly saw them to the door and asked if they knew how the scene was progressing at her shop. They radioed for information and told her she could open up again the next day.

Lilly closed the door behind them, then sighed and leaned against the door. Noley came into the foyer. "Did they have any answers for you?"

"I didn't ask. I'm sure there won't be any answers for a while. They're not even done processing the crime scene in my store yet. What am I going to do about two lost days of business?"

"Let's think about it. There's got to be some catchy phrase we can use to get people in there." She thought for a minute then snapped her fingers. "I know! How about 'We're killing the competition'?"

Lilly shot her friend an incredulous look and then burst out laughing when she realized Noley was kidding.

"You're good for my soul," she said. She couldn't help laughing so hard at such a dismal joke—it was how all her stress was coming out. She wiped her eyes with her sleeve after several long moments and heaved a long sigh of relief. Noley had watched the spectacle with a smug smile on her face. She knew just how to cheer up her best friend.

"Do you have Christmas shopping to do?" Noley asked.

Lilly rolled her eyes. "You have no idea. I haven't even started mine yet."

"Well I'm done, so I can help you. Grab your coat and let's get out of here." Lilly texted both kids to tell them to let her know when they were ready to go home. She didn't want them being in the house without her.

"You want to take Barney over to my house?" Noley asked before they left.

"No, I think he's fine here. I hope he at least made an attempt to scare the bejeepers out of the person who came into the house. Hopefully it won't happen again."

They got into Noley's car for the short drive to Main Street. Both women were quiet, pensive, on the way. Finally Noley spoke as they pulled into a parking spot, one of the only ones on the block.

"Who do you think was in the house?"

"I've been wracking my brains trying to figure it out, but I don't know. It could have been anyone, I suppose. Maybe even someone who didn't mean any harm—someone who was hungry or cold."

Noley's "hmm" made it obvious she didn't agree.

The first place they went was Dolly's Vintage Clothes. Lilly had tried to think of a way to avoid seeing Dolly, since she was well-known as one of the town's most ardent busybodies, but since her store was Laurel's favorite place to shop, Lilly didn't have much choice. Noley tried on a few dresses while Lilly chose what she thought Laurel would like best. Dolly came over during a lull in the crowd of customers.

"I'm so sorry about what happened in your store," she said in a low voice.

"Thanks, Dolly."

"Do they have any idea who did it?"

Lilly shook her head ruefully. "Not yet. I hope they have an answer soon."

Dolly lowered her voice another notch. "I'm not going to miss Eden."

"I won't either, but I would keep that to myself if I were you. You don't want to end up a suspect," Lilly warned.

"She was just so miserable," Dolly continued. "I don't think there's anyone who's going to miss her."

"It's sad when you think about it," Lilly said pensively. "Can you imagine not having anyone to miss you when you're gone?"

Dolly shook her head. "What's going on with her store now?"

"I haven't heard. I suppose it'll be sold."

"Did she have a husband or kids?"

"My son told me her son goes to his school, and I know she had a husband because he reported her missing on Thanksgiving Day."

"I suppose her husband will be the new owner of the general store."

Lilly shrugged. She had enough to worry about with the jewelry store without worrying about who was going to be the new owner of the general store. She changed the subject.

"I'm going to take this dress," she said, holding up a maxi-length dress on a hanger. "Laurel will love it. And I'll take this sweater, too." She placed a folded sweater on the counter.

Dolly rang up the sale and put the clothes in a bag. "Let me know if you hear anything," she called as Lilly walked toward the front door of the shop.

"I will. Talk to you soon." Lilly looked around at the other shoppers, hoping she didn't know any of them.

Lilly found Noley next door at the Love to Cook shop. Whenever they went shopping together Noley always spent an obscene amount of time in the cooking store.

"You have to see this pottery," Noley said as soon as she saw Lilly.

It was beautiful pottery, hand-thrown and fired locally. Lilly browsed through the collection as Noley flitted from one display to another throughout the tiny, cramped shop. "Ooh, look at this!" she squealed, pointing to a cheese-making kit. "I need to try something like this."

Lilly smiled at her friend. She picked out a tray she knew Noley would love and put it aside at the counter, winking at the saleslady and nodding her head slightly toward Noley. The lady understood and grinned. While Noley was engrossed in a conversation in the back of the store about the relative merits of immersion blenders, Lilly paid for the gift and tucked it into the bag from the vintage clothing store.

Next they went to the sporting goods store to pick out something for Tighe. Lilly always had a hard time picking out gifts for Tighe. He was a tough one to buy for. She hated giving gift cards, so she spent a crazy amount of time looking for the perfect gift. After going around and around through the camping and hiking section of the store, she finally decided on a lantern for Tighe's tent, a headlamp, and a doohickey that allowed him to carry a pouch of water on his back and drink from it while he was hiking, using a long tube like a straw.

Noley suggested they eat lunch at the Main Street Diner after their shopping was done. They sat down in one of the red vinyl booths and opened menus. The diner wasn't fancy, but it had great food. Noley wouldn't allow them to eat lunch at a place that didn't have great food. The place was packed with locals and tourists alike. A server was at their table in no time and offered coffee. They both accepted, glad to have something warm to drink.

As usual, Lilly ordered first and sat back to listen as Noley placed her order. She could only chuckle and roll her eyes when Noley started to speak.

"I'll have the club sandwich with bacon—make sure it's crispy bacon—and please bring a pot of stone-ground mustard on the side. None of that plain yellow mustard. I'll have the fries, but I'd like them fried twice." She turned to Lilly. "That makes them crispier. You'll love them." She turned back to our server. "I'd also like an iced tea, unsweetened, but please put one and a half squirts of raspberry syrup in it. You know, the stuff they use for the fancy coffees."

After the server left with a knowing smile on her face, Lilly spoke to her friend. "Aren't you afraid they're going to spit in your food or something because you're so demanding?"

Noley leaned forward. "Everyone here knows me, so they know what to expect when I come through the door. And they're good about it because I'm a big tipper." She grinned and leaned back.

"Got any ideas for making up for the sales you've missed?"

Lilly sighed. "Nope. It's a jewelry store, so it has to be classy. I can't just hang up a banner that screams 'Belated Black Friday sale!'"

"Why not? That's what it is." Noley's practicality got in the way of her small business sense sometimes.

"Because I cater to rich people who are looking for a special experience. If all they want is jewelry on sale, they can get that online. They want to be pampered and treated like royalty."

Noley smirked. "I'm glad I'm not rich. I like things simple."

Lilly laughed. "I'm glad you're not rich, too. You might not want to hang out with me anymore."

Noley snapped her fingers. "I know. Why don't you host special evening hours in the next week or two?"

Lilly thought for a moment. "You might have something there. I could serve wine and cheese and make it really special. People would eat that up. So to speak."

Noley grinned. "I'll work on a menu that will dazzle. It'll be a surprise. How can you advertise so that people know to come?"

"I could make up some classy-looking flyers and put them in the hotels and bed and breakfasts around here."

Noley was warming up to her idea. "And you could put ads online and in the newspaper. People still read newspapers, don't they? This is going to be so much fun!"

Lilly reached for her bag and took out a notebook and pen. She started making a list of places to advertise. "When should I do it?" she asked.

"How about next weekend? You could stay open late in the evenings after the rest of the stores close."

Lilly stopped writing, her hand poised over the paper. "Uh-oh. Forget it. I wasn't thinking—the other shop owners will give me so much flack that it won't be worth it."

"Why should they give you flack?"

"Because the stores on Main Street are supposed to be closed by six in the evening. And if I stay open, they're going to get all bent out of shape that I've got longer store hours than anyone else."

"Well, you're the head of the Chamber of Commerce. You ought to be able to do that if you want."

"That's just it. I don't want it to seem like I'm getting special privileges because I'm the president of the Chamber of Commerce."

"You deserve something for doing that thankless job."

"I agree, but that's not how it works. We'll need to come up with a different idea."

"Why can't all the stores be open, then? That way everyone benefits and you get to go ahead with your plan. It doesn't seem fair, though, that all the stores have to be open. Your store is the only one that lost profits because it was closed."

"I could see if that's a possibility," Lilly mused, stirring her coffee. "If I could call a vote on it in the next twenty-four hours and if we could advertise quickly enough, we might be able to pull that off."

"How do you call a vote?"

"I'll just email everyone. Voting by email is okay under the bylaws. I know everyone is in town, so it should be easy to get in touch with all the board members." She scrawled a note at the top of the paper reminding herself to send that email as soon as she got home. "I'll ask the kids to get to work on designing a flyer for the extra hours and another flyer for just my store." Laurel and Tighe made up Lilly's design team.

CHAPTER 8

T he food came and, as promised, Noley's fries were delicious. They put the plate in the middle of the table and shared them. Lilly was biting into the second half of her roast beef sandwich when an extremely tall, slender man walked up to the table. Herb Knight. Lilly suppressed a groan.

"Lilly, good to see you. I'm sorry about what happened at your store."

"Thanks, Herb. Do you know my friend Noley?"

He held out his hand and shook Noley's proffered hand. "Nice to meet you," Noley said.

"Likewise." He turned his attention back to Lilly. "So what are you going to do to make up for lost time in your shop? I noticed the police are still there."

"Actually, Herb, I'm glad you asked. I've been thinking about it and I have a proposal I'd like to make to the Chamber of Commerce."

Herb gave Lilly a wary look. "What kind of proposal?"

"I'm thinking that we have two evenings next weekend—say, Friday and Saturday—when all the stores on Main Street stay open a few hours late for shoppers."

"I don't think that's allowed under Juniper Junction ordinances."

"The ordinance states that the stores have to close at six o'clock in the evening unless there is an agreement among all the shop owners to extend that time."

"And what would this accomplish?"

There was no point in trying to convince him she was doing this out of the kindness of her heart because he'd never believe it. "Well, for one thing it might allow me to make up for some of the sales I lost because of Eden's murder. But it doesn't just benefit me—it would benefit everyone."

"I'm not sure I like that idea, Lilly. I, for one, appreciate my evenings off."

"Herb, you're a yoga instructor. Aren't yoga instructors supposed to go with the flow?" Lilly asked with a trace of annoyance in her voice.

"Not when someone is trying to take away my self-determination."

"It's just two nights, Herb, and just to give shoppers a little more time to peruse everything Main Street has to offer. And being on Main Street at night is lovely. A lot of people don't know that because the shops close and they don't come down here unless they're going to one of the restaurants."

Herb let out an exaggerated sigh. "I'll think about it. Have you told anyone else?"

"You're the first one."

"See if you can get other business owners on board and then I'll let you know my vote." He turned and walked away.

"That guy teaches yoga?" Noley asked, her incredulity evident in her eyes.

"Yes. Can you believe it? He's the most uptight guy in town. I'm surprised you've never met. He's been around for years."

"I'm not really the yoga type," Noley responded. "I'm more of the relax-in-yoga-pants type."

"I know," Lilly said, laughing. "Now finish up so we can get back to my house. I've got an email to compose." They split the bill and Noley did indeed leave a very big tip.

Back at Lilly's house, Noley packed the things she had brought over earlier and went back to her own house. Tighe texted Lilly to let her know he would be home soon, and Lilly sat down at her computer. Suddenly she was keenly aware of being alone in the house, and her heart was beating hard. She looked down at her fingers on the keyboard. They were trembling just a little. She took a deep breath and forced herself to stay calm. After all, Barney was here and he would be acting strange if anyone had been in the house in her absence.

She took her time composing the perfect email to the members of the Chamber of Commerce, acknowledging that she had lost business because of the unfortunate events at the jewelry store but also mentioning that extra shopping hours for a weekend during the holiday season would benefit all the Main Street shop owners. A half hour later she sent the email flying through the ether and waited anxiously for Tighe and Laurel to get home.

Tighe arrived first. Lilly practically accosted him at the door, telling him about Noley's idea to have extra store hours and serve customers, or "guests" as she thought of them, hors d'oeuvres and beverages. Tighe was enthusiastic about the idea and went right upstairs to design a flyer appropriate for the occasion. Laurel came home while Lilly was making dinner. Lilly had texted her several times but gotten no reply.

"Where have you been?" Lilly asked, trying to keep her voice even.

"I was at Nick's house."

"I asked you to text me."

"Sorry. I forgot."

"What were you doing at Nick's house?"

"Talking to his mom. Why the twenty questions?"

"I just told you, I asked you to text me. If you can't keep me in the loop when you go out somewhere with someone I haven't met, you're going to have to stay home." Laurel rolled her eyes.

"And don't roll your eyes at me, young lady."

"I'm sorry, all right? We just got talking and time got away from me. It's no big deal."

"It's a big deal if I don't know where you are and I can't get in touch with you!" Lilly hadn't meant to yell, but her frazzled nerves were getting the better of her. "Now wash your hands and start making a salad for dinner."

"What's the matter with you, Mom? You're being way too protective," Laurel snarled. Lilly closed her eyes and counted to ten. She didn't want to have to tell the kids about the intruder, but she might just blurt it out if Laurel kept pushing her buttons.

Laurel stomped off to the powder room and Lilly could hear the water running. She heard Laurel yell something.

"What?" she answered.

Laurel came into the kitchen wiping her hands on her pants. "Why doesn't Tighe have to help?"

"He's busy doing something else for me. He's designing a couple flyers for an event I'm thinking of holding. If you'd been home on time you could have designed the flyer and he'd be making a salad right now."

Laurel ignored the hint. "What kind of event? Here?"

"Not here. At the store. It's an afterhours shopping event."

"Sounds cool." Laurel was obviously trying to get back on Lilly's good side without actually apologizing for her behavior. Lilly recognized Laurel's stubborn streak because she had that same streak. So did Laurel's father.

They chopped and simmered side-by-side until Laurel's phone rang. She reached to answer it and glanced at Lilly. "If that's Nick, you can talk to him later."

It was Nick. Couldn't that boy leave her daughter alone for five minutes? Laurel did as she'd been told, though, and hung up the phone after promising to call him back after dinner.

Tighe came downstairs waving a sheet of paper triumphantly. "Mom, what do you think of this? It's just a draft, but I think it turned out great."

He stood between his mother and his sister and proudly thrust the paper in front of them. Lilly looked at it closely. "I think it's perfect," she said.

"Laur, what do you think?" Tighe asked. His sister peered at the paper. "I like it, but I think this part is a little hard to read," she said, pointing to the part of the flyer that listed the shop's temporary hours.

Lilly looked over Laurel's shoulder. "You know, she's right. Maybe make that font a little bigger?"

"Okay," Tighe said, and he bounded back upstairs.

After dinner Lilly took a plate of dinner over to her mother. "Hi, Mom. How's everything?"

"Everything is terrible," Lilly's mom said with a snarl.

"What's the matter?"

"That Edna Laforge came to see me today. I can't stand her, the old bat. She says Tighe makes too much noise and Barney is out barking at all hours. I told her she's crazy." Lilly turned away from her mother to busy herself at the sink, smiling.

"Why wouldn't she just come talk to me if she's got a problem with Tighe or Barney?" Lilly asked.

"Because she's passive-aggressive, that's why. I'm not letting her in the next time she comes over."

"You do what you feel is best, Mom."

"How's Billy? He didn't stop by to see me today."

"I'm sure he's very busy with the shopping season in full swing and all. Shoplifters abound."

"I think he's too smart to deal with things like that. They need to make him chief." Lilly smiled again.

"He doesn't want to be chief, Mom. Too political. He likes getting out on the street and talking to people."

"He's too smart for that," she mumbled.

"Well, if he's so smart then he needs to find a way to get the cops at my store to hurry up and get out of there." Lilly stopped short, remembering that her mother didn't know about the murder at the shop.

"What?! Why are the police at your store?"

"We had a little trouble there on Friday. It's over now, but they're still gathering evidence. They should be out of there in no time," Lilly said brightly, hoping to redirect her mother onto other topics.

But her mother had no intention of allowing herself to be misdirected. "This is why I think I should start watching the local news again," she mused aloud. "How else am I going to find out what goes on around here?"

"You hate the local news."

"I know, but if nobody's going to tell me anything, I have to find out somehow." She shook her head in disgust.

"Mom, eat your dinner. Don't worry about my store or anything else. It's nothing you need to worry about."

"I used to know everything that went on in Juniper Junction," she said. "If someone wanted the scoop, they came to me to get it."

"Believe me, Mom, you still know more than most people."

"Not the important stuff," she answered with a snort.

"Mom, I need to be at the store early tomorrow morning. Do you need anything else while I'm here?"

"No, dear. You go back home and tell Tighe to make all the noise he wants." Lilly kissed her mom goodbye and left, shaking her head and smiling. On the short drive home she wondered what other rumors Mrs. Laforge might be spreading about her little family. So much for living next door to a nice little old lady.

Tighe had finished the flyers when Lilly got home. She checked her email to see that several of the members of the Chamber of Commerce had replied with a "yea" vote for extended shopping hours the following weekend. Herb, naturally, had replied in the negative, stating his position again that this was no more than a gimmick to allow Lilly to recoup some of her losses from Black Friday.

"That old goat," Lilly muttered when she read his email.

She was getting ready for bed when the phone rang. It was Bill.

"What's up? Mom says you didn't stop to see her today."

"I've been busy at the office. I wanted to give you a heads-up."

CHAPTER 9

"That doesn't sound good. A heads-up about what?" Lilly asked, her brow furrowing.

"Your fingerprints were found on the pearl necklace that was used to strangle Eden Barclay."

Lilly felt the first stirring of unease in her stomach. "Of course my fingerprints are on it. It came from my store. I've probably put that necklace around the necks of two dozen women. How were the police able to get a fingerprint big enough? Those pearls aren't that big."

"They had enough partials to figure it out."

"Bill, you know I didn't strangle Eden Barclay."

"Of course I do, but I can't obstruct an investigation. I already told them that you're far above suspicion, but they have to go where the evidence leads. And right now it leads to your fingers being on the necklace."

"So what's going to happen?" Lilly's mouth felt dry.

"At some point they're going to want to talk to you. I don't know when. But just tell them the truth and you ought to be fine."

"Can they arrest me?" Lilly's voice sounded high to her own ears.

"I suppose they could, but they would have a hard time explaining that. I mean, your fingerprints would be expected on that necklace. In my opinion, they need to do a lot more work before they can even think about arresting you. And I don't say that just because you're my sister. I say that because it would be true of any murder and any person of interest."

"So I'm a person of interest."

"Lil, get some sleep. I just called to give you a friendly warning that the police are going to want to talk to you again. Don't give it another thought. Goodnight."

Lilly hung up. Really? Get some sleep now, after she'd just been informed she was a person of interest in a murder investigation?

But she tried. She lay back against her pillow and tried to will herself asleep, but dreams wouldn't come. She tossed and turned most of the night, wondering what would happen to her kids if she was put in jail, wondering who would run her store, how she would tell her mother. Finally, as dawn arrived and the sky brightened to a dusky gray, she fell asleep for a few minutes. The sound of Laurel going into the bathroom woke her up. She staggered down to the kitchen to make coffee and eat a muffin before getting ready for work.

Often Lilly went to church on Sunday mornings but when she woke up she felt that what she needed more than anything was to be at her store. She let the kids sleep in and she tidied up the house before going to work, still on autopilot from getting no sleep. She was relieved to see her shop empty of police officers when she arrived on Main Street, which was just beginning to come alive. The mountains behind Juniper Junction blocked the sun from reaching Main Street before eight o'clock on late fall mornings, so the snow had a purple-gray look to it. The Christmas lights still twinkled in the shop windows, giving Main Street an air of deserted festivity.

Lilly found the back door of her shop unlocked. Rats. That meant there was probably a police officer still in there.

And sure enough, when she pushed the door open a police officer rose from a chair next to her desk. She gave him a questioning look.

"The team's done in here, Ms. Carlsen. I stayed on last night just to make sure nothing else happened."

"Thank you. So I can get back to work and open the store and have customers in here and everything?" Lilly asked.

"Yup." He touched his hat as he opened the back door. "I'm sure someone from the department will be in touch."

Lilly sat down at her desk and looked around. She was so tired. All she wanted was to go back home and sleep for hours. But she knew that wasn't going to happen and the best thing for her was activity. When she had finished all the paperwork requiring her attention, she went to the front of the store, surveying the mess left by the police. The disarray looked incongruous with the Christmas décor.

This year the shop's holiday theme was "The First Noel" and she had set up a manger, groupings of small, rustic *papier mâiché* barn animals, and bright gold stars hanging from the ceiling. The lights inside, like those lining Main Street outside, twinkled a soft white. She gazed at the decorations for several moments, feeling soothed by the warmth and calm they emanated. Then she got to work cleaning up the debris the police officers had left in their wake. Finally she opened the vault and set out jewelry displays in the windows, then at the appointed hour she unlocked the front door and waited for her first customers.

She didn't have to wait long. It seemed the rumor mill had been busy over the past couple days and people were eager to visit the store to see where Eden Barclay had died. People were so morbid, Lilly said to herself more than once that day. But morbid or not, there were quite a few paying customers and Lilly began to think as the day grew long that having hosted a murder on the premises had actually been good for business.

She ushered the last customer of the day out the door just as the clock on the town square chimed six o'clock. She could hardly believe the day had passed without a special visit from the police. She hoped they were following other, more promising, leads.

She trudged through the motions of putting the jewelry back into the vault for the night, locking the cases in the front of the store, and shutting off the lights. She noticed as she closed the door leading to her office that a man was standing on the sidewalk peering into the darkened windows of the shop. Since it was already dark outside and the streetlamps only lent enough light to make Main Street pretty, she couldn't see his face. She stiffened, then recovered herself and hurried to lock the back door, double-check it, and get into her car. Normally the sight of someone peering into her shop windows after dark was a promising one, meaning she might have a customer early the next morning, but after the events of the past few days such a sight was unsettling, at best.

She was thankful that the kids had made dinner for her and taken a plate of it to her mother's house by the time she got home. The three of them ate together in the snug, warm kitchen and Lilly's exhaustion started to get the better of her.

"You kids are so good to me, making dinner and taking it over to Gran's house like this," she said, sniffling. "I just don't know what I did to deserve you two." The tears started to fall.

"Mom, what's wrong? You asked us to make dinner, remember?" Laurel asked.

"I remember," Lilly answered with a quavery smile. "I just appreciate all you do, that's all. I don't tell you often enough."

"It's no problem, Mom," Tighe answered. "I think you should go to bed early tonight." Laurel nodded her agreement.

"You look exhausted," she added. "We'll do the dishes. Why don't you go right up to bed when you're done eating?"

"I will," Lilly promised. For a fleeting moment she wondered if she would be able to sleep with Eden's murder, and the knowledge that an intruder had been in her house, hanging over her head. The thought of another night of tossing and turning filled her with dread.

CHAPTER 10

B ut she needn't have worried. Despite all the things on her
mind, Lilly fell into a deep, exhausted sleep soon after
dinner ended. She didn't wake up until the alarm startled her
the next morning. She felt much better having slept so well, and
she greeted the kids cheerfully when they came downstairs for
breakfast. She had just enough time to serve them hot chocolate
and the last of Noley's biscuits before they ran out the door for
school.

"Mom," Laurel said as she pulled the back door closed
behind her, "I'm going to hang out with Nick after school,
okay?" The door closed with a *click*.

Lilly wrenched the door open. "Laurel, wait!" she called.
Laurel was running down the driveway, probably in an attempt
to avoid answering questions about Nick, but she turned around
and waited for her mother to speak, her hands on her hips.

"What?"

"Where are you going to be after school?"

"Nick's house."

"No, you're not. Pick a public place and I'll say it's okay."

Laurel sighed loudly for dramatic effect. "All right, then. The bakery on Main."

"That's better. Have a good day." Lilly blew her daughter a kiss and went back indoors.

She drove to work that morning lost in thought about the man she had seen looking into the shop window after she closed the previous night. Would he be back? What did he want? She hoped he was a prospective customer, not some creep who just wanted to see the place where Eden Barclay had been strangled.

It wasn't long after she opened the back door of the store when a knock startled her out of a paperwork-induced trance. She got up and went to the door, feeling apprehensive.

"Who is it?" she asked.

"Police, ma'am. We'd like to talk to you for a few minutes." Lilly didn't know whether to believe the man or not. After all, there had been that man peering in the front window last night…

"Come around to the front where I can see you and I'll let you in," Lilly said through the door.

Moments later there was a knock at the front door. Lilly opened the door to her showroom just a crack so she could see who was at the front door. She let out a little squeak as she realized how nervous she had been, wondering if it was really a police officer who had spoken through the back door. She strode to the front door and opened it, stepping aside to let two officers in. She locked the door again behind them and led them to the back office. She sat at her desk; one of the men sat across from her while the other, presumably the junior officer, stood behind him.

"How can I help you?" she asked.

"We'd like to double-check the information you gave us about your whereabouts on Wednesday and Thursday," the officer in the chair said.

Why did they need to know that? "I closed the shop early on

Wednesday and finished decorating for Black Friday. Then I left. I had to go shopping for the groceries I needed for Thanksgiving," she said, trying to remember every step she had taken.

"When did you close the shop?"

"Two o'clock in the afternoon. That's when most of the shops on Main Street closed."

"And you don't remember why you might have left the back door and the door to the vault unlocked?"

"Wait a minute. I remember. My mother called me just as I was closing up the shop. She had fallen and needed help." Lilly's head snapped up. "I must have forgotten to lock the vault and the back door because I was so worried about her. She had refused to call an ambulance."

"So you left without locking the store at all." The accusation in his tone was clear.

"I must have. It's the only explanation."

The officer took up his previous line of questioning. "So you left around two o'clock. Is that when the general store closed?" The officer glanced at his cell phone.

"I assume so, but I don't know."

"So you left here and went to the grocery store. Then what?"

"Then I went home and started cooking."

"Who was at your house with you?" The officer standing up tilted his head. Lilly wondered what his role was in this inquisition.

"My kids were there with me on Wednesday afternoon."

"Were they there when you got home from the grocery store?"

"Yes." The officer standing up was scribbling in a small notebook.

"How many kids do you have?"

"Two. A son and a daughter."

"And how old are they?"

"My son is seventeen and my daughter is sixteen."

"Did you go anywhere else that afternoon or evening?"

"Yes. I went to my mother's house to take dinner to her."

"And what is your mother's name?"

"Beverly Fisk."

"Where does she live?" Lilly gave them her mother's address and hoped they wouldn't have to talk to her. She shared her concerns with the officers.

"My mother has early-stage dementia and doesn't know the extent of what took place here. I don't want to upset her. If you can avoid asking her questions, that would be good." Privately, Lilly wondered if her mother would even remember what happened the previous Wednesday. It would be just like her to say she had no idea who Lilly was or whether she had dinner at all that night, Lilly thought wryly.

"We'll see," the sitting officer said. "We may not need to check with her. Did anyone go with you to drop off her dinner?"

"Yes, my daughter went with me."

"We can talk to her, then."

"Did you go anywhere else when you took dinner to your mother?"

"No. My daughter and I went home and we watched a movie and went to bed."

"Are you married?"

"No. Divorced."

"Where's your ex-husband?"

"Your guess is as good as mine. If you find out, please don't tell me."

The standing officer coughed and looked up. Lilly ignored him. The last person she wanted to talk about was Beau.

"What's his name?"

"Beau Carlsen."

"So you went to bed Wednesday night. Then what?"

"I woke up early Thursday, went for a walk, and started

cooking again when I got home." *Rats*, Lilly thought. *I shouldn't even have mentioned going out for a walk.*

The seated officer seized on her comment. "You went for a walk. Did you go alone?"

"Yes."

"So there's no one who can corroborate your whereabouts?"

"No. Well, wait. My neighbor, Mrs. Laforge, somehow always knows what everyone in the neighborhood is doing. She might have seen me." Lilly provided the officers with Edna's address.

"Did you go out again on Thursday?"

"No. My son picked up my mother and brought her over to my house for Thanksgiving dinner."

"So you, your mother, and your kids were at Thanksgiving dinner. Anyone else?"

"Yes. My brother Bill, whom you probably know."

"Bill Fisk?"

"Yes."

The scribbling officer stopped his hen scratching and stared at me. "I didn't know Bill was your brother," he blurted out. The sitting officer turned and glared at his partner.

"Sorry," the scribbler mumbled.

"What time did you all eat dinner on Thanksgiving?"

"About five."

"Did you take your mother home?"

"No, my son drove her back to her house. I told you, I didn't leave the house again until Friday morning. I went in really early because it's such a huge shopping day and I had a lot to do, but I tripped over Eden's body in my shop while I was turning on the lights. The rest you already know."

The officers thanked Lilly for her time, told her they might have more questions for her, and left. She went back to her office and sat at her desk, lost in thought for several minutes. She was worried that the police were moving closer to declaring her a suspect, not just a person of interest, in Eden's murder. She picked up her phone and dialed Bill's cell.

"Bill, two officers were just here asking a lot of questions about where I was and everything I did last Wednesday and Thursday. Just how much of a person of interest am I?"

She could sense his hesitation on the other end of the line. "I'm not really supposed to be talking to you about this because of your status as a person of interest," he said softly. "I'm at work right now. I'll stop by your house tonight." He hung up without another word.

Now Lilly was panicked. It would be nearly impossible to wait until evening. What she needed was work and lots of it.

In addition to her job as a jeweler, Lilly also designed pieces for sale in her store. She didn't sell her creations anywhere else, so that added to their value and their caché. She yanked a sketchbook from one of her bookcases and flipped to the first blank page. Her hands trembling, she reached for a pencil from the top desk drawer and accidentally flung it across the room. Before standing up to retrieve it, she placed her hands squarely on the edge of the desk in front of her and took a deep breath, then counted to ten. When she didn't calm down, she did it again. And again, and again, until her breathing slowed and her mind was able to slow down enough for her to think rationally.

Innocent until proven guilty. The police are good at their jobs. They'll find the right person. The kids and Noley can vouch for where I was, and even Mrs. Laforge might be able to help.

When she was a little calmer, she busied herself sketching designs in her notebook. She had a small jewelry-making area in the office where she made her designs come to life. She wasn't ready to start working on any particular design yet, but it helped to sketch out her ideas. When she was drawing her mind was able to focus on the pencil strokes and banish most of the ugly thoughts until something broke her concentration.

When it was time to open the shop, she was in a slightly better frame of mind. She put the sketchbook away and went out to begin the workday. She turned the lock on the rustic wood-and-glass front door and was walking back to one of the display cases when her first customer entered the store.

She turned to greet the person and stopped short with a barely-audible gasp. She would know those blue eyes anywhere. The hair was longer and grayer, the physique a little more lumpy. But those eyes...

CHAPTER 11

"**B**eau." She said his name in a quiet voice. In order to stop herself from running toward him to beat him senseless, she made a heroic effort to remind herself that this was the father of her children and a man she had once loved.

"How's everything, Lil?" he asked, a slight smile playing around his lips.

"It's Lilly. And everything is fine," she replied in a flat voice. "What are you doing here?"

"I was in town and heard that you own this place. I just wanted to stop and say hello."

"Hello. Now, goodbye."

He ignored that. "You've done well. I'm happy for you."

"Thanks. Now, would you please leave?"

"How are the kids?" Lilly's heart jumped into her throat. She was tempted to say *What kids?* but she knew better. She wanted this man to stay the heck away from her kids.

"I don't suppose that's any of your business," she replied, lifting her chin just a little.

"They're my kids, too," he said, just a touch of annoyance creeping into his voice.

"Not really. You gave up fatherhood when you left."

"That was a long time ago."

"Exactly. You gave up fatherhood."

"Still living in the same house?" She was silent. It would be easy for him to find the house she had moved to after he left, but why help him out? If he wanted to know so badly, let him figure it out for himself.

"Okay, I get it. You're not going to answer me. That's fine. I know you moved, anyhow. I drove by the old house yesterday and there were strangers there."

This was surreal. What made him think he could disappear for fifteen years and then show up out of the thin mountain air at her store?

"What do you want?" she asked, glancing around him to see if there was anyone outside the store.

"I don't want anything. I just wanted to see you again."

"Well, you've seen me. So now it's time for you to leave."

"I'm thinking I might stick around for a while. The skiing's supposed to be pretty good here this year."

Just what I need, Lilly thought.

The bell above the door jingled and a middle-aged couple walked in, their eyes shining and their faces ruddy from the cold. Lilly gave Beau a pointed look and nodded toward the door. He must have figured there was time to come back later to harass her, so he left. As she greeted the couple, Lilly watched out of the corner of her eye as he sauntered down the street, looking back once and winking at her. She winced inwardly.

She spent the better part of an hour with the couple, answering their questions about the jewelry she designed and showing them various pieces. They left with one of her favorite pendants, one of a mountain range made of stone and edged in silver. They promised to return, too, when she had her open house the following weekend.

As soon as they left she hurried back to the office and scrabbled for her cell phone on the desk. She had kept her feelings of apprehension and dread at bay while she chatted with her customers, but now that the store was empty again her stomach was tying itself in knots and her heart was starting to pound at an alarming speed.

Bill answered on the second ring. "What's up?" he asked.

"Beau's back." Those two words had the power of silencing Bill for several long moments.

"How do you know that?" he asked slowly. He knew only too well the pain Beau had caused Lilly during their brief marriage, as well as the grief he left in his wake as she tried to divorce him without knowing his whereabouts.

"He came in as soon as I opened the store this morning."

"Why didn't you call me right away?"

"Because I had customers in here until just now. I couldn't get away to call you. What should I do?"

"There's really nothing you can do, as long as he didn't touch you or threaten you."

"He didn't. I mean, do you think I should tell the kids? Do you think I should try to find out where he's staying?"

"Whatever you do, don't try to go figuring out where he's staying or where he's been all this time or anything else. Stay the heck away from him. As for the kids, I don't know what to tell you. That's something you'll have to decide for yourself. We can talk about this when I see you tonight."

Lilly hung up bewildered and angry. How dare Beau show up after all this time, waltzing into her store like nothing had happened? Like he hadn't left her with a toddler and a baby with no money and no forwarding address? She hadn't even known if he was dead or alive. Not that it mattered. It had been years before she could even think about him without her blood boiling and even longer before she was finally able to get a court to grant a divorce.

And now he was back. Now that she had made a comfortable life for herself and Tighe and Laurel, now that she owned a successful business in Juniper Junction. She could only hope that he wouldn't stay, that he wouldn't try to make trouble for her, that he wouldn't try to contact the kids he had left behind so ruthlessly.

She was seething again. She needed something to take her mind off her troubles. She dialed Noley.

"What are you doing right now?" she asked when Noley answered.

"Trying to come up with just the right mix of herbs for a popover recipe." She must have sensed from the tone of Lilly's voice that something was not right. "What's happened?"

"Beau showed up at my store this morning." Though Noley had never known Beau, she had heard enough about him to know she didn't like him.

"You're kidding. Is he still there?"

"No, but I have this feeling I haven't heard the last of him."

"Did you call Bill?"

"I called him first."

"What did he say?" Lilly related the conversation she had had with her brother. "I'm glad he's on the force," Noley said. "He knows the history, he knows not to mess around if Beau starts to bother you. Do you want me to come down to the store?"

"If you don't have lunch plans, why don't you come down around one o'clock? I'll order something from the diner."

"I'll be down, but I'll bring lunch. Don't bother ordering anything. I need a tester for these popovers, anyway."

Lilly was only too happy to be Noley's popover tester. "See you then."

Luckily, the Christmas season rush was gearing up and Lilly was busy for the rest of the morning, helping customers who came into the shop in a steady stream. She was surprised to see Noley walk in later. "Is it one o'clock already?" she asked, incredulous.

"It is. I'll set up lunch on the back display case and you finish up with everyone in here." Lilly waited on the few remaining customers and when the shop was empty she joined Noley.

"So tell me about Beau's visit," Noley said as she handed Lilly a melamine plate.

Lilly shared the details of her ex-husband's appearance at the store. When she finished talking, she was silent for a moment, then she gasped. "You know, there was someone peering in the front window of the shop last night when I closed up," she told Noley breathlessly. "I couldn't see the person's face, but I wonder if that was him. I just figured it was someone who was hoping the store was still open." She shuddered. "To think he may have been within a few feet of me last night and I didn't realize it," she said. "I can't stand the thought of it."

Noley nodded, choosing a pickle spear from a Mason jar she had brought. "You're going to have to be aware of everyone and everything around you now," she said. "Not that you aren't normally," she hastened to add, "but with Beau hanging around you'll need to be even more alert. Not to mention the person who broke into your house." Lilly shuddered. She didn't even want to think about that.

"I just can't figure out why he's come back after all this time," Lilly mused. "There are plenty of places with good skiing in Colorado. Why pick Juniper Junction?"

"This is the only town with good skiing where *you* are," Noley said pointedly.

"He couldn't have come back because he wanted to see me," Lilly scoffed. "Not after fifteen years."

"See what Bill has to say," Noley suggested. "Now eat. I brought all this good food and you're not eating. It's insulting." She smiled, and Lilly appreciated her attempt to lighten the mood. She picked at some of the things Noley had brought, including the popovers, rounds of puff pastry spread with apricot-studded brie cheese, and edamame hummus with homemade pita chips, but her stomach was still defying any attempt to enjoy lunch.

CHAPTER 12

Noley left by one-thirty, saying she had to get back to the kitchen. Thankfully, the post-lunch crowd along Main Street included a number of people looking for unique pieces of jewelry for Christmas gifts, so Lilly stayed busy until closing time. When the last customer of the day had left with Lilly's signature silver box tied with a black tulle ribbon, Lilly closed the door, locked it, and scanned Main Street to see if there was any sign of Beau. With only the other shop lights and the twinkling Christmas lights to add illumination, Lilly couldn't see anyone loitering outside. But that didn't mean no one was there. She put the display pieces in the vault and locked it, then pulled the back door closed behind her, hopped into her car as quickly as she could, and sped off toward home. She normally liked to take her time driving down Main Street because it was so pretty, especially at this time of year, but tonight she wanted to waste no time getting home.

The kids had dinner ready when she came through the back door, stomping snow from her boots. She kissed each of them on the cheek, trying to look into their eyes to determine if anything suspicious had happened during the day. But nothing seemed out of the ordinary.

As they were sitting down to dinner there was a knock at the front door. Lilly gave a start then looked sheepishly at the kids when they both stared at her. "Mom, you're jumpy tonight," Tighe said. "I'll get the door."

"No!" Lilly said a bit too loudly. Then, in a quieter voice she said, "You keep eating. I'll see who it is."

It was Bill. In her stress-addled mind Lilly had forgotten. "Have you told the kids?" he whispered when she stood aside to let him in. She shook her head. He accompanied her into the kitchen.

"Hey, Uncle Bill," the kids said in unison. He kissed Laurel and shook hands with Tighe.

"Have you eaten?" Lilly asked. "The kids made dinner and it's delicious." Bill rubbed his hands together.

"Looks good. Don't mind if I do," he said, walking to the cupboard and helping himself to a plate and a water glass. He opened a drawer and took out flatware then sat down at the table. Lilly placed a slab of roast beef on his plate and surrounded it with vegetables that had been in the slow cooker most of the day.

"Mm. This is delicious," he said. Though he had been divorced for three years, he still hadn't learned how to cook and most of his meals were of the microwave variety. He lived alone and didn't have any kids, so he didn't have to listen to anyone complaining. His gaze went from Laurel to Tighe. "Surely your mother didn't teach you how to cook this well," he said, winking at them.

"Well, Mom and Noley," Laurel said with a smile, looking at Lilly. Tighe laughed in agreement.

"Guys, I'll clean up. You go upstairs and get your homework done," Lilly said when dinner was over. They agreed readily and left the room before Lilly could change her mind and ask them to help with the dishes.

When Lilly and Bill were alone he started clearing the table. "So tell me everything from the beginning," he said.

She went to the foot of the stairs to make sure the kids were out of hearing range then returned to the kitchen. She told him how Beau had appeared at the shop that morning, how he had not left right away despite her requests, and how he had possibly also visited the shop the night before. Bill listened without interrupting, his face grim.

When Lilly finished speaking Bill had some questions for her.

"Have you seen him around this neighborhood?"

Lilly shuddered. "No. Believe me, I would have called you the second I saw him."

"Make sure you do if he comes around. I'll tell everyone down at the station to keep their eyes open for a skier from out of town."

"You just described almost everyone in Juniper Junction," Lilly said dryly. "Do you really think he'll come around here?"

Bill shrugged. "I don't know, but it seems logical. He found your store and he went to see if you still lived in the old house. Makes sense that he might want to know where you live now. Make sure you keep the doors locked all the time. Are you going to tell the kids?"

"I'll probably tell them something just so they know it's important to keep the doors locked, but I don't think I'll tell them the whole truth." She paused for a moment, a horrid thought occurring to her. "You don't think Beau was the one who broke in here, do you?"

Bill shook his head, still chewing. When he had swallowed he said, "I doubt it. Why would he do that? Besides, I'm not entirely convinced that door handle didn't just break. That happens sometimes, you know."

"I know. Maybe that's what it was, but I can't be sure. It's totally possible that someone was in here."

Bill changed the subject. "How much do the kids know about Beau?"

"Just that he left when Laurel was a baby and Tighe was a toddler and I never heard from him again."

"Do you think they're interested in knowing more about him?"

"I don't know. I'm not interested in sharing more about him, that's for sure. There really isn't too much more to share."

Bill dried a pan and set it on the counter. "On to other matters, as long as we're done talking about Beau for now."

"I suppose we are."

"Several people in the office have mentioned to me that things may not be looking too good for you right now, what with your fingerprints being on the necklace that was used to strangle Eden Barclay and you being the one who found her."

"Yeah, but what do they expect?" Lilly asked, her hands on her hips. "Of course my fingerprints are on the necklace! I've been trying to sell it. And of course I found her! She was on the floor of my store and I open up every day!" She was getting worked up into a frenzy of anger, disbelief, and apprehension. Could they really arrest her for Eden's murder? She sat down heavily at the table. "This can't be happening. What am I going to tell the kids if the police break down my door and drag me off to jail for something I didn't do?"

"Easy does it," Bill said, sitting down across from her. "The kids know as well as I do that you didn't kill Eden. The police are just following the evidence. More evidence will turn up that points in another direction, I'm sure. But it might take a while. Can you think of any reason someone may have had it in for Eden?"

Lilly shook her head. "Nothing other than what I've already told the detectives—that Eden made everyone mad because she was always complaining about something along Main Street. Either the sidewalks weren't even or a tree branch was blocking the name of her store or any number of things like that. Little stuff."

"Make sure you call me if you think of anything else. It's important."

"Believe me, I know that. I'll call if I think of anything." She pushed her chair back and hugged her brother. "Thanks for coming over. I don't know what I'd do if you had a regular job and couldn't tell me everything that goes on in the police department."

"I can't tell you everything, but I can give you a heads-up when necessary," he said with a smile. "Make sure the doors are locked, get some sleep, and try to remember it's Christmastime. You're supposed to be happy and festive."

Lilly rolled her eyes and swatted his arm. He left and she locked the door behind him, double- and triple-checking it. Then she let Barney out and scanned the backyard carefully as he did his thing in the snow. When he came bounding up the back steps, she let him in, wiped off his paws, and locked the door, double-checking it, too. Since the locksmith had changed the lock, she felt more secure, but she still wasn't taking any chances. She tousled Barney's fur, thankful that he could be trusted to alert her if anyone came to the house who didn't belong. Beau was allergic to dogs, or so he had told her, so she hadn't gotten Barney until long after Beau left.

She and Barney went upstairs and she bid each of the kids goodnight. They were both busy doing homework, listening to music, and checking social media. Laurel was also on the phone. Lilly couldn't imagine how they got anything done, but it seemed to work for them.

The next morning Beau was on her mind as soon as she got out of bed. As she drank her coffee in the kitchen and the kids grabbed food and backpacks before leaving for school, she stopped them for a moment. "I want you both to make sure that the doors are locked all the time as soon as you get home from school," she warned. "I don't want either of you in the house without the doors being locked."

"Okay. Why the concern all of a sudden?" Tighe asked.

Lilly looked into her coffee. "No particular reason. I just got thinking that since it's Christmastime, it's prime season for burglars. That's all."

She could see Tighe watching her through narrowed eyes, but he didn't say anything. How did that kid know when she was trying to lie? She gazed into her coffee as if the future were on its surface, written in cream.

"Did you leave something for us to make for dinner tonight?" Laurel asked.

"Oh, I almost forgot. I have a Chamber of Commerce holiday happy hour tonight, so you two are on your own for dinner. Would you mind taking Gran some leftovers?"

"All right," Laurel replied. "What time will you be home?"

"I'm hoping by eight," Lilly replied. "I hate these things, so I'll try to slip out early."

Laurel grinned. "Okay. See you later." She blew a kiss to Lilly and left in a hurry.

"Bye, honey."

Tighe came over and pecked Lilly on the cheek before following his sister out the door. "Be careful, Mom."

"I will. Have a good day."

As soon as the kids left Lilly hurried to finish getting ready for work then she left, too. She gave thanks, not for the first time, that Barney was still young enough to hold his bladder until the kids got home early in the afternoon. Lilly supposed she could always ask Noley to come over to let Barney out, but she hated to impose on her friend like that.

Despite the rhythm that was returning to her days at the shop, Lilly couldn't help feeling a little jumpy every time the front door opened. It wasn't that she was afraid of the murderer coming back—she was afraid of the police coming for her. She worried that an officer would come to arrest her while she was talking to a customer or, worse, that she would be arrested at home in front of the kids. By the time evening came and it was time to lock up the shop, Lilly was ready for a drink at the Chamber of Commerce happy hour.

CHAPTER 13

L illy left the shop after checking the locks one last time, then got into her car and drove just a block up Main Street to Pine Tree Pub and Grill. She didn't usually drive such a short distance when she could walk, but she didn't relish the thought of having to return to her car alone down the alley behind Main Street after the party.

By the time Lilly walked into the pub, the Chamber of Commerce holiday mixer was in full swing. For a group of normally-staid business owners, this group could get a little rowdy when wassail and other forms of good cheer were added to the mix. She hung up her coat on an already-stuffed rack near the front door, then turned around to start greeting people.

When she faced the room she scanned the crowd quickly to get an estimate of the head count. Of course, not everyone there was a member of the Chamber of Commerce, but she knew most of them were. She was chatting with one of the owners of a floral shop when she caught a glimpse of a familiar face in the back corner of the bar, sitting alone in a booth, taking a pull from a bottle of beer. Beau.

It was a good thing she was in the middle of a conversation

when she spotted him or she might have been tempted to stride over to him and demand that he leave. Of course, she couldn't very well do that when he hadn't done anything and they were in a public place, but she probably would have done it anyway. She decided the best course of action was to ignore him and hope he left soon.

As president of the Juniper Junction Chamber of Commerce, it was Lilly's thankless job to schmooze at these mixers with all the Main Street business owners, not just the ones she liked. There was a mixer each month and though the locations rotated, the same Chamber of Commerce members were almost always in attendance. And not all of them were team players. Eden, for example, had been notorious for using the mixers to lodge gossipy complaints against her fellow small business owners. There was the year she had been miffed over one store's decision to display a menorah rather than Christmas decorations, saying the menorah looked "out of place" on Main Street. Lilly had been infuriated. There was the time Eden was angry because the sidewalk in front of her store was the last one to be cleared of snow by the public works department. That may have had something to do with Eden's earlier complaint that the members of the public works department didn't deserve holiday bonuses because taxpayers hadn't approved of such "frivolous" spending. The worst incident of all had occurred at a summer Chamber of Commerce mixer—Eden had accused the mayor of Juniper Junction of embezzling funds to build an addition on her already-large and beautiful home. Of course, there had been no evidence to suggest that what Eden said was true, but it nonetheless ruffled some very important feathers.

But Eden wasn't at this party. *Maybe*, thought Lilly, *this mixer will go smoothly since Eden isn't here. I hope so—I want to be changing into pajamas within the hour.*

She had just accepted a glass of white wine from the bartender when she spotted Herb Knight making his way toward her. He appeared a little agitated, which belied his occupation. As owner of Namaste, one of Juniper Junction's two yoga studios, Herb had discovered long ago that when a yogi loses his or her temper in public, it is not good for business.

There was something in Herb's look which warned Lilly that the conversation to come might not be entirely yogi-esque.

"Hello, Herb. I didn't get a chance to ask you at the diner the other night—how's business this season?"

"It would be better if we could get that vote on whether to allow chain stores on Main Street," he said, his voice taking on a slight edge.

"I'm not sure this is the best time or place to discuss the issue," Lilly replied lightly.

Herb gestured toward her with his drink, a clear, fizzy liquid with a lime floating in it. Herb was a teetotaler, so Lilly supposed it was club soda in the glass. "You just don't seem to understand the impact that those stores can have on the rest of us who own businesses in town."

"I understand it perfectly, Herb," Lilly said, a tinge of annoyance creeping into her tone. "But what you don't seem to understand is that those stores, while they might bring more people into Juniper Junction, would also introduce a host of problems that the town is not equipped to deal with."

"You just don't want the competition," Herb sneered, keeping his voice low. "Eden was the same way—she didn't want the big stores in here, either. I can't believe how short-sighted you are." He was becoming more agitated as he spoke. Club soda spilled from the top of his glass and he flicked droplets off his shirt.

For once Eden was right, Lilly thought with a grimace. Aloud she said, "Herb, competition has nothing to do with it. The issue is the integrity of the downtown area in Juniper Junction. National chain stores will change the atmosphere of Main Street —permanently and not for the better. Could we discuss this some other time, please?"

"We're going to have this out right here," Herb said, his voice a little louder now.

"Herb, what are you drinking?" Lilly asked. "Is that vodka in your glass?"

"None of your business, you pretentious bat." Lilly looked around for someone who could intervene and caught the eye of George Stone, owner of a men's clothing shop. George sauntered over, seeing that Lilly might need some assistance.

"Hey there, Herb. What's new?" George asked, clapping Herb on the back. Herb fixed George with a withering glare.

"This dolt won't admit the real reason for not wanting the chain stores along Main Street," Herb accused. His voice was loud enough now that people were starting to pause their own conversations to listen to what was going on between Herb and Lilly.

"Easy there, Herb," George said. He chuckled. "Isn't there some deep breathing exercise or pose or something you could do right now to calm down?"

Lilly watched as Herb put his glass down on the nearest table and took a menacing step toward George. Though he wasn't likely to do any more than that because of George's size and proportions, she hurriedly stepped between the two men. "Herb, stop it. George is merely trying to lighten this situation. You need to leave if you're going to behave this way."

Ivy Leachman, a local artist whose paint-your-own-pottery shop was located up the block from Lilly's jewelry store, walked up to the small group. "Herb is right, Lilly," she said in her high, tight voice. "We need those stores along Main Street. They can provide us with a much-needed infusion of tax dollars. Those tax dollars can be earmarked to pay for the infrastructure needs of Juniper Junction."

You've got to be kidding me, Lilly thought. *There's no way I'm going to be in pajamas by eight.* "Ivy, as I said to Herb, this is a holiday party. Let's not ruin the atmosphere by fighting over something that isn't going to happen in the near future anyway."

"But you're a big part of the reason it's not going to be happening soon," Marcia Blakely chimed in. Marcia owned a vintage record store and looked the type. With her long straight hair and rose-tinted glasses, she looked like she had stepped straight out of Woodstock onto Main Street.

Things were going from bad to worse. "Oh, my gosh. Listen, everyone. Can we have this discussion at our next Chamber meeting? This is not the place to be debating the chain store issue," Lilly pleaded. "Let's not ruin the festivities with arguments."

Ivy and Marcia turned around, grumbling, and went back to their conversations. Herb scowled at Lilly and followed the women to their table. Though she tried to ignore the three of them the rest of the evening, Lilly couldn't help noticing the dark looks they sent her way every time she was in their sight lines.

Not long after that Noley walked through the door of the pub and she made a beeline toward her. She felt a surge of relief.

"Sorry I'm late," Noley said, shrugging her coat off. "I was working on a salad dressing and I just can't seem to get it right, so I'm taking a break." Noley attended most of the Chamber of Commerce mixers because she sold her baked goods at so many of the shops in town. She was friendly with many of the store owners and liked an excuse to see them socially.

"I wish I'd been late," Lilly said ruefully.

"What happened?"

"That Herb Knight came up to me and started in again on the chain store thing. I swear, for a yogi he's the most stubborn, single-minded person I know."

"He refuses to sell my stuff in his store," Noley said. "I came up with a fantastic granola bar studded with dried fruits and nuts, then suggested to him that he provide treats for his customers for an after-workout snack, but he calls baked goods 'poison.'"

"And now he's sitting over there with Ivy and Marcia, no doubt plotting my demise," Lilly said in a low voice. "I swear, those three are a trifecta of misery."

Noley gave her friend a sympathetic smile and took her by the elbow. "You could use another glass of wine and I need something stiff," she said.

Servers from the pub were butlering around trays of small hors d'oeuvres and Lilly and Noley helped themselves. Noley bit into a tiny tomato tart and frowned. "Too much salt," she said.

"Can you ever just go out and enjoy yourself?" Lilly teased.

"No. Hence the stiff drink," Noley answered. "How long are you staying?"

"I'm going to leave as soon as I can," Lilly said. "I'm tired and this mixer has not been the festive occasion I imagined it to be." She lowered her voice. "And Beau is here. I've ignored him since I walked in." She cast a sidelong glance toward the table in the corner where she had spotted Beau earlier. He had left. "Good. He's gone," she murmured. "I feel better about leaving now. I was afraid I'd leave and he would come over and start gossiping to everyone about me."

She mingled while she waited for Noley to finish her drink and speak to a few friends, then the women left together. They parted ways on the street and Lilly drove home through the lightly falling snow, exhausted and ready to crawl into bed. When she walked inside the kids were fighting over who had to finish the dishes.

"Mom, I loaded the dishwasher. Tighe has to clean the table and the counters." Laurel crossed her arms over her torso.

"I didn't even eat the gross dinner she made. I had to eat cereal so she should have to finish the dishes herself." Tighe stuck out his tongue.

"That's stupid. It's not my fault you don't know good food when you see it."

"It's not stupid. Gran didn't even want it. She only ate it to be nice."

"You're a jerk!"

"So are you!"

"Stop it, both of you. I've had a long day and I can't listen to the fighting right now. Tighe, it couldn't have been that bad. And even if it was, you should keep those opinions to yourself."

"Yeah," Laurel chimed in.

Tighe gave his sister a look of disdain and started walking out of the kitchen.

"Wait, come back," Lilly directed. "I want you both to finish the dishes. Laurel, you clean the counters and Tighe, you clean the table."

"That's not fair," Tighe whined.

"Life isn't fair," Lilly answered. "Hustle up. Is your homework done?"

"Yes," Laurel answered.

"Nick came over and they did homework together," Tighe said with a sly glance at Laurel. She shook her head ever so slightly and gave Tighe a dark look. He smiled in return.

"Laurel, you know I don't want him here unless I'm here. You should have asked."

"If I'd asked you would have said no," she said, pouting.

"Then don't bother asking."

"But Tighe was here," Laurel said. "He was watching. All we did was homework, I swear."

"I believe you, but I need to know that you're safe here when I'm at work. I don't need to be worrying about you on top of everything else."

Just then the phone rang. Lilly glanced at the caller ID; it was her mother. She closed her eyes. "It's Gran. You two finish up and I'll talk to her."

"Hi, Mom," she answered. The kids turned away and got to work.

"You'll never guess who paid me a visit this evening," her mother began.

"Who?"

"Beau. Do you remember him? What a delightful young man."

Lilly glanced at the kids, who were not speaking to each other. She didn't want them to hear this conversation.

"Just a sec, Mom." She headed upstairs and closed her bedroom door while her mother waited on the phone. Her mother was clearly having one of her bad days. She must have forgotten, at least temporarily, that Beau had caused no end of misery while she was married to him.

Lilly sat down on her bed. Often she tried to humor her mother when she was confused, but she couldn't do it this time. "Mom," she said in a quiet voice, "you may not remember that Beau and I were married. He was not a nice person and I'm sure he hasn't changed. I knew he's come back to Juniper Junction and I'm trying to avoid him. If he comes back to your house I want you to call Bill."

"Oh, that's a good idea. Bill probably hasn't seen him yet." Lilly's mom clearly wasn't getting the message. Lilly gave up.

"You know what, Mom? You're right. It's been a long time since Bill saw Beau. I think I'll call Bill right now and maybe they can meet up to talk."

"You do that, my dear. I'll see you tomorrow." Lilly's mom hung up. Lilly flung herself backward onto her bed. Life was indeed getting more complicated.

CHAPTER 14

S he went back downstairs to put the phone on its cradle and the kids had decided they weren't mad at each other anymore. Tighe was telling an inappropriate joke and Laurel was laughing. Lilly smiled. At least one thing was going right, even if it did take an off-color joke to get them to stop fighting.

When they went upstairs Lilly opened the refrigerator door. The dinner Laurel had made sat in a glass baking dish on the middle shelf, congealing into a lumpy, chartreuse mess. Lilly wondered what it was. Against her better judgment, she took a spoonful of it, placed it on a small plate, and microwaved it for a few seconds. Tasting it, she could understand why Tighe had cereal for dinner. *Poor Laurel*, Lilly thought. *She went to all the trouble of making dinner and it turned out awful. Welcome to womanhood, my child.* How many times had Lilly made something the kids refused to eat? She smiled to herself. At some point it was every parent's joy to know that what goes around, comes around. But still, Tighe should have been nicer about it.

Lilly picked up the phone again while she was scraping her morsel of dinner into the trash. She dialed Bill and wasn't surprised when he answered on the first ring.

"What's up?" he asked in greeting.

"Beau went to Mom's house."

She knew Bill was waiting to compose himself before saying anything. After several long seconds he spoke. "When was this?"

"Earlier tonight. I just got off the phone with her."

"How did he get in?"

"I didn't ask. I'm sure she let him in. She doesn't remember that he was my husband. She called him 'delightful.'"

"I'm going over there right now. Going into a public place to talk to you is one thing, but showing up at Mom's house is another. I'll call you when I've talked to her." He hung up.

Lilly knew another restless night lay ahead. Armed with a book, the house phone, and her cell, she crawled into bed to wait to hear from Bill.

It wasn't long before he called back. "I talked to Mom," he began. "She doesn't remember talking to him. Doesn't that figure?"

"I'm not surprised. She's not having one of her good days."

"Do you suppose she *thinks* he visited when he really didn't?"

"It's too coincidental, don't you think? I mean, he shows up out of nowhere for the first time in years and suddenly she thinks he's been at her house when she probably hasn't given him a thought in the last decade? I doubt it. I'm sure he was at her house. The question is, why would he go over there?"

"I don't know. I'll be looking out for him, though, and when I find him I'll tell him to stay the heck away from you and Mom and the kids and everyone else."

"Maybe we won't see him again," Lilly said, a trace of hope in her voice.

"Don't count on it," Bill advised. "Make sure your doors are locked."

"I did. I told the kids I want the doors locked at all times when they're home, too."

"Good."

That night Lilly was haunted by a dream that had been a

recurring one a long time ago. The kids were tiny. Beau had just left and she wondered how she was going to raise her babies on her own. In her dream, the kids would both cry and Lilly couldn't get them to stop. No matter what she tried, they kept wailing. When she jerked awake from the dream, her own cheeks were wet with tears. She sighed and turned over to go back to sleep, but sleep wouldn't come. Finally she went downstairs and put on the coffee pot, then went to her desk in the den and returned to the kitchen with a sketch book. She drank several cups of coffee while new ideas for jewelry designs emerged from the tip of her pencil. This wasn't the first time she had designed jewelry in the middle of the night—in fact, some of her customers' best-loved designs were born in the wee hours of the nights Lilly couldn't sleep.

The next day Lilly got to work a little later than usual. She had drunk several cups of coffee in the night and her stomach was feeling the effects. She took an antacid when she got to work, then turned on the lights and unlocked the front door. She had turned toward one of the jewelry cases toward the back of the store when the door jingled. She turned around to greet her first customer of the day.

Her stomach sank. It wasn't a customer, but two police officers. One of them walked up to her while the other stayed at the front of the store.

"Ms. Carlsen," he began, "we'd like to ask you a few questions."

"How can I help you?" she asked, her stomach twisting.

"Do you know a Herb Knight?"

"Yes. He owns a yoga studio in town."

"Were you with him last night?"

"I saw him at the Chamber of Commerce mixer at Pine Tree Pub. Why? Is something wrong with Herb?" She swallowed hard, dreading the answer.

"He's dead."

CHAPTER 15

L illy gasped. "What happened? How did he die?"

"That's what we're hoping you can help us determine," the officer answered. "Did the two of you speak last night?"

"Yes." Lilly wrinkled her brow, thinking back to the unpleasant conversation.

"And what did you talk about?"

"Herb was angry because I'm opposed to national chain stores coming to Juniper Junction. He wants to allow them."

"So you argued with him?"

"It's more like he argued with me. I was trying to get him to stop arguing and talk about the issue at a town council meeting or a Chamber of Commerce meeting. Last night's function was really supposed to be a holiday mixer, not a time to discuss business."

"How did the argument end?"

"George Stone sort of came to my rescue. He's a pretty big guy and I think he intimidated Herb just by his physical presence. Eventually Herb stopped bothering me and he and two other women went to sit down."

"Who were the other women?"

"Ivy Leachman and Marcia Blakely. They're friends with Herb."

"What happened then?"

"I don't know, but they were shooting me some pretty hateful looks. I didn't talk to any of them for the rest of the evening."

"And how long did you stay at the party?"

"I didn't stay for much longer after that. My friend Noley came in and I waited for her to have a drink then we left at the same time."

"Where did you go?"

"I went home. I assume Noley went to her house, too."

"And you were alone when you went home?"

"I was in my car by myself, then when I got home my kids were there."

"And they can confirm this?"

This is sounding more and more like the questions the police asked when Eden died, Lilly thought. "Of course they can," she said.

"Where were you between seven and eight o'clock this morning?"

Lilly narrowed her eyes. "Am I a suspect?" she asked.

"Not at this time, ma'am, but we do need the answers to these questions."

"Should I call a lawyer?"

"That's your decision, ma'am."

Lilly thought for a minute. She didn't have anything to hide; all she could do was tell the truth.

"I was at home, getting ready for work."

"Can your kids confirm that?"

"No, sir. No one can. The kids left for school before seven."

"Neighbors? Anyone?"

For the second time recently, Lilly found herself hoping Mrs. Laforge was up to her nosy activities. "You can check with my neighbor, Mrs. Laforge. Her house is to the left of mine.

She seems to know everything that goes on in the neighborhood."

The officer made a notation in his notebook. "We'll speak to her."

"Would you mind coming down to the station to make a statement?" the officer asked.

"I can't leave my store."

"Is there someone who can mind the shop while you're at the station?"

"I don't know. Maybe my friend Noley." Lilly was starting to get more nervous now. Was she a suspect?

"Can you call her?"

Lilly pulled her cell phone from her pocket and dialed Noley's number with fingers that shook slightly. "Noley? Can you come down to the store?"

"What's wrong?"

"The police are here. Herb Knight is dead and they want me to go down to the police station to give them a statement."

Noley gasped. "Herb's dead? How? They don't think you did it, do they?"

"Yes, I don't know, and I hope not. But since he was arguing with me at the mixer last night…" Her voice trailed off.

"I'll be right there." Noley hung up.

"My friend is going to come down to watch the shop while I go to the police station," Lilly said. "She'll be here soon." The officer nodded and walked over to where his partner still stood by the front door. They were obviously going to wait there until Noley showed up.

She arrived within ten minutes. She banged on the back door and one of the officers accompanied Lilly to the office to let her in.

"I don't know anything about jewelry," Noley said.

"You don't have to do anything except talk to any customers who come in," Lilly said. "You won't be able to get into the vault to show them anything that isn't on display, but you can just show them what's in the display cases and tell them that I had to leave for an emergency. If they want to see more stuff, they can come back later today or any other day and I'll help them. You can even give them my cell number and they can call me with any questions. In the meantime, every piece on display has a tiny tag below the display telling what the piece is made of —you know, the stone, the length of the chain, et cetera."

"Gotcha," Noley said. "Don't worry about a thing."

"Can I drive my own car?" Lilly asked the officers. They nodded. One left through the front door and got into the cruiser parked out front. He drove away, presumably around to the alley in back of the store. Lilly grabbed her purse as she walked through the office, then locked the back door behind her. Sure enough, the police cruiser was making its way down the alley. He pulled up slowly next to her car. The second officer climbed in next to his partner and they waited for Lilly to pull out. Evidently they were going to follow her to the police station.

This stinks, Lilly thought. *I'm definitely a suspect. They won't even trust me to go to the police station without an escort.* Keeping an eye on the speedometer, Lilly drove to the police station. *It would be just my luck to get a speeding ticket on the way there,* she thought with a frown. *Darn that Herb Knight. Why did he have to pick a fight with me last night? It's just like him to drag me into his own death.*

CHAPTER 16

W hen she arrived at the station the officers walked in with her, flanking her on each side. They asked her to wait in the lobby. She sat down and watched as the officers disappeared into the front office and spoke to one of the clerks at the desk, who shot Lilly a quick look and nodded. All the officers disappeared into the bowels of the building, leaving the desk unattended.

While Lilly sat waiting, a wispy woman with long gray hair walked into the lobby and stood waiting at the front desk. When no one came to help her after several minutes she sat down on the floor across from Lilly. Lilly gave her a puzzled look because all the other chairs were empty, but the woman didn't see the look because she had closed her eyes and was taking a long, deep breath. She blew it out with startling force, making a loud, rather obnoxious noise. Lilly glanced at her again, alarmed.

The woman kept her eyes closed and repeated the process. Then she crossed her legs into a pretzel-looking shape and let her arms hang down at her sides. Then she opened her eyes and noticed Lilly watching her intently.

"Do you practice yoga?" the woman asked in a quiet, soothing voice.

"No."

"You should try it. It makes places like this much more bearable."

Lilly nodded. She disagreed with the woman. There was nothing short of a large measure of scotch that would make this place more bearable.

"What are you doing here?" the woman asked.

She's as nosy as Mrs. Laforge, Lilly thought. *I wonder if they're related.* "I'm here to give a statement about something," she replied.

"I'm here because I found a dead body this morning," the woman replied. She spoke in a matter-of-fact tone, as if it was a perfectly normal thing to find a dead body.

"I'm sorry to hear that," Lilly murmured.

"It was my yoga instructor. A lovely man. He just radiated joy."

There's another dead yogi? Lilly thought. *She can't possibly be talking about Herb. He was the least joyful person in town.*

"You don't mean Herb Knight."

"Then you knew him?" The woman's face lit up like the star of Bethlehem. *Please, God, don't let her start swooning.*

"I did," Lilly said.

"Then you know what a wonderful man he was," she gushed.

"Hmm," Lilly replied noncommittally.

Thankfully one of the officers came to the front to escort Lilly to an office and the clerk returned to the front desk and tended to the yoga woman. If she was enamored with Herb, then there was only one explanation: she was in shock from finding a dead body.

Lilly sat down across from the officer at the desk. He flipped on a tape recorder which sat between them and proceeded to question Lilly about what happened the previous night between her and Herb Knight. She recounted the details as she remembered them, all the while wondering what would happen if her blood pressure skyrocketed to the point where she had a stroke in the police station. It was probably just protocol to have her give a statement at the police station after the death of someone she had argued with so recently, but the stress of thinking she might actually be a suspect in Herb's death, so soon after Eden's death, was unnerving to say the least.

When she was ready to leave the station the officer escorted her to the lobby. Bill was just coming in.

"What are you doing here?" he asked in surprise.

Lilly nodded toward the officer who stood nearby. "Answering some questions about Herb Knight."

"Why?"

"I'll explain later."

"I've been out at one of the slopes all night. Seems someone deliberately jammed up the ski lift and I had to question everyone who was there, which was about a million people." He looked at the other officer. "You'll fill me in, I'm sure." The officer nodded solemnly. Bill glanced at Lilly, but she didn't return his look. She wanted to get back to the shop as quickly as possible.

When she arrived she found Noley talking to three customers at once, regaling them with stories about her experiences as a chef. Noley glanced up and saw Lilly.

"Ah, here's the woman with all the answers," Noley said, indicating Lilly with a wave of her hand. "Lilly is the owner of the shop and the finest jewelry designer you'll find anywhere. My work here is done, so I'll be off. It was wonderful to meet all of you." To Lilly she added, "I'll talk to you later."

"Thanks very much," Lilly said, giving Noley a grateful look. Then she turned to the three customers. "How can I help you?" she asked.

There were a husband and wife and a single man. The husband and wife were looking for a necklace to give the husband's mother for Christmas. Money was apparently no object, so Lilly steered them toward the more expensive items, such as the chains with diamond and ruby pendants.

Lilly had learned that, in general, the amount of time customers spent picking out a piece of jewelry correlated indirectly with the amount of money they were planning to spend. People with more money took less time to pick out what they wanted; people with less money took more time. Lilly was glad this couple was no exception to the norm, because they had left the shop within thirty minutes, having purchased a heavy gold chain with a stunning diamond pendant in the shape of a teardrop, its edges studded with tiny sapphires.

The other customer had been waiting patiently for the couple to leave. When Lilly turned to him, she apologized for not being able to help him sooner.

"That's all right," the man responded.

"How can I help you?" she asked.

"I'm Jim Barclay. Eden's husband."

CHAPTER 17

Lilly looked at Mr. Barclay in surprise. "Oh!" she exclaimed. "I'm sorry for your loss, Mr. Barclay." Her hands started to sweat. Was he here to accuse her of murder? Was he going to exact revenge? She took a deep breath. Her imagination was getting the better of her.

"Thank you. I hope you don't mind me coming into your shop. I have a couple questions for you."

Lilly was about to board the panic train when the man hastened to add, "I'm not here to accuse you of anything." Lilly wasn't sure whether she should believe him, but she listened as he continued. "What I really want to know is what the police may have told you. I'm not getting very far with them. Obviously when a married person dies, the spouse is the first one the cops think of, but I didn't kill her. They've left me alone since they confirmed my alibi, but they're not sharing any information with me."

"I'm kind of in the same boat," Lilly replied. "They're not sharing any information with me, either."

"I'm wondering if they said anything to you about Jed

Horstman, Eden's first husband." *Eden had found not one, but two, men who were willing to marry her?*

"This is the first I'm hearing about him," Lilly said.

"He's a mechanic here in Juniper Junction at Horstman Auto Repair. I haven't seen him or heard anything about him since Eden died, but there was no love lost there."

"No one has said anything to me about him," Lilly said.

Jim leaned in closer and lowered his voice. "I shared this information with the police. I just hope they're including Jed in their investigation."

"What information?" Lilly asked quickly, her body tensing.

"Jed and Eden have a son together, my stepson Davey. He's in high school."

"I know. My son mentioned that he goes to school with Davey."

"Yes. Well, Davey will be going off to college in two years. He doesn't know where he wants to go yet, but that's not really important. What's important is that the divorce decree says that Eden and Jed are to share equally in paying for Davey's tuition."

Lilly wasn't sure where this was heading. She nodded for Jim to continue.

"Jed has been harassing Eden lately about tuition. He assumes she makes—made—more than he does, so he's insisting that Eden pay more toward tuition. Problem is, he's wrong about that. I suppose you already know that the general store wasn't doing very well when Eden died. She tried to keep it a secret, but she was going to lose the store before the middle of next year if things didn't get much better. She told Jed that she couldn't afford to pay more than the divorce judge required of her, but he wouldn't listen. Said she was lying."

Lilly hadn't known about Eden's financial situation. "Okay, so Jed thought Eden made more than she did. That would have been easy enough for her to prove just by going back to court."

"But that's not all," Jim said. "Eden had a life insurance

policy in the amount of one million dollars. Davey is the beneficiary of that money."

The light was beginning to dawn on Lilly. "So if Eden died, Davey would get the million dollars and tuition might not be such a problem."

"Exactly." Jim stared at Lilly. "My theory is that Jed killed her so that Davey would get the money and Jed wouldn't have to worry about paying for Davey to go to college anymore."

"Wow," Lilly breathed.

"Eden didn't buy the life insurance policy until after we were married," Jim said. "So normally it's not something Jed would even be aware of. But here's the kicker. Jed's current wife works for the insurance agency where Eden bought the policy. All she had to do was mention it to Jed one day after work and Jed would know everything."

"And the police know this?" Lilly asked.

"I told them. Whether they followed up or not is another question. That's why I wondered if they had said anything to you about Jed."

"No," Lilly answered, shaking her head. "But my brother works on the force. I can ask him about it."

Jim pulled a card from the inside of his jacket. "Here's my contact information. If you find out anything, will you let me know?"

"Sure. Thanks for coming by."

Lilly shook her head as she watched Jim Barclay walk out the front door. *Is it possible that Eden was killed by her ex so he wouldn't have to pay for their son's college tuition? Maybe he didn't intend to kill her. But she was in this store. Whoever followed her in here meant her harm. Why did she come in here, anyway?*

Another couple came into the shop just then, interrupting Lilly's thoughts, and she spent the rest of the day helping the growing number of customers who came in as the day started to warm up outdoors.

She left the shop right on time that night and hurried home so she could call Bill. She had a lot of questions to ask him.

She called on his cell; he was at their mother's house when he answered. "I'm making dinner for Mom," Lilly told him. "Once I drop it off maybe you can come over to my house so we can talk about a few things. I don't want to talk in front of Mom."

"Agreed," he said. In a whisper he added, "She thinks I'm Dad."

Lilly grimaced. Her mother's lucid days were getting fewer and farther between. But was it really so bad that her mother thought her husband was still alive? Obviously the thought made her happy—what was wrong with that?

Lilly finished the beef and broccoli stir fry she was making then packed enough for dinner and the next day's lunch in two containers for her mother. Yelling upstairs to the kids that she would be home in a few minutes, she left, making sure the door was locked behind her.

At her mother's house she found Bill and their mom playing Scrabble on a tray in front of the television.

"Your father has never been able to beat me at Scrabble," she said proudly when Lilly walked into the living room. Lilly gave her a wide grin.

"Just wait until we play checkers," Bill said with a wink. "I'll win so fast you won't know what happened."

Their mother laughed. It was a wonderful sight to see.

"I brought you dinner, Mom. Beef and broccoli. I left it on the kitchen counter. There's another container of it in the fridge for tomorrow's lunch."

"Thank you. That sounds good. I'll go eat in a little while," Beverly said. "Now, both of you scoot. I have to watch my show." She reached for the remote next to her chair and switched the television to her favorite evening game show. Lilly and Bill both bent down to kiss their mother's cheeks and tiptoed out of the room. Beverly didn't like anyone interrupting her game show.

"Beef and broccoli, huh?" Bill asked after they had locked the door behind them and were standing in the driveway.

Lilly grinned. "I figured you'd want some. There's plenty. I'll meet you at the house." She got into her car drove away; Bill followed in a police cruiser.

Laurel was standing in the kitchen, a puzzled look on her face, when they came inside.

CHAPTER 18

"What's the matter?" Lilly asked.

"Someone just called and asked for you," she said.

"Who was it?" Lilly asked.

"Some guy. He wouldn't tell me his name. Are you dating someone and you haven't told us?" she asked, her tone faintly accusing.

"When do I have time to date anyone?" Lilly answered crossly.

"He knew my name. Well, he almost knew my name," Laurel said. Lilly had been shrugging off her coat and she stopped suddenly, her arms halfway out of the sleeves.

"What?" she asked.

"He called me Lauren. I just figured you were dating someone and you had told him about me and Tighe."

Lilly glanced at Bill, hoping Laurel wouldn't notice her sudden agitation. "It must have been someone from the Chamber of Commerce. They all know you guys," Lilly said with a nervous laugh. "Go upstairs and tell Tighe it's time for dinner." Laurel went to the foot of the stairs and yelled for Tighe.

"I could have done that myself," Lilly pointed out.

"You're welcome," Laurel said with a smirk.

Tighe came charging down the stairs. "Hey, Uncle Bill. What's for dinner, Mom?"

"Beef and broccoli stir fry. Wash your hands. You too, Laurel."

Both kids rolled their eyes and went to the kitchen sink. As their heads were bent over the soap and the faucet, Bill glanced at Lilly and gave her a *we'll talk about the phone call after dinner* look.

Dinner was delicious, though Lilly barely tasted hers. Bill helped himself to seconds, then thirds, as Lilly waited impatiently for the kids to go upstairs to do their homework. When dinner was over she offered to do the dishes.

"Thanks, Mom!" Laurel called as she ran upstairs. Tighe followed closely on her heels.

As soon as they were out of earshot Lilly fixed Bill with a jittery glare. "It was Beau. I know it was. Anyone else would have left a message or at least his name."

"I think you're probably right. I haven't been able to figure out where he's staying, but I'm going to put a guy on it at work. There's got to be a photo of Beau online somewhere. We'll find it, print it, and ask around to see if anyone recognizes him."

"And then what? He hasn't done anything technically wrong, even though he's a total creep."

"A friendly visit from a neighborhood police officer might do the trick."

"Keep me posted." She shuddered at the thought of Beau talking to the kids without them knowing who he really was.

She paused for a moment before plunging into the next topic. "Can you tell me anything about the Eden Barclay investigation?"

"I thought you'd never ask," Bill said. Then he turned serious. "You're not off the hook. Everyone on Main Street knows you didn't always get along with Eden and that she got under your skin with all her complaints. But interestingly, a passerby saw Eden and Herb talking the night Eden was murdered."

"*That's* interesting," Lilly mused. "What do you think they were talking about?"

"I have no idea. That's going to be a tough one to figure out."

"But it throws suspicion away from me, doesn't it?"

"Not exactly, but don't worry. No one is going to arrest you without evidence. Proof. They need to find a plausible alternative that has nothing to do with you."

"I've got one. How about Jed Horstman?"

"Who?"

"Jed Horstman. Eden's first husband."

"She found *two* men who wanted to marry her?"

Lilly smiled. "Yes. But that's not the point. The point is that Jed had a strong motive to kill her."

"And what was his motive?" Bill arched his eyebrows and gave her a quizzical look.

"Money. Classic motive. He knew that Eden had a life insurance policy that would pay for any college their son wanted to attend and he killed her so he wouldn't have to help pay for college."

"You know, now that you mention it, I think I did hear something about life insurance Eden had. I'll check it out. I don't know if anyone has spoken to her first husband yet."

"It's a no-brainer."

"Please don't imply the police don't have brains."

"I'm not. I'm simply saying Jed Horstman has a million reasons to kill her."

"How do you know all this?"

"Jim Barclay came by the shop to talk. He told me all about it."

"And no doubt throw suspicion away from himself," Bill added dryly.

"He said his alibi has already been confirmed."

"All right. Let me check tomorrow. In the meantime, I'm going to get online and find a photo of Beau."

"Will you recognize him?"

"Oh, I think so. I'll never forget what you said about his eyes. '*They're otherworldly. They're not the eyes of a mortal man.*'" He batted his eyelashes and spoke in a high quavery voice.

"Shut up. I was young and stupid."

"Seriously. I'll know the eyes anywhere. What else do I need to know?"

"He still looks like a skier. Long-ish hair, graying, tan, a little pudgier than he was fifteen years ago."

"Aren't we all?" Bill asked, patting his ample stomach. "I've got to go. Let me help you with the dishes and I'll skedaddle."

"No need. Just go home and find a picture of Beau. That's all I care about right now."

Bill put on his jacket and turned the doorknob. "Say, I've been meaning to ask you. Does Noley see anyone? I mean, does she have a boyfriend?"

Lilly looked at him in surprise. "No, she doesn't have a boyfriend."

"Oh. Okay. Well, I'll let you know what I find out about Beau."

"Thanks." Bill pulled the door closed behind him.

Bill likes Noley?! She thought back to the moment in the kitchen when Bill wouldn't meet Noley's gaze and Noley smiled at him like a schoolgirl. Lilly suppressed a squeal of excitement.

CHAPTER 19

T he next morning Lilly had just gotten to work and was locking the back door behind her when the phone rang. It was Bill.

"I found a picture of Beau with some bimbo in a Jacuzzi. Ski slope in the background, the whole works. God, he looks terrible. Beer belly and that pocked, veiny nose that comes from drinking too much."

Nothing else he could have said would have made Lilly happier. "Did you print it out?"

"Yup. That ugly mug is being shared with every officer in Juniper Junction as we speak. Shouldn't be long before someone spots him."

"And what happens when they do?"

"They have strict instructions to tell him to mind his own business and not to harass anyone he used to know in town."

"I hope that does the trick," Lilly fretted. "Can they find out where he's living?"

"If they ask, he doesn't have to tell them and they can't force him to answer. But it ought to be easy enough to figure it out. Maybe someone can even follow him, see where he goes."

"Thanks, Bill. I owe you one." *And I know just the thing,* Lilly thought. *A date with Noley.*

That evening Lilly had closed up the shop and was heading out to her car in the alley when she heard her name called.

"Mrs. Carlsen?" It was a quiet voice, one Lilly didn't recognize. She looked around in confusion, searching for the source of the voice.

"It's me, over here." Lilly glanced around the back of her car and there was a young woman standing there. She had short, ice-blond hair and lovely blue eyes. Lilly knew her from somewhere, but couldn't place her.

"I'm Mrs. Carlsen," Lilly said, though she never called herself "Mrs." "What can I do for you?"

"I'm Taffy. I work for Eden. That is, I did work for Eden." *That's it,* Lilly thought. *I remember her from the general store. She was always nicer than Eden.*

Taffy continued talking in a halting voice. "Now that the general store is closed, I don't have a job. Um, I came over here because I was wondering if, maybe, you know of anyone who could help me find a job. I haven't lived in town very long, so I don't really know anyone I could ask."

Lilly thought for a moment. "I don't know of anyone off the top of my head, but that doesn't mean no one is hiring. Give me your full name and your contact information and the next time I'm at a Chamber of Commerce event I'll ask around. If no one in the Chamber is hiring, maybe someone knows of an opportunity."

"I would appreciate that," Taffy said. She pulled a pad of paper and a pen out of her purse and scribbled down her name and number. Handing the paper to Lilly, she said, "It's too bad about what happened to Eden."

It took a lot of courage for this woman to come over here to talk to me in the alley, especially since I'm a person of interest in Eden's murder, Lilly thought. To Taffy she asked, "Who's taking care of the general store right now?"

Taffy shrugged. "Mr. Barclay, I guess. He told me he had to let me go because he's going to sell the store and move."

He didn't mention that to me. "Is he selling the store with everything in it?"

"I think so."

"I'm glad you came to see me, Taffy. I'm sorry that you've been a casualty of Eden's death, too. I'll do what I can to help you find something." Lilly paused, her brain working furiously. "Taffy, tell me. Have the police spoken to you about Eden?"

"Yeah, they talked to me the day her body was found."

"I know they think Eden died Wednesday night in my store. Were you at work with her that night?"

Taffy didn't seem perturbed by Lilly's questions, which was a relief. She wouldn't want to cause more grief for the woman. "We closed an hour early on Wednesday, so it was five o'clock when I left. Eden was going through the day's receipts."

Lilly nodded, hoping that her silence would compel Taffy to keep talking. It did.

"When I left the store Mr. Barclay was there. He and Eden were having such a fight."

"Really?"

Taffy nodded. "He was mad because she had lied to him about a bill and he came down to the store to have it out with her."

"A bill from the store?"

"I dunno. I got the feeling it was a bill that came to their house, so maybe not."

This *was* news. Not only was Jim Barclay was trying to sell the general store already and get out of Juniper Junction just days after Eden's death, but they had had a big fight the night she died.

"Did you tell the police about the fight?"

"Yeah." *So why hasn't Bill told me about this yet?*

"Okay. Well, I'll be in touch if I hear anything, Taffy." Taffy offered a little wave and walked down the alley while Lilly fumbled with her car keys. When Lilly saw the woman turn toward Main Street, she whipped out her phone and dialed furiously.

"Bill, someone who worked for Eden just paid me a visit."

"Who?"

"Taffy something-or-other. She says Eden and her husband were having a big fight at the general store the night Eden was murdered."

"Why do you keep talking to these people?" Bill asked after heaving an exasperated sigh.

"I don't go looking for them. She came to me. And so did Jim Barclay."

"All right, okay. Fine. Please, will you stop talking to people the minute you find out they have any connection whatsoever to Eden Barclay's death? We don't know who did it. In other words, there's a murderer out there."

Duly chastised, Lilly couldn't give up her line of questioning. "So have the police investigated the fight?"

"Yes. Jim Barclay has an alibi, remember? He told you so, and he happened to be telling you the truth. He went to some bar after the fight. He and some friend of his took a selfie that was time-stamped around the time Eden was killed. Then he stayed overnight at his sister's house. She confirmed it. Apparently he didn't want to go home after the big fight in the general store. When he got home the next morning Eden was missing. He called the police, we checked it out. It wasn't him, Lilly. I know you don't want to hear that."

"It wasn't me, either. I'm just tired of worrying that I'm going to be arrested and charged with something I didn't do."

"Let me get off the phone so I can get back to work and find out who *did* do it. And please don't go asking questions that are better left to the police."

"Okay, I'll try." That was the best he was going to get from her. "Oh, before you go, have you heard anything about Beau?"

"Nothing. But someone'll see him, don't worry. He hasn't

bothered to stay hidden since coming back to town, so I don't expect him to go into hiding now."

After she hung up Lilly drove home through the darkened streets. When she turned down her cul-de-sac she could see a pickup truck parked in front of her house. *Who's that? If Laurel has brought Nick over here without my permission, I'll let her have it.*

She pulled into the driveway and was gathering up her belongings when there was a knock on the driver's side window. Lilly jumped and let out a gasp, then looked up into the face staring back at her.

CHAPTER 20

"Beau?" She reached for her cell phone and held it in her hand while Beau held his hands in a praying gesture, obviously not wanting her to call anyone. She rolled down the window a couple inches.

"What are you doing here?" she seethed.

"I came to talk to you."

"You're not welcome here. Now get lost."

"Wait. Please, Lilly. We need to talk. Please open the car door and let me talk to you."

"You can talk to me just fine through the open window. Why are you here?"

"I thought we could get together for a bite to eat."

"No way."

"Please? We'll go somewhere well-lit with lots of people, I promise."

"No."

"I need to talk to you about something. It's important."

"There is nothing you could say to me that I would find even a little bit important."

"Please, Lilly. Hear me out." Lilly glanced at the house. No one seemed to have noticed that she was home yet. Even Barney.

"Have you been inside the house?" she demanded, her eyes narrowing.

Beau held up his hands with an *I surrender* gesture. "No. Really, I haven't."

"Then why isn't the dog going nuts that I'm home?"

"How do I know?" Taking a deep breath, Lilly rolled down the window a little bit further and sighed.

"If I go with you, will you stop bothering me?"

"It's not my intention to bother you." *A non-answer if I ever heard one.*

"Okay, then, follow me." She rolled down her window and put the car in reverse while she waited for him to get away from her car. She backed down the driveway and pulled out into the street as he ran to his car and hopped in. In just a moment he had driven around the bend of the cul-de-sac and pulled up behind her. She pulled out her phone to call the kids. Let him wait.

"Laurel? It's Mom. I'm going to grab something to eat at the diner on Main. Do you want me to pick up something for you and Tighe?"

"Just a sec. I'll ask him." Lilly could hear Laurel yelling for Tighe. They carried on a muffled conversation and finally Laurel came back on the phone.

"I'll have a roast pork sandwich with fries and Tighe wants a cheeseburger, medium well, with tomatoes. Fries for him, too. Thanks, Mom."

"I won't be late," Lilly assured her.

She hung up and drove slowly to the end of the block, remembering the nosy Mrs. Laforge just a minute too late. She hoped her neighbor hadn't snooped on the whole exchange between her and Beau and wouldn't ask the kids in the morning who the stranger in the pickup truck was.

There were parking spots in front of the diner. Lilly slid into one and Beau parked behind her. He followed her to the front of the restaurant, then hurried to open the door for her. She gave him a suspicious glance as she walked past him. She led the way to a booth as far from the window as she could get, her gaze sweeping the other tables and booths as she walked, praying she wouldn't see anyone she knew.

He sat down across from her and reached for two menus that were propped up at the end of the table. He handed one to her and opened his own.

"What's good here?" he asked. "My treat."

"Oh, no you don't. I'll buy my own dinner, thank you."

"Suit yourself," he answered with a shrug. She glanced at him over the top of her menu. *What was she doing here? She had children at home. They would not be happy to learn she was having dinner with their father, a man she disliked so much she wouldn't even talk about him.* His eyes met hers over his own menu and she quickly looked away. She said a silent prayer of thanks when the waitress came over.

"What can I get you two?" she asked cheerfully.

"Ladies first," Beau said with a maddening smile.

"I'll have a grilled cheese sandwich with a small side salad, please. And a glass of water."

"I'll have coffee and a slice of peanut butter pie."

The waitress left and Lilly put her menu down. "Why didn't you order dinner?"

"I already ate dinner."

"Then what are we doing here? I always have dinner with the kids."

"I told you. I wanted to talk to you."

"Then talk."

Beau clasped and unclasped his hands and cleared his throat. He opened his mouth to speak and then shut it again.

"Just spit it out," Lilly directed with a hint of impatience.

"I would like to be part of the kids' lives again."

Lilly didn't think she had heard him right. "You want to be a father again?" she asked, incredulous.

"Yes. I've matured a lot and—"

"I would hope so."

"As I was saying, I've matured a lot and I think I could be a good father. Remember how I was with Tighe in the very beginning?"

"Before you started running around on me and didn't have any time for him," Lilly clarified with a sneer.

"I'm not that man anymore."

"Congratulations."

"Lilly, you're not making this very easy."

"And why should I?" she asked between clenched teeth, leaning forward so other people wouldn't hear her. "What have you ever done to make things easy for me? Or the kids? And now, fifteen years later, you come back saying you've changed? I've got news for you, Beau. Everyone changes over the course of fifteen years. I changed, too—I got smarter. And I'm too smart to let you back into their lives now."

"Please just think about it," he said.

"No way. What makes you think..." She stopped talking as the waitress delivered their food. Lilly had no appetite. "Could you box this up for me, please? And I'd like to get another order for takeout. Can I get a roast pork sandwich with fries and a cheeseburger, medium well, with tomato? Fries with that, too, please." The waitress nodded and took Lilly's plate away. Beau dug into his pie and took a big gulp of coffee.

Lilly leaned back and stared at Beau as he ate. He didn't seem to notice—or if he did, he didn't seem to mind. *The nerve.* She was tempted to get up and leave him there with his pie, but she didn't know how he would react to that. She was afraid he might cause a scene. The old Beau would have done just that. Plus she had ordered dinner for the kids and she had to wait for that.

So she waited. When Beau finished his pie he wiped his

mouth and folded his napkin, placing it carefully on the table next to his plate. "So," he began. "Tell me about them. The kids, I mean."

"You've got to be kidding," Lilly said.

"No, seriously. I'm interested in knowing more about them. How's Tighe doing? Is he into sports?" Beau looked at her with an interested expression.

"For your information, he likes to go camping. And he skis, just like his dear old dad." Her voice dripped with sarcasm. She hated to tell him anything about the kids, but she supposed that if push came to shove, he could get the information in other ways. At least if she shared the information she could control what he learned.

Beau wisely ignored the jab. "How about Lauren?"

"Laurel. I'll make sure to tell her you were asking about her."

"Sorry. How is she doing? The last time I saw her she was a tiny little thing."

Lilly grimaced. "You'd be proud of her if only you could remember her name. She's smart and driven."

"What do they want to do with their lives?"

"Tighe wants to be a physical therapist and Laurel wants to be a music teacher."

"That's cool."

"Uh-huh." Lilly's gaze drifted to the kitchen area, where the waitress was no doubt taking her sweet time putting in the orders for the kids' dinners. Wouldn't that food ever arrive?

"Tell me about your shop. How long have you had it?"

Lilly waved her hand dismissively. "Years. After you left I had to make money somehow, so I had two jobs while my mother watched the kids. Eventually I saved up enough for the shop and the inventory. In my spare time I learned everything I could about jewelry, gems, stones, et cetera. I had a mentor, an older gentleman named Robert, who owned a jewelry store in town until he retired to Arizona. He was a huge help to me and in fact, I bought most of his inventory when he left. I also taught myself jewelry design. It's a great little shop; I don't know what I'd do now if I didn't have it."

"I'm happy for you."

"Thanks." The first civil words they had shared brought on an awkward silence, which was blessedly broken by the arrival of the waitress bearing three takeout boxes.

"Thank you. I'll pay for these now," Lilly said quickly. The waitress handed Lilly a check and Lilly scanned it quickly then handed over a wad of cash. The waitress took it, then asked Beau if he wanted anything else.

"No, just the check," he answered. She tore a check from her pad and handed it to him.

"Lilly, I'm not going to give up," Beau said. "I'm going to keep on you about this. I'll go to court if I have to."

Lilly rolled her eyes in response. "It won't do you a bit of good, Beau."

"We'll see."

CHAPTER 21

L illy couldn't believe she hadn't yet thought to ask Beau where he was staying. "So where have you been staying since you came back to Juniper Junction?"

But he was wiser than she expected. "Oh, a place right outside of town."

Lilly groaned inwardly and stood up, gathering the takeout boxes. "Well, I can't say this has been fun, Beau. But it was interesting."

"See you around."

"Don't count on it."

Lilly left the diner without a backward glance. The whole encounter had left her shaken and upset. So much for her detective skills—she wasn't even able to get him to divulge his address. Back in the car, she yanked her cell phone out of her purse and called Bill.

"You are not going to believe this," she greeted him.

"What now?" he asked.

"Keep it up with that tone and I won't tell you," she said.

"I'm sorry. What is it?"

"Beau and I just ate dinner at the diner on Main Street.

Well, he ate pie and I couldn't eat anything, but we sat across from each other in the same booth and I didn't kill him."

"Good. The last thing we need is for you to be a suspect in three murders. But getting back to the point, *what were you thinking?*"

"He was waiting for me at my house when I got home from work and he suggested that we get something to eat. I thought it might be a good way to get some information out of him, so I agreed."

"And did you get anything out of him?"

"Nope. He wants to be the kids' father again." There was silence on the other end of the phone. "Bill?"

"I'm here. I just can't believe it, that's all. You told him no, of course."

"Of course."

"Good. What do you mean, he was waiting for you at home?"

"He was parked out front. When I drove into the driveway he came over to my car to talk to me."

"Had he been in the house?"

"He said he hadn't."

"And based on previous experience you had every reason to trust that." Bill's disbelief was clear. Lilly chided herself for believing Beau. Her foot itched to floor the gas pedal and make sure the kids were okay.

"I called Laurel from the driveway to tell her I was going out for dinner and I took her order and Tighe's order. She didn't mention anything."

"Hopefully that means Beau was telling you the truth. We don't want him to be talking to the kids."

"I'd kill him first."

"Please, no killing talk. Like I said, you're already in enough trouble."

"Any news?"

"None."

"Has anyone talked to Mrs. Laforge to see if she can confirm my alibi?"

"Yeah. She didn't see anything."

"That's a first. Of course it has to be when I'm on the hook for two murders. But if Tighe curses even once, she makes sure I know about it."

Bill chuckled. "It's part of the grumpy old neighbor code."

Lilly sobered. "Have you talked to Mom today?"

"No. You?"

"Not yet. I'm sure the kids took a meal over to her. I'll give her a call when I get home."

"Let me know if she needs anything. I can drop it off tomorrow morning."

"Okay. Thanks." Lilly hung up with Bill and dialed Noley. As she drove home she told her the story about Beau. Noley was worried.

"Do you think he'll try to contact the kids?" she fretted.

"I've told him not to. He'll listen if he knows what's good for him. He'll have the entire Juniper Junction police force breathing down his neck if he so much as looks at Laurel or Tighe. Can you believe he didn't even remember Laurel's name? He called her 'Lauren.' What a jerk."

"Are you going to tell the kids about him? Maybe they should know he's back in town."

"I'm afraid to tell them anything because I don't want them to get the urge to see him or talk to him or want to know more about him. I've been pretty successful at keeping his personality flaws to myself, but they still know I can't stand him. And I don't know what I would say if they asked to see him. I mean, he's still their biological father and I can't blame them for being curious. I think I would feel obligated to let them at least meet him."

"Too bad he ever came back," Noley said. Lilly was pulling into the driveway.

"I'm home now, so I've got to run."

She was met at the door by two hungry kids. "Did you bring dinner?" Laurel asked before Lilly could get fully inside.

"Yes," she said with a laugh. "Sorry it took so long."

"Who'd you go to dinner with?" Tighe asked. He had become more and more protective of Lilly as he had gotten older.

"An old friend," she answered, hoping her evasiveness wasn't too obvious.

"A friend who's old or someone who's been a friend for a long time or someone who used to be your friend?" he asked. Lilly rolled her eyes.

"You'd make a good lawyer, you know that?"

"I know. I also realize you didn't answer the question."

"Who cares?" Laurel asked. "Leave her alone. Every woman is entitled to some privacy. Right, Mom?"

"Yes. But you are not a woman yet, so don't try to trick me. I still want to know what you're doing all the time."

"Mom..." Tighe's voice held a hint of impatience.

"All right. I went out to dinner with someone I was friends with a long time ago."

"Thank you. Was that so hard?" Tighe asked.

"No. And you're not my father, young man," Lilly said, pointing her finger at her son. He smiled at her.

"So who was it?"

Lilly let out an exasperated sigh. "No one you'd remember. Now would you stop it with the third degree and eat your dinner?"

"Uncle Bill called and said to keep an eye on you."

What's it called if I kill my own brother? Fratricide? Aloud, Lilly said, "Don't worry about me at all. I'm just fine. Bill's worried because Eden Barclay and Herb Knight are dead. Police officers are like that—they worry about their families all the time. I'm fine, trust me."

She changed the subject, hoping Tighe would leave her alone. "Did you two check on Gran today?"

"Yeah," Laurel replied. "She was wearing a bikini when I got there. If I ever wear a bikini at that age, I want someone to shoot me."

"A bikini? Why?"

Laurel shrugged. "I don't know. She said she was going swimming."

The thought of her mother outside in the cold wearing nothing but a bikini bathing suit spurred Lilly into immediate action. She grabbed her purse and rummaged through it for her phone while she grilled Laurel.

"Did you tell her to change her clothes?"

"Yes, but she said she was plenty warm and didn't want to put anything else on."

"How long did you stay?"

"About a half hour. She stopped talking about going swimming, so I figured it was okay to come home."

"And she was still in her bathing suit when you left?"

"Yeah."

Lilly was dialing her mother's house. It rang six times, then the answering machine clicked on. Lilly hung up and called again. Six more rings, then the answering machine. Lilly grabbed her car keys and dialed Bill's number as she pulled on her coat.

"Bill, Laurel told me Mom was wearing a bathing suit earlier tonight, talking about going swimming. Have you talked to her?"

"No. Did you call her?"

"Yes. No answer. I'm going over there."

"I'll meet you." He hung up and Lilly yanked open the back door.

"Want us to go with you, Mom?" Laurel asked. Her eyes were wide, her mouth drawn. She was probably afraid her grandmother had gone out in the cold after she left.

"No, you stay here in case Gran calls. I'll text you if I need you to come over. Lock the door." Lilly pulled the door closed behind her and left in a hurry.

She pulled up to her mother's house in just a couple minutes. The lights were off and her mother didn't answer her repeated loud knocks on the door. Lilly ran back to her car and rifled through her glove compartment for her set of keys to her mother's house. She ran back up the front steps and was trying to open the door with trembling fingers as Bill's police cruiser pulled up next to the curb.

He ran up the walk and Lilly turned to him in frustration. "I can't get the key in the lock!" she cried. "She's not answering when I knock."

"Calm down, Lil. You're not helping anyone by getting upset. Give me the key," he said, holding out his hand. She handed him the key and he slipped it into the lock. He unlocked the door and pushed it open, calling, "Mom? Mom, are you home?"

No answer.

CHAPTER 22

"Bill, we need to find her. If she's outside in a bathing suit she could freeze to death." Bill pulled his radio out of his coat pocket. It squawked as he spoke into it, alerting any officers to keep watch for their mother. He described her as "possibly dressed in a swimsuit."

He turned to Lilly, who was still wearing her coat. "I'm going to check inside. You get in the car and go up and down the streets in the neighborhood. Check with a couple neighbors, ask if they saw her leave."

"What kind of neighbor would watch an old lady in a bathing suit wander down the street in the snow and not do anything?" Lilly asked in exasperation.

"I don't know, Lilly. I'm just trying to keep us both busy until she's safe." The edge in Bill's voice betrayed his concern.

Lilly nodded. "I'll call if I learn anything."

She ran out to the car and drove off slowly, scanning each side of the street for her mother or any sign that she had been outside recently. She didn't see any footprints in the fresh snow, but it was dark outside and the streetlamps weren't very strong. Besides, she couldn't see the sidewalk clearly from the inside of the car. She turned a corner and stopped in front of a small Craftsman-style bungalow where her mother's friend Joyce lived. She ran up Joyce's steps and rapped on the door.

Tiny, scared eyes peered through the curtain covering the window set in the front door and the porch light came to life.

"It's me, Joyce. Lilly Carlsen, Beverly's daughter. Remember?" Three locks clicked and the door opened slowly.

"Joyce, have you seen my mom?" Lilly asked breathlessly.

"No, my dear. I haven't talked to her today. She's missing?" Joyce's hand flew to her mouth.

"We can't find her," Lilly explained. "I'm going out to look for her. If you hear from her or see her, would you please call her house? My brother is there waiting for news."

"Of course," Joyce answered, but Lilly was already down the front steps, running back toward her car. She had left it running.

She slid into the front seat and had put the car in gear when her cell phone rang. It was Bill.

"Did you find her?" she asked.

"Yes," he said, his voice low. "She was sound asleep in the spare room in the basement, still in her bathing suit."

"Is she awake now?"

"Not yet. I didn't want to wake her up until you got here."

Lilly heaved a sigh of relief. "I'll be back in just a minute." She hung up, got out of the car again, and went up Joyce's front steps. Joyce had been watching from the living room window and opened the door before Lilly could knock.

"Did someone find her?" she asked, her voice quavery with anxiety.

"Yes. Bill found her. She was asleep in the spare bedroom in the basement. I guess she couldn't hear the phone or us knocking on the front door. But she's all right, so don't worry about her."

"I'm afraid this is going to be happening more often," Joyce said with a sad shake of her head. "She's failing."

"I know," Lilly replied quietly. "We'll deal with that. I'm just glad she's okay."

Joyce put her hand on Lilly's arm. "She doesn't want to go into a nursing home."

"I know that, too. Bill and Mom and I are going to have to examine our options. You get back inside, Joyce. It's cold out here. I'm sure Mom'll call you tomorrow."

She returned to her car more slowly, her happiness at knowing her mom was safe dampened by Joyce's words. Her mother's friend was right—this was going to happen more and more as her mother's dementia worsened. It was not a reality she was ready to face and not a conversation she was ready to have with anyone, and least of all her mother.

When she pulled up in front of her mom's house, there was another police cruiser parked behind Bill's. She suddenly felt very weary, as if she just couldn't make it up the front steps of the house. She closed her eyes and leaned her forehead against the steering wheel. How long would she and Bill be able to take care of their mother without around-the-clock help? She couldn't keep relying on the kids to take care of her—within two years they would both be leaving for college, God willing.

Taking a deep breath, she got out of the car and went inside. Bill was sitting on the couch in the living room talking to an officer who sat in Mom's favorite chair.

"Hi," Lilly said, walking over to him and extending her hand.

"Gary, this is my sister, Lilly. Lilly, Gary Fields." Lilly sat down heavily next to Bill.

"Is Mom all right?" she asked.

"She's fine. She's certainly in much better shape than either you or I. I asked Gary to come over because he was in the neighborhood and he's been going through this with his father."

"How's your father now?" Lilly was almost afraid to hear the answer.

"He's living in an assisted living facility. Loves it."

Gary's words did nothing to soothe Lilly's fears. She didn't want to put her mom anywhere. She nodded and looked at Bill, wanting nothing more than to change the subject. "Should we go wake her up?"

"I guess so. I don't want her to wake up in the morning by herself and not know where she is. Besides, she must be freezing in that getup."

Gary smiled. "My dad used to go outside in his underwear in the winter. He always swore he wasn't cold."

Bill chuckled. "If the whole thing weren't so serious, it would be comical."

Gary stood up to leave. "Let me know if you need anything. You know, there's a company that sells scent bottles for elderly people. They ship you a sterile bottle and all you have to do is swab your mom's skin with a cloth they provide. You know, arms, legs, torso, neck. Then you put the cloth in the bottle and seal it up. That way if your mom ever does actually leave the house and go missing, police dogs have a scent they can follow to find her. I've heard it works really well."

Bill shook Gary's hand. "We'll definitely look into that. Thanks for coming over."

Gary left and Bill followed Lilly down to the basement. She opened the door to the spare bedroom and had to smile when she saw her mom lying on the bed, no covers, clad in only a bikini with red ruffles.

Lilly leaned over her mother and shook her shoulder gently. "Mom?" she said. "Mom, Bill and I are here to get you upstairs and in your bed."

Beverly groaned and turned over, her arm lying over her eyes. "Why is it so cold in here?"

Lilly and Bill grinned at each other. "You're wearing nothing but a bathing suit, Mom. You must be freezing."

Beverly pushed herself into a seated position. "Oh, that's right. Now I remember. I was going to go swimming but my friend cancelled."

"Who were you going swimming with?" Bill asked. Something in his mother's tone must have alerted him that she didn't imagine the swimming.

"That nice young man. What's his name...Oh. Beau. He called and asked if I'd like to go swimming in the pool by his house. He's such a delight."

"Beau asked you to go swimming?" Lilly asked, her voice doubtful.

"Yes. He was going to pick me up, but then he called and said he was having car trouble and we would have to reschedule. I hope he gets his car fixed."

Bill shot Lilly his typical *We'll talk about this in private* look, then he took one of his mother's arms and Lilly took the other. Together the three of them managed to get up to Beverly's bedroom on the second floor of the house. Bill went downstairs to wait while Lilly helped her mother into a nightgown and made sure she had everything she needed for the night. Then she joined her brother in the living room.

"He's done it again," she seethed. "How dare he contact her? She's practically helpless!"

"Shh," Bill cautioned. "You don't want Mom to overhear you. Let's think about this for a minute. This could be the information we needed. If Beau really did invite Mom for a swim, I'm going to assume it's at an indoor pool. There aren't too many apartment complexes around here with an indoor pool. If we can get that information we should know where Beau is staying."

"So he did us a favor." Lilly still couldn't believe he had the nerve to contact her mother again.

"Possibly. Let's go with that for now and get furious with him once we find out where he lives."

"Do you think Mom should have some kind of alarm system?" Lilly asked.

"If she had all her mental faculties, I would say yes. But with the problems she's been having, I'm not sure that's such a good idea."

"You're probably right," Lilly mused. "I just can't stand the thought of Beau in this house. And she *likes* him! That's the kicker."

"Maybe we can just talk to her and remind her that he's not a nice guy and we don't want her talking to him."

"That won't work. I've already tried it."

Bill shrugged. "Worth another try."

After making sure Beverly was asleep Lilly and Bill checked the deadbolt and chain on the back door then left the house, locking the front door behind them and double-checking it, too.

When Lilly got home the kids were clamoring to know about their grandmother. Lilly tried to make light of it, telling them that she had, indeed, been in a bathing suit when Bill found her, but the truth was that she was worried. She should have known better than to try to trick the kids into thinking everything was all right.

"Mom, I'm worried about Gran," Laurel fretted.

"Me, too," Tighe chimed in. "She's getting more and more confused all the time."

"I know it," Lilly said, placing her purse on the counter. "Uncle Bill and I are going to have to talk to Gran one of these days and decide what the future is going to hold for her."

"You mean like putting her in a nursing home?" Laurel asked. The worry and disdain were evident in her voice.

"I hope not," Lilly answered. "But that is an option. I don't think she's ready for a nursing home yet. But maybe assisted living."

"Could she live here?" Laurel asked. "Tighe and I could help take care of her."

Lilly reached out and squeezed Laurel's hand. "You're sweet to suggest that. But I'm not sure that's the answer, either. You and Tighe will be moving on to college before we know it and I work full time. No one would be around to help Gran if she needed it."

"We need to think of something," Tighe said. "I can hold off for a year on college, even."

"Oh, no you can't, young man." Lilly was firm. "You're going to college three months after you graduate from high school. Gran would tell you the very same thing."

"I can help," Laurel offered. "I'll be here for a whole year after Tighe leaves. And Nick can help, too."

Nick again. "I'm not sure Nick wants to take care of an old lady during his senior year of high school."

"He's so nice. You'll see. He wouldn't mind at all." Nick was the last person Lilly wanted to discuss.

"Uncle Bill and Gran and I will talk about it and see what can be done," Lilly said, putting an end to the conversation. "Now you two scoot and get your homework done." The kids tramped upstairs and Lilly poured herself a healthy measure of wine. She sat down next to the fireplace and sipped the wine, thinking that she should look for an assistant to help at the store so she could spend more time at home, looking after her mother and enjoying the time with her kids and maybe even taking Barney for a walk now and then. She had owned the store for several years—maybe it was time to admit that going it alone was getting harder than she had imagined.

CHAPTER 23

T he next evening it was almost closing time when the bell above the door jingled. Lilly turned to greet the newcomer.

It was a tall man with black eyes and olive skin and hair the color of obsidian. He wore a plaid flannel shirt and jeans. He extended his hand in greeting.

"Are you the owner?" he asked.

"Yes. I'm Lilly Carlsen."

"I'm Hassan Ashraf. I'm vacationing in Juniper Junction and I saw your lovely shop last night after you were closed."

"Thank you." Lilly was trying to figure out his accent. It was ever so slight, but it was there. He looked Middle Eastern. Perhaps that's the accent she was hearing?

"I am a jewelry collector of sorts," Hassan explained.

"Oh?" Lilly asked, waiting for him to elaborate.

"Yes. Jewels fascinate me." *Not much of an elaboration*, Lilly thought.

"Can I help you find anything in particular?" she asked.

"No, thank you. I'd just like to look around, if you don't mind."

"Not at all. Please enjoy," Lilly said, waving her hand around the shop. He wandered toward the front display case, seemingly absorbed by everything he saw. Occasionally he would turn to ask her a question about one of her gems and the depth of his knowledge was evident from his queries.

"Do you know where this particular lapis lazuli was mined?" he asked.

"That came from Afghanistan," she answered. "I don't know the exact location, but I'm sure my supplier does." Mr. Ashraf said something to himself, but Lilly didn't catch it.

"And this?" he asked, pointing to a particularly large piece of citrus-hued tourmaline. "Where did this come from?"

Lilly wondered about his interest in the provenance of the gems and stones. She was getting a little annoyed by his questioning.

"The tourmaline is from Sri Lanka, I believe," she replied.

"Sri Lanka is a beautiful place," he said, nodding. "Some of the best tourmaline comes from Sri Lanka."

"Have you been?" she asked, her curiosity getting the better of her.

"Oh, yes. Many times."

"And where are you visiting from?" she asked.

"Minnesota."

"We don't get too many people from Minnesota around here," she said. "Most people who live in cold climates don't want to go to another cold climate for vacation."

Mr. Ashraf smiled. "I am here at the insistence of my family. It was their choice."

"Do they ski?"

He nodded. "A little. Me? I like to cross-country ski and the trails are beautiful around here."

Their conversation lagged at that point and Lilly didn't know what else to say. She turned back to her tasks as Mr. Ashraf continued to browse. She wondered if he wanted to buy something.

Finally he turned his attention away from the display cases. "Thank you for allowing me to look around," he said. "You have some beautiful stones here."

"Thank you," Lilly replied. He left the store and she locked the door behind him. *Was he here to case the store? What brought him in here?*

The shoppers along Main Street were thinning out as people began to return to their hotels or go into the restaurants for dinner. She made sure the vault was locked and headed home, happy to be leaving at a decent hour.

When she got home it was as if all the planets had aligned to give her the evening off. Tighe had pulled a frozen casserole out of the freezer and baked it. Laurel had taken a plate of it over to her grandmother for dinner. Lilly called her mom when she got home and was pleased to listen as her mother recounted, with perfect lucidity, what she had done that day. Lilly and the two kids worked on a crossword puzzle after dinner and then the kids did homework while Lilly read a book in pajamas with a cup of tea at her side. She sighed contentedly as she crawled into bed a little early—*this is the life*, she thought. *The kids didn't fight, Mom had a good day, I got home from work on time, and there was already something in the freezer for dinner. If I had an assistant I could experience this more often.*

CHAPTER 24

The next day began with a pre-dawn phone call from her mother.

"Lilly, I can't find my glasses."

"Mom, you don't wear glasses."

"Yes I do. And they're missing."

"I'll come over before I leave for work and help you look for them," Lilly offered.

"I'm afraid I won't be able to wait that long. I have an appointment."

"Where could you possibly have an appointment before I leave for work?"

"The hairdresser."

"Mom, the hairdresser doesn't even open until ten o'clock, and your next appointment isn't until next weekend."

"I wish I could find those glasses." From the rustling noises in the background, Lilly surmised that her mother was rummaging through something to look for her imaginary glasses. She tried a different tack.

"Mom, your hair looked lovely when I saw you the other night. I don't think you need an appointment yet."

"How would you know? You haven't been here in weeks." Her mother's voice sounded angry.

"Mom, I was there thirty-six hours ago. Remember? You were asleep in the basement. You were wearing a bathing suit."

"Pshaw. I was doing no such thing. I'm not complaining, mind you. I'm just stating a fact. I know how busy you are at the shop."

Ah, there's nothing quite like a passive-aggressive phone call to start the day, Lilly thought. *It's too early for this.*

"Have you called Bill? Maybe he knows where your glasses are," Lilly suggested. She knew an impossible request to find nonexistent glasses was not how Bill wanted to start the day, but she figured it was only fair. She tried to ignore the guilt that crept into her conscience.

"I already tried him and there was no answer. He's probably working, poor thing. He works so hard."

And I don't? Lilly suppressed an exasperated sigh and sat up in bed.

"I'll be over to help you find your glasses as soon as I get ready for work," Lilly said, placing a slight emphasis on *ready for work*. She hung up, took a quick shower, and left a note for the kids to let Barney out before school and to lock the door after he came back inside.

She drove over to her mother's house in the lightly falling snow. When she arrived, she found her mom in the kitchen drinking a cup of tea.

"I'm glad you could come over to chat, Lilly."

"What about your glasses?" Lilly asked.

Her mother gave her a funny look. "You know I don't wear glasses, dear." She chuckled and shook her head. "No, I've never had to wear glasses. Your father had terrible eyesight, but mine has always been pretty close to perfect."

Suppressing a sigh for the second time that morning, Lilly accepted a cup of tea from her mother. They sat in silence at the kitchen table, Lilly watching the steam curl upward from the cup and her mother looking out the window at the snow, which had started to fall more thickly.

"What's going on today, Mom?" Lilly asked, breaking the silence.

"Oh, I think I'll call Joyce and invite her over for lunch. Then I have an embroidery project I'm working on and I might go outside for a walk in the snow. It's so beautiful this time of year."

Lilly gripped her teacup a little harder when her mother mentioned going outside for a walk. "Why don't you wait until Joyce gets here and you can go for a walk together?" she asked. "It's always nice to take a walk after lunch."

Her mom nodded. "I think that's a good idea. I'll stay indoors until Joyce gets here."

Lilly closed her eyes in silent gratefulness for her mother's quick agreement with the plan.

Lilly rinsed out the teacups while her mother got dressed for the day. She wanted to be sure her mother was busily engaged in some activity before she left for the shop. When Beverly came downstairs dressed in comfortable slacks and a large cardigan with lots of pockets, Lilly smiled. This was her mother's favorite sewing outfit. Beverly smiled.

"Don't worry about me, Lilly. I have plenty to keep me busy. I'll call Joyce and get to work on my project as soon as you leave for the shop."

Lilly hugged her mother. These lucid moments were worth celebrating. She thought again of how nice it would be to enjoy more time like this with her mother, something she could do if she had an assistant at the shop.

When she got to work she set out the displays and had time to look over some recent designs she had created, tweaking a few until they were just the way she wanted them.

When she opened the shop, there were two customers standing on the sidewalk in the falling snow waiting for her to unlock the front door. She recognized one of them.

"Good morning, Mr. Ashraf. You're back."

"Yes, Ms. Carlsen. I was hoping to have a word with you."

"Certainly. Let me take care of this woman first," Lilly replied, nodding toward the woman who had preceded them into the store," and then I'll be happy to talk to you."

The woman had heard of Lilly's collection of jewelry designs and had come into the shop to look at pendants. She wanted something unique for her sister for Christmas. While Lilly showed the woman a large selection of her personal designs, she noticed Mr. Ashraf out of the corner of her eye. He seemed intrigued by the designs but obviously didn't want to be nosy. Lilly spent quite a long while with the woman and was pleased when she chose a medium-sized pendant made of granite that had been mined in Colorado. Lilly had shaped the stone into a heart and its veining and colors were magnificent. The woman seemed thrilled with her purchase.

After the woman left Lilly turned to Mr. Ashraf, who had been waiting patiently, just browsing around the store.

"How can I help you this morning, Mr. Ashraf?"

He looked down at his feet and around the store before answering. He avoided eye contact when he cleared his throat and spoke.

"I noticed last night and this morning that you do not wear a wedding ring. I thought perhaps you would like to have dinner with me some evening while I am still in Juniper Junction. That is, if you are in fact not married. It's just that I don't often find female jewelry shop owners who are so charming and attractive."

Lilly felt herself blushing to the very tips of her ears from his compliment, but her stomach immediately began churning. She wasn't used to being asked out. *What should I say?* Her mind raced until, unbidden, an image of Noley appeared. The imaginary Noley shook her finger at Lilly and said *If you don't say yes, I will never listen to you complain about men again.* Lilly smiled. "Thank you, Mr. Ashraf. That's very nice of you. I would like that."

He beamed. "Thank you. What evening would you be free?"

Every night of my life, if we're being honest. "Tomorrow evening works for me if that's all right with you." She didn't want to seem desperate.

"Tomorrow evening will be perfect," Mr. Ashraf said. "And please call me Hassan. Shall I pick you up here when the shop closes?"

"That would be fine, yes," Lilly said, still blushing. She was already worrying about what to wear to work the next day.

"My family and I have visited several good restaurants in town since getting here. Is there one in particular you like?" he asked.

Lilly named a restaurant at the far end of Main Street, a quiet place with large picture windows overlooking a small river.

"That sounds very nice," Hassan said. "You close the shop at six?"

Lilly nodded.

"I'll see you then." He gave her a slight wave and left the shop, turning around once and smiling at her from the sidewalk. She pulled out her cell phone.

"Noley, guess what," she said when her friend answered.

CHAPTER 25

"Beau's in jail?"

"I wish. No, some guy just came in here and asked me to go to dinner with him tomorrow night."

Noley squealed. "And you said yes, right?"

Lilly laughed. "I said yes."

"So tell me all about him."

"His name is Hassan Ashraf. He looks Middle Eastern and speaks with a slight accent, but I can't figure out what accent it is. He's visiting Juniper Junction with his family. He's from Minnesota."

"Skier?"

"No, but he said he likes to cross-country ski."

"That could be a romantic thing to do."

"Noley, we're only having dinner. Let's not worry about future romantic outings. He's not from around here, after all."

"What's he do?"

"Like, for a living?"

"Yeah."

Lilly shrugged as if Noley could see her. "I don't know. He

didn't say. He seems to be very interested in jewelry, though. Maybe he's a jeweler. Or an appraiser. I'll ask him tomorrow."

There was silence for a moment. "Noley?" Lilly asked. "You still there?"

"I just had a thought. Now don't get worried, it's just a thought. But you don't think his sudden appearance has anything to do with the murders of Eden and Herb, do you?"

Lilly had to admit she hadn't thought of that. She chided herself for being so careless about accepting an invitation from a stranger. Hadn't she spent the last seventeen years warning her kids about such things?

"What if you're right?" she asked Noley. "Ooh, the thought of it sends chills up my spine. Do you think I should cancel?"

"Now don't go off the deep end. I told you, it was just a random thought. I probably shouldn't even have mentioned it to you. This guy's probably legit, but you have to be aware, that's all. I'm sure you're going somewhere public, right? Not back to his hotel room or anything?"

"We're going to the Water Wheel Restaurant."

"That's certainly public enough. He's not going to try anything in a restaurant full of people. Just don't go anywhere alone with him. Are you meeting him there or is he driving you?"

"He just said he would pick me up at the shop at six."

"That probably means he's planning to drive you. Okay, so just tell him you prefer to drive yourself because you want to have your car with you after dinner so you can get right home."

"Do you really think I should be worried?" Lilly asked, her hands sweating.

"No. I shouldn't have said anything. I'm sure he wants to take you out to dinner because he thinks you're hot."

"Now I know you're lying."

Noley laughed. "No, seriously. I shouldn't have said anything. You'll have fun."

"I hope so. I can't even call to cancel or anything because I don't have his phone number and I don't know where he's staying."

"Take notes. You'll have to remind me what it's like to be on a date." Noley laughed.

I've got to set her up with Bill.

When Lilly woke up the next morning she was grumpy from a lack of sleep and the headache that resulted from tossing and turning all night. All she could think of was going back to bed. She told the kids she would be home a little late that evening and they didn't ask why. Even that made her mad. Didn't they care where she went after work? Weren't they concerned about her with a murderer on the loose in Juniper Junction? God knew she spent enough time worrying about them.

Before she left for work Barney had an accident on the kitchen floor, further deepening Lilly's dark mood. Trying to clean it up in a hurry, Lilly knelt in dog urine and had to change her pants.

This does not bode well for a pleasant day, she thought with a groan.

When she got to work she found three people waiting to get in. She checked her watch and sure enough, it had stopped. *It figures.* She apologized profusely for being late to open the shop and led the customers in. It wasn't until she had helped all three pick out pieces of jewelry that she realized she had buttoned her blouse wrong and the buttons weren't lined up. She rolled her eyes. What those customers must have thought of her! It was a miracle they stuck around to buy anything.

She had barely enough time to worry about her date that evening with the Christmas customers coming in all day long. It was about five thirty when someone tapped her on the shoulder as she was rearranging a display and she shrieked and spun around.

"Hassan! I'm so sorry about that." Apparently her subconscious had been at work, worrying, while she waited on customers.

He looked taken aback. "No, it's my fault. I shouldn't have tapped you while you were busy. Please forgive me." He held out a gorgeous bouquet of winter greens and tiny rosebuds.

Lilly blushed. "These are beautiful. Thank you very much. It wasn't your fault I jumped—I've just been a little on edge, that's all."

"Do you still want to go to dinner with me?" he asked, his eyebrows furrowing. "I would understand if you'd rather not go or if you'd like to go some other time."

"No, no. I'll go. It'll do me good to get away from this place," she said with a smile. "Let me put the flowers in some water and I'll be right back. Oh, do you mind if I drive my car? You can follow me. I want to have my car with me so you don't have to bring me back here when dinner is over."

He looked disappointed for a brief moment, then smiled. "Of course that's fine. I'll just browse in a couple of the shops nearby until you close up."

Lilly left the bouquet on the counter until six o'clock, when Hassan came back to the shop. She suggested that he get his car and wait for her in front of the shop and then he could follow her to The Water Wheel. She locked the door behind him, made sure the vaults were locked, and left through the back door, again checking the lock. If there was one positive thing that had come out of everything that had been happening since Black Friday, it was that she was more mindful of security and keeping doors locked.

She drove her car around to the front of the store and saw Hassan. She slowed and waved to him and he pulled out behind her.

She drove to The Water Wheel and parked in the pine-needle-strewn lot. Hassan parked next to her. As she was gathering her purse and car keys she noticed he had hurried around to her door to open it for her. She unlocked it so he could lift the door handle. He held out his hand to help her out of the car.

Flushing, she took his hand and stood next to him while he closed her door.

Inside the restaurant, they were shown to a table in the back, overlooking the lamplit garden and the swiftly rushing river. After they were seated, Lilly pointed out the window and said to Hassan, "This building used to be a mill. It used a water wheel for power, hence the restaurant's name. The water wheel is still out there, but you can't see it in the dark."

Hassan followed her gaze. "I do love to visit places with an interesting history. I would like to see the water wheel in the daylight."

They perused their menus. Lilly already knew what she wanted, but kept her gaze on the menu because she didn't know what else to say to Hassan. She was struck with a feeling of dread, wondering how she was going to make it to the end of dinner. How long had it been since she'd been on a date? She shuddered to think. Years. Did people even date the way they used to?

Luckily Hassan had thought ahead and was keen to talk about jewelry.

"So how did you get involved in the jewelry business?" he asked after the server had poured two glasses of sauvignon blanc.

"It all came about when I needed a job following my divorce years ago," Lilly said. "I found work in a jewelry store owned by a nice old man who eventually became a sort of mentor to me."

"And?" Hassan prompted.

"And when he retired I had enough money saved up to rent a place and open my own business. I've never looked back. I think jewelry is fascinating."

"And how did you become interested in jewelry design?"

"I had one customer, an elderly woman who used to vacation several times a year in Juniper Junction. Every time she was in town she would visit my mentor, Robert, when he was still in business. After Robert retired she started visiting my shop. One day she brought her daughter in to purchase a piece, but I didn't have anything the daughter was interested in. She liked more modern pieces. Her mother asked if I could design something and I said "yes" without even thinking. Then I had to teach myself." Lilly chucked fondly at the memory. That daughter had since become one of her best customers.

"I am quite impressed," Hassan said, leaning back in his seat and swirling his wineglass. "That's not an easy thing to learn, and it takes a special eye for design."

"Robert taught me everything I know about creativity," Lilly replied.

"Oh, I think creativity is inherent. Robert may have coaxed it out of you, but it must have been there all along."

Lilly glanced down for a moment, embarrassed by his praise. "What about you? You seem to know a lot about jewelry," she said.

"I've been in the jewelry business a long time," he said. "As was my father before me, and his father before him."

"I knew it. You have such a keen interest in jewelry that I knew you were involved in the business somehow. Do you have a store back in Minnesota?"

Hassan shook his head. "I am not in the business that way. I am a gem hunter."

CHAPTER 26

L illy's eyes widened. "A gem hunter?" she repeated. "That's incredible!"

Hassan laughed softly. "I've been hunting gems since I was a little boy. My father used to take me with him on trips."

Lilly's head was reeling with questions. She had never met anyone who actually went hunting for the gems that were sold by jewelry stores. She only dealt with the suppliers.

"Wow. There are so many things I want to ask you," she said. "First, what kinds of gems do you hunt for?"

"My favorite stone is lapis lazuli, but I look for everything from rubies to sapphires to diamonds to jade to citraline to tourmaline. Everything, really."

"Where do you look for the stones?"

"I go to Afghanistan as often as I can. That's where I find the best lapis lazuli. And Sri Lanka, all over the Middle East."

"I can't believe what an incredible job that must be," Lilly said, not even trying to mask the awe in her voice.

"It's a fascinating way to make a living, that's for sure," Hassan said with a smile.

"So tell me what you do when you go hunting for lapis lazuli."

"The lapis lazuli is getting harder and harder to find. The best places I've found are in caves in very remote parts of Afghanistan. Of course, much of Afghanistan is very remote. But it takes several days to get to the caves and it can be treacherous. There are certain times of year I can't go because of the weather or because of tribal fighting."

Lilly shook her head in disbelief. "So how much time do you spend actually hunting for gems?"

"The time I spend actually traveling, several months out of the year. Time spent actually gem hunting, many weeks. I have contacts all around the globe who help me suss out the best places to find quality stones."

"That's so exciting. So tell me—where are you from? I can detect a slight accent, but I can't identify it."

Hassan chuckled. "It's a British accent, but it's not very strong. That's probably why you couldn't identify it. I'm originally from London, but I moved to the United States when I was quite young."

"Have you lived in Minnesota since then?"

"My family has moved around, but mostly we've stayed in the Midwest. We have family there and my parents wanted to live with other Muslims."

Lilly hoped her eyes didn't betray her surprise. Had she ever even known a Muslim?

"So what made you decide to come to Juniper Junction?"

"My sister was put in charge of finding a place this year. We usually vacation together as a family, and when I say "family," I mean aunts, uncles, and cousins. There are about twenty-five of us."

"Where are you staying?"

"We have rented several places near each other on the outskirts of town."

"What a fun way to vacation. My kids and I rarely go on vacation, but when we do it's just the three of us."

"Sometimes it's a good way to spend a vacation; other times it's not," Hassan said with a smile.

"I think I know what you mean. I don't have a large extended family, so even if we went with the whole family it would still be a small group."

"How old are your children?"

Lilly told Hassan all about Tighe and Laurel. He seemed interested in knowing about them and their interests—sports, hobbies, everything. The more interest he showed in the kids, the more Lilly liked Hassan. She found herself wondering over a bite of steak if they would be going out again.

It wasn't until Hassan asked if Lilly had any pets that she blurted out Beau's name by mistake, thereby ruining her own appetite and, she thought ruefully, probably Hassan's.

"I got Barney when Beau left," she began. Then she set down her fork abruptly and said, "I'm so sorry about that. I didn't mean to mention his name—my ex-husband, I mean."

"That's all right. He was part of your life at one time so I assume he'd be a part of some of your stories." Lilly smiled, pleased that Hassan didn't seem to mind the mention of Beau.

"Anyway, when he left we lived in a house that was in the middle of nowhere. It was just me and the kids in the house, and they were just babies at the time. I couldn't afford to move, but the more time passed, the older the kids got, the more isolated I felt out in the country. I felt we needed some kind of protection. I couldn't afford an alarm system, but I could afford a dog from the pound. So that's how I got Barney." Lilly gave a wistful smile at the memory. Barney had been with her since Tighe was seven—ten years.

Hassan asked to see a picture of Barney and Lilly was only too happy to oblige. After an appropriate amount of time spent oohing and aahing over several photos that emerged from Lilly's purse, Hassan pulled out his wallet and showed Lilly photos of his own dog, Dusty. Hassan spoke of Dusty, a French bulldog, fondly.

"Who takes care of Dusty when you're not home?" Lilly asked. Noley often looked after Barney when Lilly was away, but Hassan's whole family had come with him.

"There is a dog sitter near my home. I leave Dusty with her. Dusty thinks of it as a vacation, I'm sure. The dog sitter ends up watching Dusty whenever I travel because my family are all cat people." He smirked. "They do not appreciate the beauty of coming home to a dog every day."

Lilly grinned in perfect understanding. The kids might get mad and her mother might be ornery, but Barney was always happy to see her, always ready to display unconditional love.

Talk turned again to gem hunting. "I think it must be such an exciting job," Lilly said.

"It can be," he agreed, "but often it's just digging through rock where I may or may not be rewarded with anything but cuts and bruises."

"Tell me about a recent trip you took," she suggested. "Where you went, what you found, what you did with the gems once you found them, that sort of thing."

"I went to Afghanistan late last fall," Hassan replied. "I was searching for lapis lazuli." His eyes took on a faraway look. "I have a team I work with when I'm there, and they met me in Kandahar and took me up into the mountains. We had to complete the trek before winter weather set in because it can be so treacherous there once the snow falls. It would be almost impossible to get out of the area before next spring."

"How big is the team?"

"Between the drivers and the guides, there are six or seven of us, depending on the day. They are very loyal to me, so they know the best places to search for lapis lazuli and they don't share the locations with other hunters."

"Believe it or not, I never really thought too much about

where the gems that I sell in my store actually come from," Lilly said, shaking her head. "It's fascinating."

"The best part is getting to meet people from the mountainous areas of Afghanistan and other countries," Hassan said. "They are the most hospitable, kind people you'll ever meet. And though many of them are poor beyond measure, they take pride in welcoming me into their homes and serving food and drink to me and my team. We bring them things, of course, like school supplies for their children and eyeglasses that have been donated to us, so there's a reciprocity in our dealings."

"That's wonderful. Does your father go with you?"

"I used to accompany him, but he has gotten too old to make those long, dangerous treks into the caves of Afghanistan. I keep in close contact with him when I travel, though, because he knows the people and the business better than anyone. Better than I do, certainly, but I'm learning."

"He must have some incredible stories to tell," Lilly said.

"He does. I hope you'll get to meet him before we have to return to Minnesota." He grinned at Lilly and she blushed.

CHAPTER 27

Too soon, they were done eating and Hassan asked if Lilly would like to go for a walk in the gardens behind the restaurant before going home. She didn't hesitate for a moment, though she wondered what Bill would say to such a thing. He'd be beside himself, she was sure. But the gardens were not large and were in full view of the windows in the back of the restaurant.

Hassan held her coat as she slid her arms into the sleeves, and a warm feeling spread through her. Beau had never done such a gentlemanly thing. She shook her head to rid herself of the thought of her ex-husband. Hassan saw the movement.

"Is everything all right?" he asked.

"Yes," she said with an embarrassed laugh. "Just trying to clear my head."

They walked outside, where the sudden blast of cold air took Lilly's breath away for a second. She had more questions for Hassan, this time about Minnesota. Most of all, she wanted to know how anyone could live in a place that was even colder than the Colorado mountains.

Hassan let out an easy laugh. "In the winter, I long for

warmer places. Minnesota is at its best in the summertime. My vote for the tropics was ignored when my sister was looking for input for vacation ideas, but," he added, glancing sideways at Lilly, "this spot is turning out better than I expected."

Lilly smiled at him, not trusting herself to say anything. She was afraid one of two things would happen: either she would put her foot in her mouth or mistakenly blurt out how attractive she found Hassan.

Hassan had lots of questions about Colorado—how long winter lasted, what it was like in the summertime, and when the slow season was for tourists in the Rocky Mountains. Other than her children and her dog, Lilly's favorite subject was Colorado, and Juniper Junction in particular. She waxed poetically about her state and the reasons it was her favorite place in the world, and Hassan seemed intrigued by her descriptions of a Rocky Mountain summer.

"If what you say about Colorado in the summertime is true, this might be a place I should visit once the weather is warmer," he said.

"I'm sure you'd love it," Lilly replied.

"How safe is it in Juniper Junction?" Hassan asked. "I've been reading the newspaper since we've been on vacation and there have been two murders in town. It doesn't seem like a dangerous place to me, but the stories in the paper suggest otherwise."

A groan escaped from Lilly's lips. "I was hoping you wouldn't mention those, since I seem to be involved with both," she said ruefully. "The first victim, Eden Barclay, was found strangled in my shop. The second victim, Herb Knight, was found dead the morning after he had a big argument with me at a holiday party."

Hassan stopped walking and looked at Lilly, his eyes wide with surprise. "You're kidding me."

"I wish. But it's all true. I can't think why Eden would have been in my shop after I closed it. And as for Herb, he was a hotheaded yogi. Someone killed him right in his studio."

"But they obviously don't believe you committed either of those murders," Hassan said.

"Unfortunately, I haven't been cleared yet. I don't have an alibi for either murder that can be confirmed by anyone."

"That's simply unbelievable," he said, shaking his head. "So you haven't been cleared. But are you an actual suspect?"

Lilly shrugged. "My brother, Bill, is on the police force here in town and he's trying to get police to move quickly to find the murderer or murderers, but they can only go so fast when there aren't any clues to be had."

"I'm sorry you have to go through this," Hassan said quietly.

"I'm just hoping it will be over soon," Lilly said with a sigh. "It hangs over my head every minute of the day." She looked over at him. "That's part of the reason this evening has been so nice. It's allowed me to get away from the drama for a little while and have a grown-up conversation that doesn't involve motive or opportunity." She gave him a wan smile.

"In that case, perhaps you'd like to go back to the house where I'm staying and meet my family," he suggested.

"I would like that, but I really should be getting home," she said. She was sorry to decline the invitation, but she wanted to get home and see the kids before they went to bed and she wanted to talk to Bill to see if there had been any progress in finding Beau. Though she had been dying to pull out her phone and check her texts while she and Hassan ate dinner, she felt it would be too rude. Now that the evening was drawing to a close, she was feeling anxious again and as much as she had enjoyed herself, she needed to get home.

"If you would like to go out again, I would consider it my duty to keep your mind off your troubles," Hassan said with a grin as they made their way through the parking lot. She unlocked her car door with the key fob and he opened it for her. She stood in front of him nervously. Was he going to kiss her?

Worse yet, was he going to shake her hand? She thought she would pass out wondering.

He gazed at her for a moment, the expression on his face unreadable, then he leaned toward her. She closed her eyes and took a deep breath, but he surprised her by kissing her cheek. She opened her eyes and he was grinning at her.

"I hope you don't mind me doing that," he said. *Mind? A kiss on the lips would have been nice, but I'll take what I can get,* Lilly thought. She smiled at him and shook her head.

"Not at all," she answered.

"If it's all right, I'll stop by your shop in the next couple days and perhaps we can go out again," he said.

"I'd like that."

She slid into the driver's seat and he closed the car door with a gentle *thud*. Then she pulled out of the parking lot while he was getting into his car. He watched her drive away and in her rear-view mirror she saw him waving.

CHAPTER 28

W hen Lilly got home she chatted with the kids before they went to bed, then she took out her phone and texted Bill. She had been surprised that he didn't text her while she was at dinner, so that probably meant he hadn't located Beau yet.

"Hi. Nothing to report," he greeted her. He must have known what she was going to ask.

"How can it be so hard to find an apartment or condo complex with an indoor pool?" she asked in frustration. Bill might have called it "whining."

"We've just got a couple places still to check out. Hopefully we'll get a lead on him at one of those places."

"You'll let me know, right?"

"Of course. You'll be my first call if I find him."

"Did you talk to Mom tonight?"

"Yeah. She was fine. How was your date?"

"I had a great time. Hassan is charming."

"Hassan? That's not a name you hear around Juniper Junction very often. You're more likely to hear "Chip" or "Flynn." Is he Muslim?"

"Yes. Normally I save my heavy personal questions for the second date, but he did mention it." As Bill shared Lilly's parents, he also shared her sarcastic tendencies, so he wasn't ruffled by her response.

After Lilly hung up she immediately called Noley. She told her friend all about her date with Hassan.

"Hassan sounds hot," Noley said.

Lilly laughed. "How can you tell?"

"I don't know. He just does. When do I get to meet him?"

"Let's see if we go out again before we go making plans to meet the family," Lilly answered dryly.

"Did he kiss you?"

"On the cheek."

Noley let out a sigh. "How romantic and old-fashioned."

"Do you think? Maybe I just don't appeal to him."

"He wouldn't have kissed you at all if you didn't appeal to him. He would have shaken hands instead. Plus he would have sent you on your way after dinner instead of suggesting a walk in the snow. It's all just too romantic."

"Easy there, tiger."

"So he's a gem hunter. That's got to be the coolest job in the world."

"I agree."

"So you two have a lot in common. I'm so excited!" she squealed.

When Lilly hung up with Noley she found she was too excited to sleep. It had been ages since her last date, and this one had been so... so... invigorating. She had enjoyed every minute she spent with Hassan. She hoped he would call back. Soon.

The next day was the Main-Street-open-late celebration that was supposed to help make up for Lilly's Black Friday sales. Lilly was busy in the shop from the moment she unlocked the front door and was glad she had spent so much time decorating the displays for Christmas. She got rave reviews for how lovely the shop looked. And true to her promise to surprise Lilly with a dazzling menu, Noley had made finger foods: cheese straws, sun-dried tomato and goat cheese palmiers, roasted shrimp cocktail, rum balls, and lots of cookies. Lilly had decided wine created too much liability, so Noley had made a nonalcoholic punch. That way Lilly wouldn't have to deal with anyone who had celebrated a little too much.

The sales were fast and frequent that evening and Lilly was busy with customers while Noley made sure they were well-fed as they waited their turn to speak to Lilly and part with their credit card numbers. When Lilly finally closed and locked the front door at ten o'clock, she and Noley flopped down on two chairs in the office and ate what remained of the hors d'oeuvres while they talked.

"I was surprised Hassan didn't come in," Noley said between mouthfuls. "I was so hoping to meet him tonight."

"To tell you the truth, I hoped he would come in, too. But he's on vacation with his entire family, so maybe they had plans." *I hope that's what happened and that his plans weren't to take someone else to dinner,* Lilly thought to herself with a miserable twinge of jealousy.

"I know what you're thinking," Noley chided her. "You're thinking he's out to dinner with someone else. Quit worrying."

"You know me too well," Lilly said with a laugh.

After they had cleaned up the food Noley went home. Lilly stayed for a little while to tidy up. It was close to eleven o'clock when she looked at her watch and yawned. *This could have been done in half the time if I had someone to help me,* Lilly thought. *I'd be in bed by now.*

She snapped her fingers. "Taffy!" she exclaimed to herself. Why hadn't she thought of Taffy? She wondered if Eden Barclay's former employee had found a new job. She vowed to call the woman first thing in the morning.

When she arrived home the kids were already asleep, but there was a note from Laurel on the kitchen table. "Look in the fridge!" it read. Lilly opened the refrigerator door and gasped when she saw a gorgeous bouquet of pine boughs, red berries, pinecones, and little white rosebuds. The vase was encircled with at least two dozen candy canes held in place with a red velvet ribbon. There was a card attached to a pick in the bouquet.

"*Thank you again for a lovely evening yesterday. I wanted to visit your shop tonight for the Main Street celebration, but my aunt insisted on taking everyone to dinner.*

Hassan

So she had been right. Hassan's other plans for the evening had included his family, not some leggy blond. She grinned to herself as she set the vase in the center of the kitchen table. Things were looking up.

True to the promise she had made to herself, she called Taffy the next morning as soon as she got to the shop.

"Taffy, this is Lilly Carlsen from Juniper Junction Jewels. I don't know if you remember me."

"Sure I do. I asked if you knew of anyone hiring. Have you found something?"

"Actually, I think I have. Would you have any interest in coming down to my shop for an interview?"

There was the briefest of silences, then Taffy gushed, "I'd love that! Thank you so much for the opportunity. When should I be there?"

"Are you free today?" Lilly asked.

"Yes."

"Then come down to the shop anytime today and we can talk then. You might just have to wait a few minutes if I'm busy with customers."

"That's okay. Gee, thanks for thinking of me. I'll see you later today."

She was, indeed, busy with a customer when Taffy came into the shop later that afternoon. Lilly noticed her out of the corner of her eye and gave a little wave, then she returned to her customer and Taffy waited patiently until Lilly had concluded the sale.

"Hi, Taffy. Thanks for coming in," Lilly greeted her.

"Thanks for calling me. I was beginning to think I would never find a job," Taffy said. Lilly could hear the relief in her voice.

"So what can you do?" Lilly asked.

"At the general store I waited on customers, answered the phone, opened up some mornings, locked up at night sometimes, and counted the cash register and credit card receipts at the end of the day. I used to have a small store when I lived in Missouri, so I'm familiar with everything that has to be done."

Lilly nodded. "All that would be useful here, but I also need someone who knows at least a little about jewelry and gems. Do you know anything about them?"

Taffy shook her head. "Not really, but I'm a quick learner," she answered. The eagerness in her voice was apparent, and Lilly decided on the spot to give Taffy a trial run.

"Okay, that works for me. I have some books in the back office that you can take home. Spend some time looking through those and hopefully they'll get you acquainted with some of the things you'll need to know to work here. When can you start?"

"Today, if you want me to."

"I'll tell you what. You can start tomorrow, but I'll pay you for the time you spend looking through those books today."

Taffy gave Lilly a bright smile. "Thank you! That'll be great. How much time should I spend on the books?"

"Just learn what you can from them and I'll pay you for eight hours of work."

"That's really generous of you, Ms. Carlsen."

"And please call me Lilly."

"Okay, Lilly."

CHAPTER 29

S he beckoned Taffy to follow her as she went back into the office and selected several thin volumes from one of her bookshelves. She handed them to Taffy.

"These are great for people who are just learning about gems and jewelry," Lilly said. "They'll give you a good background."

Taffy thanked her again and left through the front door of the shop.

Lilly smiled to herself after Taffy left. Not only would she get some help around the shop, but having an assistant would enable her to spend a little more time at home with the kids and with her mother. And maybe Hassan, too, she hoped.

She told Laurel and Tighe about Taffy when she got home that night. They greeted her news with relief.

"Mom, you work so hard. I'm glad you've finally hired someone to help you," Tighe said.

"Yeah. Does this mean we can go on vacation sometimes?" Laurel asked.

"I don't know about that yet," Lilly cautioned. "I'll have to see how Taffy works out. I'm not ready to leave my store in someone else's hands just yet. For one thing, I hardly know her. I've only met her twice. And for another thing, it's still my store. I can't just leave it to other people to handle for me."

"But you can take a break sometimes, can't you?" Tighe asked.

"Of course. That's why I hired Taffy."

"Where should we go first when we go on vacation?" Laurel asked.

"I vote for Hawaii. I want to learn how to surf," Tighe answered.

"I vote for Paris," Laurel said.

"Um, kids, there's no more money to take an extravagant vacation than there was yesterday," Lilly reminded them, her eyebrows arched. "Less, in fact, because now I'm paying an assistant."

"Ugh. Au revoir, Paris," Laurel responded. Tighe nodded his agreement.

Lilly smiled. She would miss this type of banter when the kids were in college. A twinge of sadness—or was it despair?—rose up in the back of her mind. She wouldn't think about the kids leaving for college right now.

"We can at least go out for dinner to celebrate," Lilly said. "Get your coats on and we'll go."

"I can't," Laurel said. "I told Nick I would meet him at the library."

"Oh, Nick, I've missed you so much," Tighe teased in a high voice. Laurel swatted his arm.

"Can't you postpone it an hour?" Lilly asked.

"Can I invite him?" Laurel countered.

Lilly sighed. She supposed it was the only way she was going to spend time with her daughter. And it was probably time for her to meet Nick.

"All right. But hurry up. I'm starved."

Laurel ran upstairs and came down talking into her cell phone. She clicked it off and turned to her mother and brother.

"He's coming. He'll meet us wherever we go and he and I can drive to the library after dinner. Where are we eating?"

"How about the Route Ten Diner?" Tighe suggested.

"Sounds good to me," Lilly said. "Laurel?"

"Okay. Let me text Nick." Her fingers flew across the keys as she told Nick where to meet them.

"We should take Gran with us," Laurel said.

Great. All I need is to go out for a nice, relaxing dinner and end up with Nick the phantom boyfriend and my mother, who may or may not decide to wear any clothes, Lilly thought with a grimace.

"Uncle Bill and I will take Gran out for dinner sometime soon," Lilly said. "I just wanted to spend time with you guys."

"And Nick," Tighe said, grinning.

"And Nick. Of course."

The three of them piled into Lilly's car and she drove them west out of town to the Route Ten Diner. As always, the parking lot was full of pickup trucks and motorcycles. It was a popular place with locals. They went inside and sat down at a booth by the window, but since it was dark outside they could only see their own reflections.

They had been there about ten minutes when Laurel's face lit up. She was seated where she could watch the diner's front door and Lilly assumed Nick must have walked in.

A moment later Lilly was shaking hands with a shockingly tall young man with light brown hair that needed cutting. He grinned when Laurel introduced him as her boyfriend.

CHAPTER 30

"I t's nice to meet you, Nick," she said, gesturing for him to sit next to Laurel. Nick slid into the booth, his hands under the table. Lilly assumed one of his hands was on her daughter's knee and she wanted to smack him. She put both of her own hands on the table in a not-so-subtle effort to get him to follow suit.

But he chose not to take the hint. Or maybe he just didn't get it.

Nick liked talking about himself. In the first five minutes after his arrival at the diner, Lilly learned that he was an avid skier and wanted to be a ski instructor after he graduated from high school. *So much for my daughter marrying a surgeon,* Lilly thought with an inward groan.

"Wouldn't you like to go to college first?" she asked. Laurel kicked her under the table.

"Nah," Nick said. "It's a little-known fact that good ski instructors can make as much as a CEO."

I have a feeling I know why that's such a little-known fact, Lilly thought. *Because it's a crock.*

"That's funny. I was married to a ski instructor—Laurel and Tighe's father—and he never made that much."

Laurel and Tighe both fixed her with blank stares. "Our father was a ski instructor?" Tighe asked, his eyes wide.

Lilly hadn't meant to let that information slip. Damn that Nick. He was bringing out the worst in her.

"Yes, he was," Lilly said matter-of-factly. "A good one, too," she added with a glance at Nick. "But he never made as much money as any CEO I ever heard of."

"Even so," Nick said after taking a long slurp of soda, "good instructors can make good money."

"And then what do they do in the summertime?"

"There are plenty of opportunities for someone who's willing to work." Nick smiled broadly. "Like me."

"So, what's everyone ordering?" Laurel asked, giving Lilly the evil eye.

"Mom, Laurel wants you to change the subject," Tighe said, his eyes twinkling. Lilly would have sworn he was trying not to laugh.

Nick appeared oblivious to the barely-concealed family argument that was fomenting around him. Laurel leaned into his shoulder and whispered something to him, studiously ignoring her mother. Then she pulled out her phone, turned toward the corner of the booth so no one could see what she was doing, and let her fingers fly.

It wasn't long before Lilly's phone buzzed. Laurel made a point of scanning the menu with hawk-like concentration and Lilly knew who the text was from. She decided to make another point rather than looking at her phone. She could read a snarky text from Laurel anytime.

"It's rude to use your phone at the table, Laurel. Haven't we spoken about that many times before?"

"Yeah," came the surly reply.

"Then please leave your phone in your pocket while we're eating."

"We haven't even ordered yet."

"Then please leave your phone in your pocket while we're in the restaurant."

"It's barely a restaurant."

"That's enough, Laurel," Lilly said in her best warning voice.

Laurel rolled her eyes and Lilly made a mental note to remind her daughter that boys did not find disrespectful girls attractive. Or did they? At any rate, she was going to have to remind Laurel who the adult was in the family, at least for the time being.

The waitress came to take their orders just in time to stop Laurel from saying anything else. Lilly waited while Nick ordered a shrimp cocktail and a prime rib platter and Laurel and Tighe ordered club sandwiches, then she ordered a cheeseburger and fries. Settling back into the booth after the waitress left, she asked Nick if he played any sports.

"Yup. Basketball," he said. Lilly smiled.

"I should have guessed that. How tall are you?"

"Six four," came the answer.

"He scored the most points all season last year," Laurel said proudly, clearly more pleased with the direction of this conversation. Nick preened.

"I did," he said, making a valiant attempt to sound self-deprecating.

"That's wonderful. What do you like to do in your spare time?" Lilly asked.

"Mom, he isn't interviewing for a job," Laurel said in a warning tone.

"I know. I'd just like to get to know him a little better. After all, he's dating my daughter," Lilly answered with a wink.

The eye-roll again. Laurel's earlier pleasure at the direction the conversation was taking evaporated quickly.

"I like to play video games, skateboard, stuff like that," Nick answered.

"Where do you live?" Lilly asked.

"In one of the condos off Deer Run Road," he answered. "I want to move. I can't park my truck there because there are only two parking spots for each condo and my parents each have a car."

"So where do you park your truck?"

"I just park in other people's empty spots."

The waitress brought Nick's shrimp cocktail and he devoured it in a matter of two minutes. He offered one shrimp to Laurel, but she wrinkled her nose at him. He grinned.

An uncomfortable silence lingered at the table while the foursome waited for the rest of the meal to arrive. Lilly's phone rang.

"It's not polite to answer your phone in the restaurant," Laurel said pointedly.

"It's okay if you're a mom," Lilly retorted. She excused herself from the table and answered the call. It was Bill.

"Did you find him?" she asked, walking to the vestibule of the diner.

"Sure did. Found his truck, ran the plates and everything."

"Where's he staying?" Lilly asked.

"If I tell you, do you promise not to do anything stupid, like showing up at his place?"

"Of course," she answered, exasperated. "Why would I do that? He's the last person I want to see."

"Okay. He's staying at a fancy-schmancy complex outside of town, on Route Nineteen. He's got himself a big two-bedroom right next to the clubhouse, which incidentally has an indoor pool and hot tub. I can just imagine Mom in there having a soak."

Lilly let that image flee her mind before speaking. "Thanks, Bill. Has anyone from the police station talked to him?"

"Not yet. We just got confirmation on the whereabouts of his apartment."

"Okay. I'm at dinner with the kids. We're celebrating because I hired an assistant today."

"That's great. Maybe you can take some time off now."

"That's my plan. The kids have already placed their orders for trips to Hawaii and Paris." Bill let out a loud laugh.

"Let me know when you're leaving and I'll hide inside one of your bags."

"You got it." Lilly hung up with a smile. Somehow it was comforting to know that the police knew where Beau was staying. Not for the first time, she felt a sense of security knowing that Bill was looking out for her.

She didn't spot Beau until she was making her way back to the table. He was standing at the counter, probably waiting for a to-go order. He was talking to one of the waitresses and not looking in her direction. Instinctively she turned her head away from him, hoping he wouldn't turn around and see her.

But her wishing was for naught. She sat down at the table next to Tighe and put her phone on the table next to her.

"Who was that?" Laurel asked.

Lilly glanced at her, warring with herself over whether to answer the question that was clearly none of Laurel's business. She decided not to pick that battle and answered, "Uncle Bill."

"What did he want?" Laurel asked.

Lilly glared at her daughter for a moment. "Nothing," she finally said. Laurel locked eyes with her mother in a silent test of wills and Lilly felt a slight thrill of triumph when Laurel looked away first.

But the sense of triumph, however small, dissipated immediately when Lilly looked up and noticed Beau walking toward her table. She busied herself rummaging through her purse, praying that Beau hadn't seen them and that he was just visiting the restroom.

No such luck. Beau stopped at her table and looked down at her. "Hi there, Lil. How's everything?"

"Fine, thanks."

"Who've you got with you tonight?" he asked, as if he didn't know.

"These are my children, Tighe and Laurel," she answered, not making eye contact with her ex. Then she gestured toward Nick. "And this is Laurel's friend."

Beau was silent for an awkward moment, though it seemed to Lilly like an eternity and she used the time to pray that he wouldn't announce to everyone at the table that he was the kids' father. Somewhat to her surprise, he didn't reveal the secret.

"Nice to meet you, kids," was all he said. Lilly breathed a quiet sigh of relief. She had dodged a bullet—this time. He turned to leave and winked at her. She ignored him, hoping the kids hadn't noticed.

She needn't have worried; Tighe was looking at the dessert menu that was printed on a framed postcard propped on the table and Laurel and Nick were nudging each other and giggling like little girls.

"Want anything for dessert?" she asked. Laurel shook her head and looked at Nick. Much to Lilly's surprise, he declined. She glanced at Tighe, but he put the menu back on the table and said, "Nah. They don't have anything but banana pudding and ice cream. If they had chocolate cake I would have some."

Lilly signaled for the bill and walked up to the cash register at the front of the diner to pay, then she waited for the kids to gather their coats and the four of them walked outside. Lilly's eyes scanned the parking lot, but Beau had apparently driven off.

Laurel and Nick had decided to skip the library. Lilly and Tighe sat in the car waiting while the two lovebirds said good-bye, as if they might not see each other for the next six months instead of at school the next day, then Laurel joined them and they drove home.

Laurel scooted upstairs as soon as they went in the house and Tighe stood at the kitchen counter, opening and closing cupboards for no apparent reason while Lilly refreshed Barney's water and fed him.

It was clear Tighe wanted to talk about something. Lilly turned to him when she was done feeding Barney.

"What's up?" she asked, cleaning a couple mugs that were in the sink. She didn't face Tighe, thinking that he would prefer to talk if she wasn't looking at him. She had learned a thing or two about teenage boys in the past several years.

And she was right. Tighe shuffled his feet while she watched him out of the corner of her eye. Finally he spoke. "Who was that guy who came over to our table at the diner?"

CHAPTER 31

The smart thing would have been to act nonchalant, continue washing the mugs, but Lilly froze and Tighe noticed.

"What's the matter?" he asked.

"Nothing. He's just someone I used to know."

"Laurel looks just like him."

The realization that Tighe had probably figured out who Beau was hit Lilly like a fist.

"You think so?" was all she could summon the courage to say.

"Yeah. Is he our father?" Tighe had stopped shuffling and stood still now, staring at Lilly. She couldn't lie to him and she couldn't avoid answering the question.

"Yes." She met his gaze but her voice was barely audible.

"I knew it. Why didn't you guys say something?"

"That wasn't the time or the place."

"Does he live in Juniper Junction?"

"I hope not. He showed up in town recently and I assume he's not planning to stay."

"Why's he here?"

Lilly shrugged. She couldn't tell her son that Beau wanted to be his father again.

"Where's he been all this time?"

"You mean, since he left us?"

"Yeah."

"I asked him the same thing. He said he's moved around a lot. He goes where the jobs are, it seems."

"What's he do?"

"Like I mentioned earlier, he's a ski instructor. I don't know what he does when there's no snow."

Tighe smiled. "I wondered why you freaked out when Nick said he wants to be a ski instructor."

"Was it that obvious?"

"Yeah. But I don't blame you. I think he's a loser."

"I have to agree with you there, but let's keep that between us for now. I don't want to come right out and tell Laurel what I think of him. I'm hoping she'll come to that realization on her own."

Tighe nodded. "Hopefully they won't get married before she realizes it." He looked up and saw his mother wince at his words. "Sorry. That didn't come out right."

"That's okay. I know what you mean. I definitely should have done some serious thinking before I married your father. I would have come to the same conclusion as I hope Laurel will."

"Did Gran like him?"

Lilly grimaced. "She didn't when we were married, but apparently she thinks he's just wonderful now."

"What do you mean?" Tighe had been looking down at his fingernails but Lilly's mention of his grandmother snapped him to attention. Lilly immediately regretted saying anything.

She tried a breezy approach. "Oh, it's no big deal. He just stopped by to say hello to her for old time's sake."

"And she liked him?" He sounded incredulous.

"She told me she did."

"I can't believe he would go see her. Does Uncle Bill know

about it?" There was that protectiveness again. Lilly felt another pang of sadness at the thought of her son leaving for college.

"Yes," she answered, nodding. "As you can imagine, Uncle Bill was not happy to hear about that. He and every other police officer in Juniper Junction has been trying to figure out where Beau's staying."

"What was he like?" Tighe asked. The questions were slipping into untested territory for Lilly. She had never said much to the kids about their father except to tell them that he had left when they were very young, and as they got older they had learned that questions about Beau were not met with eager communication.

"He was very exciting when I met him. He was athletic, a great ski instructor, and he had all kinds of plans for the future. He was going to go into the construction business with a friend and make his fortune that way. But he got sidetracked with the ski life and his interest in going into business waned. Eventually he got itchy feet and wanted to move around to other ski meccas, like Utah and Vermont. He apparently didn't feel like he could take a wife and kids with him to explore a lifestyle like that, so he left. I never did find out where he went. After he had been gone and I hadn't heard from him for a certain number of years, I got a court order to declare us divorced." She deliberately didn't mention Beau's indiscretions with other women.

Lilly took a deep breath. She had just shared with Tighe more about Beau than she had ever said about him in the past fifteen years.

"Wow. So he's just a loser, too. Like Nick."

"I'm probably the wrong person to ask if you want an unbiased opinion about Beau." Tighe smiled at her.

"He left you, he left me and Laurel. That makes him a loser," he said. His voice was firm and strong.

To her astonishment, Lilly started to cry. She hung her head and the tears started flowing as if someone had turned on a faucet.

"Mom, what's wrong?" Tighe hurried over to Lilly and wrapped her in a big, warm hug. That only made her cry harder.

"I just don't know what I've done to deserve you and Laurel," she said through her sobs. "I'm going to miss you both so much when you go to college."

"Well, at least me," he said. She laughed.

"Laurel, too," she said with a hiccup.

"I know. I'm just kidding. I'm sorry if my questions made you upset. We don't have to talk about Beau anymore."

Lilly pulled herself away and looked at her son with eyes that glistened from tears. "You know, I actually feel better after talking about him."

They both turned when they heard a noise on the stairs.

"Mom, why are you crying?" Laurel had come into the kitchen with an empty water glass. "Tighe, what's wrong?" Her voice was rising as she approached them.

Lilly looked at Tighe and smiled. "Tighe figured out something at dinner and I'm just relieved about it, that's all."

"What did you figure out?" Laurel asked, turning to her brother.

Tighe gave Lilly a questioning look. "I'll tell her," she said. She took a deep breath and spilled the secret that she had been hiding—that Beau was back in town and that Laurel had met him earlier that evening.

Laurel was speechless. She looked from her mother to her brother in wide-eyed disbelief, making sputtering noises for a few moments before being able to form words.

CHAPTER 32

"That long-haired guy at the diner was our *father?*" she asked.

Tighe broke in. "Mom, I'm going upstairs. Goodnight."

Lilly hugged him again and turned to Laurel. "You want to sit down?" Laurel nodded. They pulled out chairs at the kitchen table and sat across from each other. Lilly repeated to her daughter the story she had shared with her son. Laurel's reaction was similar to her brother's.

"How come he came back after all this time?" she wanted to know.

This wasn't the time to reveal that Beau had professed his desire to give the whole fatherhood thing another whirl.

"I don't really know," Lilly answered. After all, it *was* the truth. She had no idea why Beau had come back with such a preposterous notion. "But what's important to know is that nothing is going to change with us."

"Is he going to be coming around?" Laurel asked.

"I've asked him not to, and Uncle Bill is keeping an eye out for him because he doesn't want him bothering us or Gran."

Laurel's eyes widened. "Do you think he would actually bother Gran?"

"He's already paid her a visit or two and we don't want that to continue. She's too confused sometimes to realize that he does nothing but cause pain wherever he goes."

"Maybe one of us should stay with Gran all the time to make sure he doesn't bother her." Lilly gazed at her daughter. She might be a contrarian, but her heart was in the right place. Lilly couldn't be more proud that both her kids had reacted with a protectiveness toward their grandmother when faced with the prospect of her being hoodwinked.

"Hopefully your Uncle Bill will be able to dissuade Beau from vising Gran anymore. But if we find out that Beau's gone over to her house again, we should think seriously about your idea. Maybe you and Tighe could take turns with me and Uncle Bill spending nights with her. And hiring an assistant at the shop will give me more time to spend with Gran, too, so I can keep a better eye on things."

Laurel looked down at her intertwined fingers. "You didn't like Nick, did you?"

Lilly was surprised by the abrupt change of subject. "He was all right, I suppose. I just want more for you, that's all. He doesn't seem to have much ambition and I want the best for you."

"Were you thinking about Beau when you heard that Nick wants to be a ski instructor?"

Lilly gave a tiny chuckle. "I suppose I was. I don't associate ski instructors with stability and happiness, and I suppose I projected my disappointments onto Nick. I'm sorry if I did that, but I *do* wish he had a bit more drive."

"Just because I'm dating him doesn't mean we're getting married, Mom."

Lilly sat back and fixed Laurel with an intense gaze. "You know, you're absolutely right. I guess I've been thinking long-term and it never even occurred to me that you might not be thinking the same way I do."

Laurel rolled her eyes and grinned. "Mom, I rarely think the same way you do." Lilly had to laugh.

"Go to bed," she told Laurel. "Don't worry about Beau. Uncle Bill and I will take care of him."

Laurel kissed her mother's cheek and hurried up the stairs. Lilly smiled to herself, a calm settling on her now that Laurel had told her that marriage to Nick wasn't on her young mind.

Lilly was getting ready for bed when there was a knock at the front door. She froze in the middle of pulling on her pajama pants, wondering who could be at the door. Bill or Noley would have texted first. Barney, cooped up in Lilly's bedroom behind the closed door, jumped around as if his tail were on fire. When Lilly opened the door for him, he raced down the stairs at top speed, skidding into the front door on all fours. Lilly wasn't far behind. She pinched the curtain on the sidelight, trying to peer outside to see who was there.

It was Mrs. Laforge. Lilly opened the door and Barney bounded around Mrs. Laforge's legs as the neighbor stepped into the foyer and Lilly tried to shush Barney. Finally she offered him a piece of cheese and shooed him out the back door. Mrs. Laforge followed her into the kitchen.

"Is everything all right, Mrs. Laforge?" Lilly asked. Though the older woman was nosy and could be miserable, Lilly felt a bit protective toward her, as she lived alone in the big, rambling home next door.

"I'm here to tell you that that daughter of yours brought her boyfriend right into the house while you were at work the other day." Lilly suppressed a groan.

"Don't worry, Mrs. Laforge. I've met Nick and he's a nice boy," she said, making a mental note to read Laurel the riot act before she left for school the next morning. "I'm not concerned about them as long as Tighe's here."

"But Tighe wasn't here," Mrs. Laforge noted, a triumphant smirk on her face.

"Well, thank you for bringing it to my attention. I'll be sure to speak to the kids in the morning. Is there anything else I can do for you?"

"No. I just thought you deserved to know what your kids are up to while you're always at work."

Lilly had an uncharitable urge to strangle Mrs. Laforge's chicken-like neck, but refrained. Instead she pasted a wide smile on her lips and shared her good news with her neighbor. "You'll be happy to learn, then, that I've hired an assistant at the shop. That should give me more time with the kids and with my mother."

Mrs. Laforge nodded. "Good. Your poor mother deserves better."

Lilly opened the back door, hoping Barney would drape himself over Mrs. Laforge with snowy, frigid paws, but Mrs. Laforge turned around to head toward the front door.

"No need to show me out, Mrs. Carlsen. I know the way."

"Good," Lilly muttered. "The sooner the better."

"Oh, I almost forgot." Mrs. Laforge's voice grew louder again as she was apparently making her way back to the kitchen. Barney turned from where he was gobbling a biscuit Lilly had placed in his dish and raced over to Mrs. Laforge. She looked at him with disdain.

"There was a man parked outside your house for a long time yesterday. In a dark blue pickup truck. Unsavory-looking sort."

"Did he have longish blond hair?"

"Yes."

Beau. Lilly shivered at the thought of him sitting outside her house when no one was home. Wait—what if someone *had* been at home?

"Do you happen to remember what time this was, Mrs. Laforge?" Lilly asked in her sweetest tone.

"Sure do," the neighbor said, nodding. "It was eleven thirty in the morning. I know because I wrote it down." So the kids would have been in school. Lilly didn't know whether to feel relieved or even more creeped out.

She writes stuff down? Lilly couldn't help smiling as she pictured Mrs. Laforge, using ream after ream of paper to take notes on the various comings and goings of each neighbor. *I probably have my own file at her house,* Lilly thought with a grimace. *Like the FBI.*

Barney was snuffling around Mrs. Laforge's feet and apparently the woman couldn't stand it any longer. Lilly knew her to be a lover of cats, and it was probably taking every ounce of willpower she possessed to be in Lilly's house with a slobbering dog. She smiled at Mrs. Laforge again and waited for the woman to leave. "Thanks again, Mrs. Laforge!" Lilly called behind her as she returned to her own house through the snow. Lilly made sure Mrs. Laforge was safely inside her own house before shutting her own front door and going upstairs to bed.

"Who was at the door, Mom?" Tighe asked, coming out of the bathroom.

"Mrs. Laforge."

"What did she want?"

"To tattle on your sister and Nick. And you."

"Why me? I didn't do anything."

Lilly sighed. "I know. You weren't home when Laurel brought Nick to the house, that's all."

"I'm not her babysitter."

"I didn't say you were. But apparently Mrs. Laforge thinks you should be. Go to bed and don't worry about her. She's lonely and has nothing else to do than spy on the neighbors."

"When you put it that way I feel sorry for her."

"Yeah, I know. Feels better to be mad at her, doesn't it?" Lilly smiled at her son and snapped off the light.

CHAPTER 33

Taffy was waiting when Lilly arrived at work the next morning. Lilly showed her the office, the location of the vaults, and showed her how to work the copy machine. Taffy was eager to show Lilly how much she had learned by reading the books Lilly had sent home with her.

"I never knew there were so many kinds of gems," Taffy said as she followed Lilly into the front of the shop. "I think my favorite is tanzanite. I always loved sapphires before this, but tanzanite is only mined in one place in Tanzania, so that makes it rarer."

"Tanzanite is a beautiful stone," Lilly agreed.

"Is there any in the shop?" Taffy asked. "I'd like to see it for real. Not just in a picture."

"No, we don't carry any right now. If someone comes in with a question about it, I could always order a few pieces. But people tend to prefer the better-known stones, so I only discuss it with people if they ask about tanzanite specifically. Same with spinel and a few others. I really should order some, because they *are* beautiful. But I have to cater to what people want, and that's mostly diamonds, rubies, and sapphires. And gold and silver, of course."

"And you design jewelry, right?"

"Yes, but I like to use stones that are local to the Rocky Mountain region. They don't have to be from Colorado, but my customers prefer that they come from the western part of the United States." All this talk about gems and stones was making her think about Hassan. When would she hear from him again? She shook her head to dislodge that thought and turned her attention back to Taffy.

"Sounds like you learned a lot and that you enjoyed it," she said, smiling at her assistant.

"Yeah. This is going to be different from working for Eden because it was boring there. She just carried normal stuff, like first aid supplies and toys and stuff." She stopped talking and the silence widened between them in the wake of her mention of Eden's name.

Lilly finally broke the silence. "Taffy, I'll set you up at my desk so you can fill out the employment forms and then I'll show you around up front."

Taffy followed her to the back, where Lilly gave her a small pile of papers to fill out. The store wasn't open yet, so Lilly stayed in the back going through invoices while Taffy worked. When both women had finished, Lilly stuffed the papers into a mailing envelope and texted her accountant to come pick them up. Then she led Taffy to the front, showed her how to lock and unlock the front door, and showed her the proper way to hang necklaces and bracelets for display. Taffy was a quick learner and asked if she could set up the displays in all the glass cases.

"Sure," Lilly said. "Just remember to face the price tag away from the customer."

Lilly busied herself with other paperwork on top of one of the display cases while they waited for the first customer. Lilly had explained to Taffy that her job was only to watch Lilly interact with customers on this first day on the job, but beginning tomorrow she would be able to take care of customers under Lilly's watchful eyes.

The first person who came through the door was an elderly man who needed a new watch. Lilly showed him the watches she had on display, then waited patiently as he tried on one after another. Taffy stood by her boss the entire time, watching Lilly's movements and noting which watches Lilly showed the man and in what order.

While other customers came in to browse, Lilly left Taffy in charge of the man trying on watches and it wasn't long before Taffy approached her to notify her that the man was buying one of the more expensive watches he had tried on. Lilly smiled and introduced her to a couple who were looking at bracelets for their daughter for Christmas. She asked Taffy to assist them while she took care of wrapping the man's watch and taking care of the payment details.

She kept her ear cocked while she waited on the elderly man, listening to what Taffy was saying to the couple. Apparently she was about the same age as their daughter, so they were asking her advice about what styles were popular with young women and which design Taffy thought their daughter might like. She was doing a great job.

Lilly thanked the man for shopping in Juniper Junction Jewels and was holding the door for him when her cell phone rang. It was Tighe. The last time Tighe had called her during school hours it was to announce he had broken his wrist playing tennis in gym class. She answered the phone with a breathless "What's wrong?"

"Take it easy, Mom. No big deal, but I left school to go to the diner for breakfast during second period and the car wouldn't start when I left the diner."

Lilly breathed a sigh of relief. No injuries.

"What did you do? Where are you calling from?"

"I'm calling from school. The tow truck guy gave me a ride back here after he dropped my truck off with the mechanic.

Can you pick me up later today and drive me over to get the truck if they can fix it?"

Lilly glanced at Taffy. She wasn't ready to leave Taffy in charge of the shop while she left. She was working toward that goal, but Taffy wasn't ready to run the shop by herself.

"It may have to wait until this weekend, or maybe Uncle Bill could take you over. That might even be a good thing. If you show up in your uncle's police car, maybe the mechanic won't overcharge you."

"I won't know until later today how long it'll take to fix the car. I might not even be able to pick it up today. I was just checking since you got that new assistant."

Lilly lowered her voice. "I don't think I want to leave her alone in the shop just yet. I barely know her. I'd hate to come back and have the place cleared out of all my inventory."

"Oh. That makes sense. I'll call or text you when I know about the car and maybe Uncle Bill will be free later."

Lilly hung up and walked over to where Taffy had indeed helped the couple choose a bracelet for their daughter. It was a gorgeous tennis bracelet with alternating diamonds and sapphires. It happened to be Lilly's favorite piece in the store, other than her own designs. She was thrilled that Taffy had sold it, but sorry to see it leave the store.

"Taffy, you're a born saleswoman," Lilly said when the delighted couple had left the store.

"Thanks. I just have a special connection with people, I guess," she answered.

An odd way to phrase "people person," Lilly thought. Aloud, she said, "Whatever it is, I'm impressed." Taffy grinned at the compliment.

It was a quiet day in the store. Taffy left for a half hour at lunchtime and when she returned Lilly sat at her desk to eat the sandwich she had brought from home. She sat back, trying to remember the last time she had enjoyed lunch at her desk.

Normally she ate it standing up at one of the display cases. This assistant idea of hers was a gem. So to speak.

Despite Taffy's success, however, when Tighe called later that afternoon to tell Lilly that his truck would be ready early that evening, Lilly wasn't ready to leave Taffy in charge of the shop while she took Tighe to the mechanic. It wouldn't be fair to Taffy, either, to ask her to mind the shop alone on her first day at work.

"Can we pick up your truck early tomorrow morning?" Lilly asked Tighe. "I can drive you over there early and you can still be at school on time."

"That's fine."

Lilly sent Taffy home an hour before closing and locked up the shop herself. She hoped it wouldn't be long before she could let Taffy do the end-of-the-day work and she could get an afternoon off once in a while. But the holiday season was not the time to start easing up—it was the time to work longer hours, to try to benefit from people's generous spirit of giving.

Lilly went home to a deliciously-scented dinner of pork tenderloin in the crock pot. She had slathered it with a maple-bourbon glaze and set the timer to cook the pork all afternoon. Laurel had baked some potatoes for the three of them and Gran, so all Lilly had to do was whip up a Waldorf salad to round out the meal. Before they sat down to dinner Tighe drove her car over to her mother's house and dropped off dinner.

"How's Gran today?" Lilly asked when Tighe had returned home and the little family was sitting down to dinner.

He shrugged. "Can't we get her a kitten or something? She seems lonely."

Lilly felt a pang of sadness for her mother, who had spent years caring for her own children, husband, and countless friends and family who were always coming through the door. She had always found enough food to feed anyone who happened to be at the house at dinnertime and she did every-thing with a cheerful smile. She hated to think of her mother, now aging, living alone and depending on others for the things she used to do for herself and her own family.

On the other hand…a kitten? Bill would flip.

"That's a great idea!" Laurel said, the excitement shining in her eyes. "Please, Mom? Can we surprise Gran with a kitten?"

"I don't know," Lilly answered slowly. "Let me think about it." Did she really need to be worrying about her mother with a kitten on top of everything else?

CHAPTER 34

The next morning Lilly and both kids left the house well before the usual time so they would be able to pick up Tighe's car and everyone could get to work and school on time. Lilly sat behind the wheel of her car, ready to pull out of the driveway, and it occurred to her that she had no idea where the tow truck driver had taken Tighe's car.

"Where are we going?" she asked.

Tighe glanced at a sheet of paper he was holding. "Horstman Auto Repair."

Lilly knew that name. From where?

Then it dawned on her. The owner, Jed Horstman, had been Eden Barclay's first husband. Lilly suddenly felt a reluctance to pick up Tighe's car, and it showed in slow pace of her drive to the body shop.

"Mom, we're going to be late to school," Tighe said, a hint of impatience in his voice.

"I'll write you both an excuse if you need one," was her uncharacteristic response. Tighe, who was sitting next to her in the front seat, turned around and raised an eyebrow at Laurel.

She finally pulled into the cramped parking lot of Horstman Auto Repair. Between the rusting metal shells of former cars and the piles of used tires, Tighe's truck sat waiting for the ride to school. A single bulb burned in the office, a pinpoint of light in the early-morning charcoal darkness.

Tighe got out of Lilly's car, followed by Laurel; Lilly brought up the reluctant rear. A large man in denim dungarees streaked with grease looked up from the desk where he was pecking away at the computer.

"You must be Tighe Carlsen," he said, standing and extending a rough hand. Tighe returned the handshake, nodding.

"Yes, sir," he said. "Came in to get my truck."

"And you must be Mom," the man said, turning to Lilly. "Jed Horstman."

"Yes, I'm Lilly Carlsen. Good to meet you, Mr. Horstman. Thanks for fixing Tighe's truck so quickly." Under the light of the single bulb, she could see that Jed Horstman carried a small paunch inside the overalls. He was of medium height with light brown hair that was a little too long and looked greasy in the dimness. Maybe it was just wet from showering.

"No problem," he answered, then ran his hand through his hair. "Carlsen. That name sounds familiar to me for some reason."

Lilly took a deep breath. She had seen this coming. "I believe you were Eden Barclay's first husband? I'm the owner of the jewelry store where her body was found. I'm sorry for your family's loss, Mr. Horstman."

He gazed at her for a moment while her heart thudded. How would he react? Was he going to haul off and punch her? Was he just going to continue staring at her? Would he order her out of the office?

None of the above, as it turned out. "Oh, yeah. I guess. Actually, I think it's because my son, Davey, goes to school with

Tighe here," he said, nodding his head in Tighe's general direction.

Lilly could have kicked herself. She had gotten so worked up about having to talk to Eden's first husband that it had never occurred to her that he might not miss his ex-wife as much as she thought he would. *I'm keeping my big fat mouth closed after this,* she thought.

Tighe confirmed that for her after they had each paid half of the bill for the truck repairs. "Mom, you're not a movie star. You don't have to introduce yourself as the owner of the place where a murder took place."

Lilly felt her face grow hot, whether from embarrassment or anger she didn't know. "I know that," she answered testily. "Normally I wouldn't, but he was Eden's ex-husband."

"We're going to be late, Mom," Laurel said, turning to Lilly. Lilly gave them each a kiss goodbye and they clambered into the truck and drove away.

Lilly turned toward her own car, thinking she had plenty of time to stop for a coffee before going into work. The door to the body shop swung open and Jed Horstman waddled toward her.

"Wait a minute, Mrs. Carlsen," he said, and she was struck by a stab of fear. She should have gotten into the car faster. What could he possibly want with her?

"Yes?" she replied, her voice noticeably higher than it had been just thirty seconds ago.

"So you're the one in the paper—the one the police have talked to about Eden's death." It was a statement, not a question. Lilly nodded, trying to judge the distance to her car. She cast a doubtful glance toward him. He looked even fatter than he had in the office. Could he really run fast enough to catch her if she made a break for it?

Ridiculous. *Stand still and quit being stupid,* she told herself. *He's just curious. After all, his son's mother is dead.*

"What do you know about Eden's murder?" he asked. Though it was a perfectly reasonable question, the blood rushing in Lilly's ears lent a menacing sound to Horstman's voice.

"Not much," she squeaked.

"Aren't you a suspect?" he asked, leaning a bit closer.

"No," she managed.

"Then why would Eden die in your store?"

"I don't know." Her voice was a little stronger. She was beginning to feel the stirrings of anger toward this man. How dare he imply that she was responsible for Eden's death just because the woman's body was found in Juniper Junction Jewels?

"Were you friends with her?" Horstman asked, his tone challenging.

"We were acquaintances," she answered. "I didn't know her very well."

"Are the police telling you anything?"

"No. And I don't quite understand why you're questioning me, Mr. Horstman," she replied, her courage having returned and her ire up now.

"Easy does it, Mrs. Carlsen," he said, holding up his hands defensively and taking a step backward. "I just want to know what they're saying about Eden, that's all." Lilly was sure he had been seeking more information, but backed down once she regained her mental footing. Who was he to ask questions of her when he was the one who allegedly wanted to use Eden's life insurance proceeds to send Davey to college? She decided not to give voice to her thoughts.

"I don't know any more than anyone else in Juniper Junction," she replied primly. "Now I have to get to work." She turned and walked toward her car, resisting the urge to break into a run and lock herself into the vehicle. She started the engine and looked up; Horstman was staring after her. He gave her the creeps.

She drove straight to work, opting not to stop for coffee. After the experience with Jed Horstman, she figured the last thing her jangled nerves needed was caffeine. She unlocked the back door and eased herself into her office, locking the door behind her. Early morning in the shop felt almost luxurious. Lilly had plenty of time to pull out her sketchbook and work on jewelry designs while she waited for the sun to come up and for Main Street to come alive with holiday shoppers.

CHAPTER 35

The town tree lighting was that night, and it was a tradition Lilly looked forward to every year. The entire town gathered in the public square to sing Christmas carols and partake in hot chocolate and cookies provided by the historical society. Santa made the rounds, too, though it wasn't ideal for picture-taking because it was dark outside. Lilly and the kids always went, and every year they invited Noley and Bill and Beverly to go with them. No one needed an invitation, but Lilly liked to make sure no one stayed home for the festivities.

Taffy got to work right on time and Lilly opened the store. Sales were slow that day, probably because people were planning on going out later in the evening for the tree lighting.

"Are you going to the tree lighting?" Lilly asked Taffy when Taffy returned from lunch.

"I don't know. Where is it?" she asked.

"I forgot you're relatively new in town. It's on the public square. Everyone goes. You'll love it. In fact, you're welcome to join my family if you'd like."

She felt for a second like she'd overstepped her employer-employee bounds by inviting Taffy to join her family at a social event, but Taffy didn't seem to notice.

"That's okay. My boyfriend can go with me. His name is BJ —at least, that's what I call him. Thanks for the offer, though," she said with a smile.

Late that afternoon Hassan stopped by the store. Taffy was clearly intrigued by his exotic, Middle-Eastern good looks and faint accent. Lilly introduced them and Taffy's eyes widened when she heard he was a gem hunter.

"You actually dig gems right out of the earth?" she asked in awe. Hassan laughed.

"Yes, but the way you say it makes it sound far more appealing than it actually is," he answered.

Taffy shook her head. "Wow. That's all I can say."

It was Lilly's turn to laugh. "That's how I felt at first, too, Taffy. It's a pretty amazing job."

Hassan pulled her aside. "I was hoping you don't have a date for the tree lighting tonight," he said, his dark eyes twinkling.

"As a matter of fact, I have lots of dates," she said with a grin. "My kids, my best friend, my mom, and my brother. Would you like to join us?"

"Most definitely," he said. "I'll have most of my family in tow, but I think we can lose them if we run fast enough." He winked and Lilly felt her stomach flutter. She laughed nervously.

"Shall I come for you here at closing time?" he asked.

"That would be great," she said. Bill was picking up their mother and bringing her so he could park the police cruiser close to the square, and Noley was picking up the kids and bringing them. The fewer cars to park, the better. Lilly would leave hers in the alley behind the shop and walk with Hassan. She advised Taffy to do the same; the public square was just a few blocks up Main Street.

At the appointed hour Lilly closed the shop, turned off all the lights except the twinkly white ones that hung over her First

Noel displays, and she and Taffy left through the front door after making sure the back door was locked.

"See you over there," Lilly called to her assistant as Taffy walked down the street. She turned around, giving a little wave and a smile.

Hassan sauntered up a few minutes later. He offered Lilly his arm and they walked slowly toward the public square, admiring the lights, the garlands, the wreaths, and all the other decorations that made Main Street such a special place at Christmastime.

"This is a beautiful place," Hassan said in a quiet voice, matching the calm that had settled over the town like snow.

"That's part of the reason I love it here," Lilly replied.

"I hate to leave after New Year's," he said.

Lilly cast a quick glance at him, but he was staring at the sidewalk in front of them. She didn't even know him that well, but already she didn't like the idea of him returning to Minnesota after the holidays.

The crowd was beginning to gather when Lilly and Hassan got to the public square. Lilly stood on her tiptoes looking for Tighe and Laurel or Noley, but she didn't see them. They were supposed to text her when they arrived and she hadn't gotten a text yet, so she and Hassan wandered around to look at the displays various vendors had set up under large tents. There was something for everyone looking for Christmas gift ideas—local honey, handmade wooden Christmas ornaments, birdhouses, soaps, and anything else someone could want.

They had enjoyed their first cup of hot chocolate when Laurel texted Lilly to tell her they were by the apple cider doughnut stand. Lilly was surprised to find that she was suddenly nervous about introducing Hassan to her kids. Her forays into romance since her divorce had been scattered and unsuccessful, so this was the first time in many years the kids were meeting a man their mother was dating. In fact, it had been so long since her last romance that the kids probably didn't even remember it. Heck, even Lilly barely remembered it.

When Lilly and Hassan got to the line for apple cider doughnuts but before she spotted the kids, Lilly extricated her arm from Hassan's. She didn't want the kids to see any public displays of affection, even one so mild as her arm in his. She could feel her heartbeat increasing and her breath was coming in shorter spurts.

Hassan noticed.

"Are you all right?" he asked, those gorgeous eyes full of concern.

"I'm fine," she answered, then she gave a nervous titter. "It's just that I haven't introduced my kids to a man in a very long time."

"You don't have to introduce me if you don't want to," Hassan answered quickly. "I don't want you to feel uncomfortable."

"No, no, it's okay. I want to. Really," she insisted when he raised his eyebrows at her. *Am I fifteen?* Lilly asked herself. *It's not as if I'm marrying the man. I'm just introducing him to Tighe and Laurel. Lighten up, for Pete's sake.*

She saw Tighe before she saw Laurel, and was relieved to see that Nick hadn't joined the party. She beckoned to Hassan and made her way to the kids through the throngs of people waiting for doughnuts. Noley was a few feet away them, watching them like a mother hen, and she beamed when she saw Lilly with Hassan in tow.

Lilly hugged her friend when she reached Noley and thanked her for picking up the kids. Tighe and Laurel were sprinkling cinnamon sugar on their doughnuts, so Lilly introduced Hassan to Noley first. Noley shook his hand firmly. Tighe and Laurel came over, each biting into a doughnut. They looked at Lilly with surprise when Lilly gestured toward Hassan and introduced him to them.

Tighe was the first to recover. He wiped his sticky fingers on his jeans and shook Hassan's hand. Laurel followed suit, though she used a napkin to wipe the sugar from her hand. Once the introductions were complete, the group stood in an awkward circle until Lilly finally broke the silence.

"What time is the tree lighting?" she asked, as if she didn't know the answer already.

"Seven thirty," Noley answered.

"What shall we do until then?" Lilly asked.

The kids looked at each other and shrugged. "How about the snowball target game?" Tighe suggested.

They all nodded their agreement and Tighe and Laurel led the way to the area of the square where all the wintry games were set up. They divided themselves into two groups—the adults against the kids. Tighe and Laurel stood in one line and Lilly, Noley, and Hassan stood in another line. When they all got to the front of the two lines, they took turns throwing snowballs at the large blue and white snowflake targets set up thirty feet away. They had three minutes to throw as many snowballs as they could make, and the winning team was the one to hit the snowflake target the most.

The kids won.

The adults didn't feel the shame for long, though, since there was spiked cider for the over-twenty-one crowd. By the time Lilly and Noley and Hassan had warm cider in their gloved hands and the kids were sipping hot chocolate, the group had grown much noisier and more energetic. Hassan was regaling Tighe and Lilly with stories of outwitting bandits in the mountains of Afghanistan and they were wide-eyed with rapt attention.

CHAPTER 36

"M om, he is *amazing*," Laurel whispered when Hassan had paused his story to answer one of Tighe's many questions. Lilly grinned.

Just then Lilly's phone rang. It was Bill.

"Where are you?" she asked.

"In the doughnut line with everyone else in Colorado. How about you?"

"We just got spiked cider. Want some? I can get some for you and Mom and we'll come find you. You'll be in line much longer than we will."

"Sure."

Lilly and Hassan, each holding a steaming cup of spiked cider, threaded their way through the crowd followed by Noley and the kids. Bill looked relieved when he saw Lilly. He shook his head almost imperceptibly and gave a slight nod toward their mother, which Lilly took to mean that she was having one of her bad days.

Beverly was watching the couple in front of her argue about what to give the man's father for Christmas. Lilly introduced Bill to Hassan; Beverly didn't even notice. Finally she spoke to the people in front of her.

"You know, all your ideas are terrible. What men want is good scotch."

The man stared at her in surprised silence while his wife replied with, "Never thought of that."

"You see? Ask the old ladies what men like," Beverly responded with a wink. "Though, of course I can't say in polite company what men *really* want for Christmas."

"Mom!" Lilly exclaimed.

"Okay, thank you for the suggestion," the husband said in a sing-song voice, taking his wife's arm and turning her to face the other direction. The wife giggled.

"She's right, you know."

Beverly had diffused an argument between strangers. Maybe she wasn't having such a bad day, after all.

Bill and Lilly had been listening to the exchange. "Mom," Lilly began, drawing her mother's interest away from other people, "I'd like you to meet my friend Hassan. Hassan, this is my mother, Beverly."

Beverly looked Hassan up and down, squinting. "I don't know you, do I?"

"No, ma'am."

"Mom, I just introduced you," Lilly said.

"Where are you from?" Beverly asked.

"Minnesota."

"Didn't expect to hear that," Beverly mumbled.

"Mom," Lilly warned.

"What?" Beverly asked, her voice challenging Lilly to disagree. "He looks like he's from the Middle East."

"My family is originally from Afghanistan, that is correct," Hassan said, smiling over Beverly's head at Lilly. Lilly was mortified.

"What's that accent?" Beverly asked.

"It's British."

"So are you British or American or Afghani?"

"Mom!" Lilly was almost shouting, drawing the attention of the previously-arguing couple standing in front of Beverly. She lowered her voice. "Mom, enough of the questions."

"It's all right," Hassan assured her. "Believe me, I would rather people just ask me than make assumptions about me."

He spoke to Beverly. "I was born in Britain to parents of Afghan descent. I came to the United States from Britain years ago."

"Are you a citizen?"

"Yes, ma'am, of both the United States and Britain."

"So you're not a terrorist."

"Mom, time to talk about something else," Lilly said firmly, taking her mother's arm.

"No, really, it's okay," Hassan said, holding up his hand. He turned to Beverly. "I am not a terrorist, I can promise you that."

If Lilly could have evaporated, she would have disappeared right then. "For God's sake, someone give Gran a doughnut," she said crossly to the kids. Laurel handed her grandmother what was left of the bag of doughnuts. Beverly munched away happily, seemingly oblivious to the stir she had created.

"I'm so sorry, Hassan," Lilly murmured, leaning toward him. "My mother has obviously lost her filter."

He grinned. "Like I said, people make assumptions about me because of my skin color and hair, but it's always better to ask. That way any misunderstandings can be cleared up right away."

If he'd asked, she would have married him on the spot.

Beverly swallowed a bite of her doughnut. She wasn't done with the humiliating remarks yet.

"Why isn't Beau here with you?" she asked Lilly.

"Because I divorced him fifteen years ago."

Beverly seemed surprised by this. "He was a lovely young man," she said wistfully.

"Mom, he was a jerk."

"Well, this is the first I'm hearing about it," Beverly replied. Lilly rolled her eyes and silently pleaded with Bill to do something about their mother. He grinned and walked over to Beverly.

"Mom, how's that doughnut? Have another bite."

Beverly gave him a withering look. "I know what you're trying to do. You're trying to get me to stop talking to this man," she said, gesturing toward Hassan.

"No, I'm trying to get you to stop talking, period. If you can't say something nice, you really shouldn't say anything at all."

Beverly turned to Hassan. "Did I say anything that wasn't nice?"

"Not at all."

She smirked at Bill. Thankfully, before she could say anything else, the public address system crackled and came to life.

"Please begin making your way to the Christmas tree in the middle of Public Square," a voice said. "The lighting festivities will begin in fifteen minutes."

"Thank God," Lilly muttered. The kids and Noley had watched the entire exchange with smiles, but remained silent. Now Tighe and Laurel stepped forward.

"Gran," Laurel said, "come with us. You already ate a doughnut, so you don't need to stand in line any longer. We'll find a good place to watch the tree lighting." She glanced at Lilly and smiled. Lilly could have hugged her. The two people who seemed to be able to do no wrong in Beverly's eyes were Tighe and Laurel and if they suggested something, Beverly usually complied.

She did this time, too. She gave Laurel her hand and Laurel led her away from the doughnut line. Tighe followed. Lilly shrugged and managed a tired smile. "Shall we go with them?" she asked the others.

Hassan nodded. He didn't seem fazed by meeting Lilly's

family. He vacationed with his own extended family, so he was probably familiar with frustrating conversations.

It was as if he could read her thoughts. Taking her by the arm, Hassan whispered, "She's nothing compared to my parents. They ended up staying in tonight, though, so you don't need to worry about them."

It was just the right thing to say to get Lilly laughing. She couldn't imagine it, but she was glad she and the rest of her family weren't alone.

CHAPTER 37

While she and Hassan talked on the way over to the big tree, Lilly noticed that Noley and Bill had lagged behind and were engaged in an earnest conversation. She would have invited them to catch up, but they seemed lost in their own world and she didn't want to interrupt. Besides, it gave her a chance to talk to Hassan alone. Or as alone as they could be in a crowd of thousands.

"So this is an annual event?" Hassan asked.

"Yes," Lilly replied. "I look forward to it every year. It's one of the few public events I can attend without having to do something official for the Chamber of Commerce. I think that's part of the reason I like it so much."

"What do you do for the Chamber of Commerce?"

"I'm the president this year, so that means I have to make an appearance at most of the events, plus I have to come up with ways to make Juniper Junction appealing to tourists and business owners alike. Often those interests are the same, but sometimes they're at odds. For example, recently there's been an argument among the business owners about allowing big chain stores onto Main Street. Some of the shop owners think it's a good idea because it will bring more people into their shops, but others don't want it because chain stores will take away from their business."

"I suppose that's an issue every small town has to deal with," Hassan said.

"Probably, but my only concern is this small town," Lilly said with a smile. "I'm in the group that opposes the big chain stores because many of them sell jewelry. It's nowhere near the quality of the stuff that I sell, but it's cheaper. Some people don't care about quality if the price is right."

"But are those the people who shop in your store?"

Lilly thought for a moment. "Yes, I think so. But that's not the only reason I don't want the big stores coming into our downtown. There's a certain ambience that people love about Main Street in Juniper Junction. They like that they're supporting local businesses and there's a charm and beauty to Main Street which you won't find in other towns that don't care who sets up shop."

"Is that part of the reason you think Eden Barclay was killed?"

"I really don't know. Eden wasn't a nice person and she tended to be an equal-opportunity bully. As far as I know, Eden agreed with me that the big chains don't belong in Juniper Junction."

"So they really don't have any idea who killed her?"

Lilly didn't like the direction this conversation was taking. She thought the tree lighting might be a cozy, romantic way to spend the evening, but it was turning into an inquest.

Hassan seemed to sense her agitation. "I hope you don't mind talking about it," he said. "It's just that I'd like to introduce you to my parents and the rest of my family. Because we're all involved in the gem business, they've been following the story with interest. To my family there are few things more exciting than a murder in a jewelry shop. I'm just thinking when I introduce you they'll recognize your name and pepper you with a million questions. I'm just trying to get an idea of your part in the story, that's all. Please forgive me if I sounded accusatory. Their questions will be worse than mine, I guarantee it. Remember I told you your mother has nothing on my family?" he concluded with a grin.

Lilly nodded solemnly. "I remember, though I'm not sure how that's possible," she said, her lips curving into a small smile. "I was just beginning to get the feeling you actually thought I did it."

"Oh, no. Of course I don't think that. It's just my way of preparing you to meet my family."

"Are you sure you want to introduce me to them?" Lilly was suddenly nervous. The last family she met, Beau's parents, hadn't liked her and made that plain.

"Of course. You introduced me to your family and your best friend. Why shouldn't I do the same?" He tucked her arm under his and they continued walking. They had reached the place where the tree sat proudly in the center of the crowd, protected by a makeshift split-rail fence. A huge lever was stationed nearby and, following decades-old Juniper Junction tradition, the family who had won the town's contest for the best-decorated house was gathered around it to flip the switch and turn the tree lights on at the appointed time. The atmosphere was festive and the falling snow and cold only added to the sparkle of the evening.

Lilly was standing where she could see Tighe and Laurel flanking their grandmother to keep her from being jostled by the crowd. Looking around, she noticed that Bill and Noley had caught up and were standing just behind her and Hassan. Her world felt complete.

Buzz was building among the crowd as the time grew closer for the tree lights to be flipped on for another holiday season in Juniper Junction. Hassan reached for Lilly's hand and she squeezed back, thinking how nice it was to have someone to share the experience with her this year—someone other than family, that is.

The mayor of Juniper Junction stood and the crowd quieted as she made some brief remarks about the town and the beauty of the Christmas season in the Rocky Mountains, then issued a reminder to shop locally for the best gifts. She introduced the family to her left, the lucky family that would be lighting the giant tree that stood proudly just twenty feet away, its branches swaying in the stiff mountain wind.

The Juniper Junction custom was to turn off all the lights on the public square just seconds before lighting the tree. It made the tree lighting more dramatic when the only lights were the twinkling colored bulbs coming from the branches of the huge Douglas fir standing in the crowd.

The mayor counted down from ten and the crowd joined in. "three...two...one!"

Hassan bent his head and kissed Lilly's lips the moment the tree lit up with thousands of fairy lights of every color. The experience would have been near-perfect without the kiss, but when he stood up straight again all she could think was that this had been the best tree-lighting in the world.

CHAPTER 38

Nearby she heard the crackle of Bill's radio, which he still wore even though he wasn't on duty. He listened for a moment, then tapped Lilly on the shoulder. "There's a skirmish over by the chocolate shop. I'm going to go check that out. Can you take Mom back to my car?"

"Sure." Lilly was still floating in her own perfect world, one filled with Hassan and Christmas trees and twinkly lights. She would have done anything anyone asked.

"Come on, Mom." She made her way to the kids and her mother, then reached for her mother's hand and started walking in the general direction of Bill's car. The kids were going home with Noley. Hassan walked on one side of Beverly and Lilly walked on the other, making sure she didn't stumble.

It wasn't until they got to Bill's car that Lilly realized he hadn't given her the keys. She looked around for him, wondering what she should do. The later it got, the colder it would get. She didn't want her mother standing around, freezing, until Bill was done with whatever he was doing. She tried calling his cell, but it went right to voice mail. She cursed him silently.

She made an executive decision. "Hassan, would you mind waiting here with Mom while I run back to Main Street to get my car? I shouldn't be too long."

"I don't mind as long as your mom doesn't," he said with a smile at Beverly. "What do you say, Beverly?"

"That's fine with me," she said. "I'll hang around with a handsome man anytime."

"Mom!" Lilly scolded her.

"I call 'em the way I see 'em, Lilly," Beverly replied. Hassan blushed slightly, but wore a broad grin.

Lilly sped off in the direction of Main Street, but soon had to slow her pace because she was getting out of breath. She hadn't gone far when she spotted Taffy, moving through the crowd.

"Taffy!" Lilly called. "Wait up!"

Taffy turned around in surprise, then smiled when she saw Lilly approaching.

"Were you at the tree lighting?" Lilly asked.

"Yes. It was beautiful!" Taffy replied.

"Where are you headed?"

"Back to Main Street to get my car. BJ is waiting for me."

"Do you and BJ want to come over to my house?" Lilly asked. "I've got a couple friends coming over for dinner, plus my kids and my mom."

Taffy looked startled by the invitation and Lilly worried for a second time that she may have overstepped the employer-employee bounds. But Taffy recovered quickly. "That's nice of you, but we should probably just go home tonight. I'm so tired. I think I could use a good night's sleep so I can be ready for work in the morning," Taffy replied with a wan smile.

"I understand perfectly," Lilly said.

Taffy's car was parked along Main Street a few blocks from the jewelry store. She said goodbye and Lilly continued walking.

When she got to her own car she cranked up the heat so it would be nice and warm when her mother and Hassan joined her. She drove toward the square, then threaded her way through the people who were still standing around until she saw Hassan, standing half a head taller than anyone else nearby. She beeped lightly and Hassan looked in her direction. She got out of the car and waved at him, hoping he had seen her. He saw her and took Beverly by the arm, steering her toward Lilly. Lilly went around to the passenger side and opened the door for her mother, who climbed in wearily.

"Can you just take me home, Lilly?" she asked. "I'm so very tired. This young gentleman has been very entertaining, but I'm afraid I'm just want to go to bed."

"Sure, Mom." Lilly looked at her mother in concern, then took her by the arm and helped her into the front seat of the car. Hassan hopped in back.

When she pulled up in front of her mother's house, Hassan was quick to get out of the car and help Beverly out and up the steps to the porch. With cold fingers Lilly fumbled to unlock her mother's front door.

They all went inside where the only light was blinking red and came from the answering machine on a side table in the living room. Lilly hurried to switch on a lamp and the lights in the kitchen.

"You've got a message, Mom," she said. Beverly sat down on the couch, still in her winter coat, and pressed the Play button.

"Hey, Bev. It's Beau. Are we still on for lunch tomorrow? Give me a call." He rattled off his number.

"What?!" Lilly exclaimed, her voice strident. "Mom, are you meeting Beau for lunch tomorrow?"

"Yes. He's a nice young man—he's even offered to help me around the house. We're meeting for lunch to discuss his payment and what I need done around here."

"Oh, no you're not," Lilly said, shaking her finger.

"Don't you shake your finger at me, young lady," Beverly said. "I'll hire whomever I please to help me around here."

How could her mother slip so seamlessly from confusion to

lucidity to back again? Maybe it was the stress of being in a big crowd, followed by a long wait in the cold for Lilly to get the car. Whatever the reason, Lilly wasn't about to let Beau work for her mother. She looked at Hassan and threw her hands in the air.

"We'll talk about this later, Mom. For now, please promise me you won't call Beau."

"I will do no such thing."

"Then I'll call him myself," Lilly said, striding over to the answering machine. She punched Play and grabbed a pen from the end table. Listening to the message again, she scribbled his number down on the palm of her hand, then she whipped out her cell phone. Beverly gave Lilly a withering look. Hassan looked from one woman to the other.

There was no answer, so Lilly left a message. "Beau? It's Lilly. I've just heard the message you left for my mother on her answering machine. I don't know what you're up to, but I'm warning you to stay away from her." She hung up.

"Mom, he hurt me, he hurt the kids, he hurt all of us. Why would allow him to come around here? To let him in your *home*, for God's sake?"

Beverly remained silent, pressing her lips together in a thin line.

Lilly shot her a look of disgust. "Bill agrees with me." Beverly finally spoke.

"You two don't let me have my own life anymore," she said, her lips trembling.

Hassan's eyes widened as he realized he was about to be in the middle of an emotional mother-daughter conversation; Lilly could practically smell his fear. She turned to him. "Would you mind waiting for me in the car? Turn on the heater if you're cold. I won't be long."

He nodded and said goodnight to Beverly, who returned his words with barely concealed incivility. He closed the door behind him and through the filmy white curtains in the living room window Lilly could see him walk down the steps to the sidewalk.

She turned back to her mother. "Mom," she said, her voice softer now, "it's not that Bill and I don't want you to have your independence. We do. But we also want to make sure you're okay. And if we know you're planning on hiring someone who has hurt you in the past, we have an obligation to make sure that doesn't happen so he can't do that to our family again."

"But it's my house and he's a very kind young man."

"Mom, he's tricking you. He's not kind. I wish you could remember how he used to be. Do you remember that he and I were married?"

Beverly shook her head, looking at the floor. "Sometimes there's a lot I don't remember."

"I know. That's how dementia works. That's why you have to trust Bill and me to veto decisions you make that might be dangerous."

Beverly stood up, her shoulders slumped and her mouth turned downward in a look of abject sadness and realization. Lilly tried to swallow, but the lump in her throat made it almost impossible.

"I'm sorry, Mom. I wish it weren't this way."

Tears glistened in the corners of Beverly' eyes. She blinked hard and they rolled down her cheeks. Lilly tried blinking back her own tears while she gathered her mother into her arms and held her there. Her mother's soft white hair tickled her neck.

"It's so hard to get old," Beverly whispered into Lilly's neck.

"I know, Mom. I know."

CHAPTER 39

T here was a knock at Beverly's front door and it opened before mother and daughter had time to step apart. It was Bill.

"What's going on? Mom, what's wrong?" he asked, glancing at Lilly.

"Mom's tired," Lilly said.

Beverly nodded and pulled a tissue from her pocket. She dabbed her eyes and blew her nose. Bill put his arm around his mother's thin shoulders and squeezed.

When Lilly and Bill left a few minutes later they made sure Beverly locked the front door behind them, and Lilly suggested that Bill drive over to her house where Noley and the kids were waiting. She slid into her own car, where Hassan had his eyes closed and was leaning against his headrest.

"Sorry about that," Lilly said.

"Don't be sorry. How's your mom?"

"Weepy. She's having a hard time giving up some of her independence. Has that happened to your parents?"

"Not yet, but I expect it will happen someday. When it does, I hope I'm as patient with them as you are with your mother." He smiled at Lilly and touched the back of her hand.

"Thank you. I wish I could take all the hurt away." The words hung in the air, both of them knowing it was impossible, but wishing for it nonetheless. Lilly changed the subject.

"Want to come to my house? No doubt Noley has whipped up something for dinner while we've been over here. She's a great cook. Bill's coming, too."

"I'd like that."

They drove to Lilly's house, where they were met with a fire in the fireplace, a delicious scent wafting from the kitchen, and Noley and the kids playing a noisy board game in the living room. Bill was hanging his coat in the closet when Lilly and Hassan walked in.

Lilly lifted the lid from a pan on the stove, breathing in the heady scent of homemade tomato soup. "Noley, did you make this?" she called into the living room.

Noley and Laurel and Tighe had adjourned their game for a while, so all three wandered into the kitchen, followed by Hassan and Bill.

"No, Laurel did," Noley answered.

Lilly looked at her daughter in surprise. "This smells wonderful! Thanks for making dinner for everyone." Laurel beamed.

"I found the recipe online and it was really easy," she replied.

"I can't wait to try it," Lilly said.

They all sat down to eat once the kids had chosen eggnog to drink and the adults each had a glass of red wine.

Laurel beamed under the lavish praise that everyone heaped on her over dinner. The tomato soup was delicious and just the perfect comfort food everyone needed that night. Talk over dinner turned to the weather, as it invariably did at dinner tables all through the Rocky Mountains. Everyone wanted to talk about a blizzard the meteorologists had been discussing.

"I hope it turns into a huge blizzard," Laurel said. "They'll have to close school for that." She wrinkled her nose. "I read online that in Georgia they close schools for a *forecast* of snow."

"Well, I hope the blizzard doesn't materialize," Bill said. "It's always a headache going out to find the idiots who didn't stay home and end up stranded."

"It would be bad for business, that's for sure," Lilly said.

"It wouldn't bother me," Noley said. "I do all my work in the kitchen and on the computer."

When dinner was over Hassan helped Lilly with the dishes while Bill and Noley remained at the table talking to the kids. Bill was asking Laurel all about her boyfriend.

"Nick's a senior. He's going to be a ski instructor."

Bill glanced over at Lilly and they locked eyes for a moment. Lilly gave a quick shake of her head. Bill knew better than to press the subject of ski instruction.

"Where does he live?"

"In a condo just outside of Juniper Junction."

"What do his parents do?"

"His mom works at the primary school and his dad works for the electric company."

Bill nodded. "Sounds like a fine young man. He wouldn't be dating you if he weren't, I'm sure." He winked at Laurel and she grinned.

"I should be going," Noley announced when the kids had gone back upstairs. "I have to get up early. Lots to do tomorrow."

"I'll walk you to your car," Bill offered. He stood up from the table and kissed Lilly's cheek.

After Bill and Noley left and the dishes were done Lilly poured two more glasses of wine. She and Hassan took the glasses and sat down on the couch together in the living room. Lilly leaned her head back and sighed. "This has been such a wonderful evening. I mean, except for my mom getting upset and the discussion of Laurel's boyfriend and the fact that I'm still a person of interest in two murders. You know, minor stuff."

"Well, unfortunately, there's not much you can do about your mom. And I don't know your daughter or her boyfriend and I don't have children of my own, so I can't offer any words of wisdom. But as for the murders, let's think about this. What do we know about the first victim?"

"Eden Barclay. She owned the general store on Main Street, she wasn't doing well financially, and her ex-husband knew about a life insurance policy that would pay for their son to attend college. Oh, and she and her current husband had a fight the night before Thanksgiving. He's now in charge of the store and rumor has it he's selling it and moving away," Lilly said, ticking off the facts on her fingers.

"And what about the second victim?"

"Herb Knight. He was a yoga instructor who owned his studio. I don't do yoga, but I understand he was a great instructor. Not a very nice guy, though. Bill said someone saw him talking to Eden the night she was killed, but didn't remember it until after Herb was dead. So the police never got a chance to question him about it."

"So we know Eden didn't kill Herb. But could he have killed her?"

"I suppose that's possible. But why? As far as I'm aware, Herb didn't have any reason to kill Eden."

"Does your brother have any ideas?"

"Not that I know of. I think he's busy just trying to keep my name off the suspect list."

"I hope he's successful at that," Hassan said with a smile. He put his arm around Lilly's shoulders on the back of the couch and she leaned her head toward his. It was comfortable like that.

They sat in silence like that for a few minutes, then Lilly spoke. "I forgot you don't have your car here. I can take you downtown any time you're ready."

"Are you trying to get rid of me?" he asked, grinning.

"No! I mean no, I was just putting the offer out there."

"You're right—I should probably get going. My sister and I have to get up early tomorrow because we're heading to Denver to have a look around."

"You'll like Denver."

"That's what I hear. How long will it take us to get there?"

"About an hour and a half. More if the roads are bad, but I think they should be okay."

"Good to know. Why don't I walk back to Main Street and you stay inside where it's warm?"

"No way. I'm driving you."

Hassan stood up and pulled Lilly to her feet. They stood for just a moment facing each other, then he leaned down and kissed her lips gently. "We should do this more often."

Lilly smiled and held out her hand. He took it and followed her into the kitchen, where she put the wine glasses in the sink and turned to face him. He kissed her again, longer this time, but they pulled apart when they heard someone coming down the stairs.

"What's up?" Tighe asked, coming into the kitchen.

"We were just leaving. Hassan left his car on Main Street, so I'm going to drive him to pick it up. I'll only be gone for a few minutes. Lock the door behind me."

Tighe rummaged through the contents of the refrigerator, emerging at last with a jar of green olives and a container of whipped cream cheese. Hassan gave him a quizzical look.

"I put the cream cheese on a cracker and top it with an olive," Tighe explained. "It's delicious."

"I'll have to try that," Hassan said. He extended his hand toward Tighe, who returned the hearty handshake. Lilly felt a little thrill of happiness sweep through her. *A good sign,* she thought.

She and Hassan drove through the quiet streets of Juniper Junction on their way to Main Street, commenting on how pretty the houses looked decked with twinkling lights and garlands. There were no people outside—it was quiet and peaceful.

Lilly pulled her car next to Hassan's and he gave her another kiss before getting out. She couldn't help the wide smile that spread across her face when he leaned back, and she was even more pleased that her smile matched the one on Hassan's face.

CHAPTER 40

"Have fun in Denver tomorrow," she called as he got into his own car. He waved and she drove off.

Tighe was waiting for her in the kitchen when she got home. "So how did you meet this guy again?" he asked.

"What guy? Do you mean Hassan?"

"Yeah."

"He came into my shop to look around. We got talking and he came back the next day to ask me to dinner."

"Do you trust him?"

"Sure," she answered. "Why shouldn't I?"

"It's just that two people have died recently and he's been in town recently."

"Oh, Tighe. That's just a coincidence. There are a lot of people who come to Juniper Junction around the holidays. It's a nice place to be for people who like outdoor activities and for people who like to shop and relax and go to nice restaurants."

"It's just something I was thinking about, that's all. As long as you trust him, I trust him," Tighe replied.

"I trust him."

"Then so do I." Her son came over and gave her a hug

goodnight, then disappeared up the stairs. She had been wiping the counter mindlessly while they talked, and now she threw the dishcloth into the sink with uncharacteristic vehemence.

Now why did he have to go and say those things? Hassan is too nice to be subjected to suspicion like that.

But what if Tighe's right?

Lilly let Barney out, then double-checked the locks, turned off all the lights, and went upstairs to bed. She tried to read, but Tighe had put her in such a foul mood that she couldn't concentrate on the story. She wanted to be mad at him, but she knew he was just trying to protect her. She wanted to be mad at Hassan, but he was completely blameless. She wanted to be mad at the police for failing to find the murderer or murderers who had been plaguing Juniper Junction, but she knew they were doing their best to solve the crimes. She had no choice but to accept that anger wasn't going to solve anything. She wanted to believe that her instincts were right, that Hassan was the man she thought he was, but she'd been wrong about a man before. Very wrong.

The thought of Beau made her even more angry. He had come back into town at just about the same time as the murders began, too, come to think of it. And she already knew he was a snake—he could be behind these killings just as easily as Hassan. In fact, that scenario was far more likely.

Surely the police were looking at both locals and tourists and wanderers like Beau as suspects in each of the killings. She was tired of not knowing whether she had been discounted as a suspect.

Lilly fell into a fitful sleep, punctuated by long minutes of staring at the ceiling in despair.

Lilly got to work early the next morning and spent an hour trying to put her ideas for new jewelry designs onto paper. When there was a knock at the back door she lifted her head, startled. She glanced at her watch and was surprised that it was already time to start setting up displays so the store could open on time.

She peered through the peephole in the back door. Taffy was standing there. Lilly opened the door and stood back to admit her assistant.

"Sorry if I startled you," Taffy said in greeting. "I tried knocking on the front door and there was no answer. It didn't seem like you to be late for work." She grinned.

"I've been working on some jewelry designs," Lilly explained. "I guess the time got away from me." Taffy waited as Lilly put her sketches away, then both women hurried to set up the jewelry displays before they unlocked the door for the day.

One of the first customers of the day had heard about Lilly's prowess at designing jewelry and wanted to commission her to design a special pendant for his wife. Taffy took care of other customers while Lilly and the man discussed how he wanted the pendant to look. He was buying a cabin in the mountains as a surprise for his wife and wanted the pendant to reflect the view from the front porch of the cabin. He had taken photos of the mountain peaks in the distance at different times of day. His favorite was the photo in which the mountains appeared almost purple in the light of dawn.

"I think I can come up with some ideas you'll like," Lilly said excitedly. This was precisely the type of assignment she liked best—a design which was for a specific person with parameters that allowed her creative freedom but still gave direction to her work. She promised him she would have several sketches within a week and suggested that he return to the shop to look them over. He agreed, thrilled to have found someone to make his ideas come to life, and left the shop.

Juniper Junction Jewels was busy all day long. Lilly was exhausted by the time she and Taffy took down the displays and left for the evening. She loved days like this, meeting new customers and chatting with old ones, but she was always drained when she went home. Noley was at the house and had brought over dinner for Lilly and the kids.

"What did I do to deserve the royal treatment?" Lilly asked as she hung up her coat.

"I just had such a nice time last night with Bill that I decided to thank you by bringing dinner over. I'll join you, if you don't mind, since I didn't have time to make anything for myself." She grinned.

"Of course you'll join us! What did you make?"

"Salmon with a maple vinaigrette, maple butternut squash, Brussels sprouts, and Parker House rolls. The salmon is a recipe I'm developing, so you'll be helping me out, too."

"So we're your guinea pigs?" Lilly teased.

"Who else would be so willing?"

"Bill would," Lilly answered with a wink. Noley grinned.

"I'll definitely make it for him sometime, but it has to be perfect. That's why I need guinea pigs."

Tighe came into the kitchen. "Who's a guinea pig?"

"We are," Lilly said. "Noley made us dinner. Call Laurel down here and we'll eat."

"Laurel's not home yet."

"Where is she?"

CHAPTER 41

Tighe didn't answer at once. And his brief silence told Lilly everything she needed to know—Laurel was somewhere with Nick.

"I don't know," came Tighe's answer after a long moment.

"Okay, then we eat without her. She knows to be home in time for dinner. Sit down, you two." She pulled out a chair and Tighe and Noley followed suit.

They carefully avoided any talk of Laurel while they ate the five-star meal Noley had prepared.

"I'll be your guinea pig anytime, Noley," Tighe said as he finished dinner. "Mom, why don't you cook stuff like that?"

Lilly smirked. "Because I need a job I can actually make money doing. I have a child going off to college soon and one going a year after that. And it's possible that I'm not as good a cook as Noley."

Tighe hooted. "That's for sure." Lilly shot him a withering look and he held up his hands in surrender. "Sorry," he said with a wide grin.

Barney let out one bark and the door swung open. A gust of

wind whooshed into the warm kitchen, bringing with it a bedraggled-looking Laurel.

"You missed dinner."

"I know. I'm sorry, Mom. Nick and I were at the library and lost track of time." Lilly couldn't believe Laurel could say such a thing with a straight face.

"Uh-huh."

"It's true."

"Then you won't mind if I call Mrs. Ledbetter. You remember her—she used to live a couple houses down and she works the checkout desk. She would have seen you."

"All right," Laurel said with a sigh. "I was at Nick's house."

"Why did you lie?"

"Because I know you don't like Nick and I figured the library sounded better."

"Were either of Nick's parents at home?" Lilly was pressing her fingernails into her palms to keep from blowing her top.

"No."

"You're grounded until next Monday." Lilly turned away from Laurel.

"But Mom…" Her voice trailed off. She knew better than to argue—this was an argument she wasn't going to win.

"Sit down and eat dinner," Lilly said over her shoulder. Noley and Tighe, who had been silent while Laurel and Lilly talked, got up to help with the dishes. With a long sigh, Laurel sat down by herself.

"Why don't you like Nick?" she finally said in a whiny voice.

"It's not that I don't like him, though I don't think he's the most thoughtful of boys," Lilly said. "It's that you can do better."

"You're just upset because he wants to be a ski instructor and you weren't able to make marriage to a ski instructor work." Lilly whirled around to stare at her daughter. She could tell from the look in Laurel's eyes that the girl knew she had overstepped her bounds.

"You have no idea what my marriage was like," Lilly said, her voice hard. "You have no right to make statements like that. I don't know what's gotten into you, Laurel, but you'd better snap out of it because you and I aren't going to be able to coexist peacefully if you can't be respectful." She turned on her heel and left the room, leaving Noley and Tighe staring after her, astonished at her outburst.

She went to her bedroom and closed the door, then lay face-down on the bed and began to cry into her pillow. She was thankful she had been able to hold it together until she was in the privacy of her room.

She cried long and hard until, after about fifteen minutes, she was all cried out. She sat up on the bed, sniffling, her hair a tangled mess, and stared out the window. It was dark, and the snow was falling thickly. The streetlamp lent a serene, almost vintage look to the view from the bed, belying the pain Lilly felt in her mind and heart.

She hadn't cried like that in a long time. The last time it had happened, she had been under a tremendous amount of stress and she knew that this crying jag stemmed from the same thing —stress.

She could identify most of her stress—her mother, Laurel, Nick, her nerves about Tighe going off to college in less than a year, being a person of interest in two murders, and the never-ending stress that a small business owner feels.

But there was also stress she couldn't name. It was a feeling of dread, of hopeless malaise, that arose from all that had happened in Juniper Junction. Not only had there been two killings since Black Friday, but she had a general sense that the peace and quiet of the little mountain town had been shattered. Hopefully not forever.

Then there was Hassan. She liked him and she liked the way he made her feel. But after Tighe asked her whether she really trusted Hassan, she had been harboring doubts about him. He *had* come to town around the time of the murders and he *was* a stranger in Juniper Junction.

And what if he was completely innocent of any crimes, which she fervently hoped was the case? Well, he still lived in Minnesota and she wasn't inclined to become embroiled in a long-distance relationship. So he would leave after the holidays ended and she would be left alone again, missing him.

It was all very disheartening.

There was a knock on her bedroom door.

"Come in," Lilly said.

Noley peeked around the door. "You all right?"

"Yeah," Lilly said with a sigh. "Sorry about that. All of a sudden I couldn't take it anymore. I see Laurel headed for the same mistakes I made and I just can't watch that happen."

"I know. It doesn't help when she's kind of snotty about it, too." Lilly nodded her head ruefully.

"It's not just Laurel, though. It's everything that's been happening around here. Beau coming back, Mom's problems, the murders, me being a person of interest, the police not making any progress, and Hassan."

"What about Hassan?"

"I like him. A lot. But Tighe asked me something that made me second-guess myself and now I'm not sure about anything."

"What did Tighe ask?"

"He asked if I trust Hassan." Lilly put her chin in her hands.

"And you do, of course."

"Well, I thought I did until Tighe brought it up. But two murders have taken place since Hassan came to town. What if that's not just a coincidence? What if Hassan has something to do with them?"

"Hassan doesn't strike me as a killer."

"Me neither, but would I know a killer if I saw one? I doubt it."

"The murders have taken place since Beau came to town, too. There are probably a lot of people in Juniper Junction who've been here since Thanksgiving. It's a popular holiday spot. Anyone could have killed those two. They were both awful. And who says it has to be someone who is just passing through? It could be someone who's lived here for years."

"Is that supposed to make me feel better, considering that I've lived here for years?" Lilly asked. She chuckled wryly and hiccupped.

"I guess that's not very comforting, is it?"

"I just want the police to get my name off the list of the people of interest. I'm a nervous wreck about it."

"Just be patient. I'm sure they will. And you know I'll help you however I can. Now, I didn't tell you this before, but I brought dessert over, too," Noley said with a sly smile.

"Why didn't you say so? Here I am blubbering away, completely oblivious."

"Come on," Noley said, standing up and offering Lilly her hand. "You've got one more guinea pig job tonight."

CHAPTER 42

Noley led the way downstairs and ordered Lilly to sit down at the table. Laurel was still there, pushing food around on her plate.

"Don't you like salmon, Laurel?" Noley asked.

"It's okay."

Noley took Laurel's plate away and put it in the sink, yelling for Tighe as she did so. He came bounding down the stairs.

"What?" he asked.

"Dessert."

"Cool. What is it?"

"Poached pears with honey-ginger syrup," Noley answered.

She brought four dessert plates to the table and after just a few moments everyone agreed that the dessert was light, perfectly spiced, and great for a snowy evening.

"Noley, you should write a cookbook," Tighe said in between bites.

"Yeah," Laurel agreed. "This is delicious."

"Maybe I will," Noley said.

When everyone was done eating, Lilly shooed the kids

upstairs and she did the dishes while Noley leaned against the counter nearby.

"Help me take my mind off everything," Lilly told her. "Tell me what you think about Bill."

She glanced at Noley, who blushed. "I like him. I don't know why I never really thought about him before. He's kind and thoughtful and brave and he appreciates good food."

"I assume you're interested in seeing him again?"

"Of course."

"I'll see to it, then."

Noley pushed herself away from the counter. "Thanks. Don't make it too obvious, though. I don't want to seem desperate."

"Leave it to me."

When Noley had left, taking all her clean serving dishes with her, Lilly settled down to sketch for a few minutes before getting ready for bed. Drawing quieted her mind, and she often turned to pencil and paper when she was trying to empty her head of thoughts that wouldn't leave her alone. She tried a few variations of the design her new client had in mind and slipped the papers into her purse when she was finished. She went upstairs and knocked on Laurel's door.

"Can I come in?" she asked.

"Yeah."

Lilly opened the door and stuck her head into the room. Laurel was sitting at her desk. "I just wanted to make sure we're okay after our discussion earlier."

"Yeah."

Lilly walked into the room and sat down on Laurel's bed. She wanted to talk to her daughter, to think of something that would bring them closer, but she couldn't think of anything that wouldn't upset at least one of them. She sat in silence for several long moments while she thought. Laurel remained silent.

"I thought we'd decorate our Christmas tree this weekend."

"Okay."

"That's always a nice thing to do. We'll have Gran and Bill come, and maybe Noley."

"Can Nick come?" Laurel asked, glancing at her mother.

Uh-oh. I should have seen this coming, Lilly thought. Aloud she said, "I'd rather he didn't, since it's just a family thing. I'm sure he would understand. I wouldn't expect his family to invite you to trim their tree."

"Well, they did."

That came as a surprise. Lilly wasn't ready to back down on this, though. "It'll be nice, I promise, and then you can go out with Nick right afterward. How does that sound?"

Laurel shrugged. "All right, I guess, as long as you're not going to let him come over."

"Thanks." Lilly didn't trust herself to say anything else. She planted a kiss on Laurel's cheek and left the room, closing the door softly behind her.

She went downstairs, let Barney out, and together they went back upstairs to bed. Lilly's faithful friend snuggled up to her feet and both of them were sound asleep almost immediately. Lilly's tears had tired her out; Barney was tired from protecting the house all day.

The first customer in the store the next morning was Hassan.

"How was Denver?" Lilly asked.

"We loved it," he said with a broad smile. "I wanted to call you on our way back to Juniper Junction last night, but I thought I might wake you up. We were pretty late."

"What did you do there?"

"We took a tour of the State Capitol building and the US Mint, we went to the art museum, and took a brewery tour. We ate at a couple great restaurants, too. I'd love to take you there sometime."

"I'd love that, too." To her own ears, Lilly sounded like a schoolgirl who didn't know how to converse with a grown-up. She grimaced.

"Is something wrong?"

"No, not at all. I was just thinking about my last trip to Denver," she lied.

"What happened?"

"I got lost." That much was true. She vaguely remembered a trip several years previously, when she had the flu and had to drive her mother to the airport because Bill couldn't leave work.

"There's so much that we didn't have a chance to see," Hassan continued. "Maybe we could head into the city between Christmas and New Year's. What do you think of that idea?"

"I think that sounds great. I always close the shop during that week because people don't do much jewelry shopping right after Christmas. And we're not planning to go anywhere this year, so that would be nice."

"It's a date, then." Hassan kissed her cheek and squeezed her hand. "What did you do yesterday?"

Lilly liked the sound of that. She had finally found someone who was interested in her days and she fought back the stabbing reminder that he would be leaving after New Year's.

CHAPTER 43

"I'll have to show you. A man came in yesterday asking me to design a pendant for his wife. He had something specific in mind, but he asked me to do something creative with it. My sketches are in the back.

"Taffy, can you watch the front? I want to show Hassan some sketches I did yesterday."

"Sure."

Lilly took Hassan's hand and led him to the back of the shop.

She withdrew her sketch book from one of her bookshelves and opened it to the first page of new sketches. Slowly she and Hassan flipped through the pages of drawings. Hassan was quiet, contemplating each sketch. When Lilly got to the last one, Hassan looked up at her from where he was sitting.

"You have a great talent. These are incredible designs."

"Thank you," she said, blushing. "I've got a few more at home, but I think most of these are better. I'm going to choose a few and let my customer decide which one he wants to use."

"Do you mind if I help you choose? I assist jewelry store owners quite often with design ideas since I supply the raw materials for those designs, and I've got a pretty good handle on what stones and gems look best in certain designs."

"I'd love for you to help, thank you."

"Did your customer mention whether he wants particular stones in the pendant?"

"Not really. I usually work with materials that are endemic to Colorado or the Rocky Mountains, but he said that wasn't the most important consideration. The most important thing, he said, was to get a design that looks like the mountains."

"I only ask because I have some lapis lazuli that would be perfect for part of the mountains. It's a deep blue with spidery white veins."

"That sounds great. Can I see it?"

"Sure. It's back at the house where we're staying. Why don't you come by after you close up tonight and I'll show it to you? You can meet my family, too, since we never saw them at the tree lighting."

Lilly had been turning pages back to the front of her sketch book and her hand froze in mid-turn. "Your family?"

"Sure. Show me yours and I'll show you mine, as they say," he answered with an impish grin.

"Well, I guess that would be fine. After all, I've inflicted my mother on you, so I suppose it's only fair."

"I thought your mother was charming."

"Oh, she can be. She just turns on a dime sometimes."

Hassan wrote down the address of the place where he was staying and Lilly promised to stop by after six o'clock. He was planning on spending the day cross-country skiing so she told him to get out there while it was still pristine after the new snow-fall. He kissed her goodbye and left the shop.

"He seems really cool," Taffy said after he left. "Where did you meet him?"

"Right in here," Lilly replied. "Who'd have thought it, huh?"

Taffy laughed. "At least you knew right from the start that

you two have something in common. I met my boyfriend at a bar."

Two customers came in just then; Lilly helped one and Taffy the other. After a half hour of browsing, asking to see pieces from the vault, and discussing price, Lilly's customer bought a pair of earrings for her mother. Taffy wasn't so lucky. She spent nearly the same amount of time with an elderly man who opted not to purchase anything.

"I wish I could learn to sell the way you do," Taffy told Lilly.

"Don't forget, I've been doing this a while. I'm sure you'll start to make more sales the longer you're at it." A fleeting remembrance of Robert crossed Lilly's mind; she loved the idea that she might be someone's mentor as Robert had been to her.

"Working here is so different from working for Eden," Taffy said. "She didn't really interact with customers too much and I spent all my time in the back storeroom. I prefer working like this. It got so boring to work there."

"This store is fundamentally different from Eden's store. With her store, people went in knowing what they wanted. In here, they often come in with nothing more than the thought that they'd like to buy a piece of jewelry for themselves or someone else. It's a more personal thing to buy, so it requires a more personal approach to selling."

"You're lucky to live in a place where people have a lot of money to spend."

"We're lucky to live here for lots of reasons, but that's certainly one of them from a small business perspective." Lilly grinned. "I don't think this store would do nearly as well if there were no ski resort or summer festivals nearby."

"BJ and I have been talking about moving back to Missouri," Taffy said.

"Really? Why?"

Taffy shrugged. "Mostly because my family is there. His parents are dead and he doesn't have any siblings, so he doesn't really care where we live."

"I would be sorry to see you leave," Lilly said. She had grown fond of having an assistant in the store—someone to talk to during the day and someone who could take up some of the slack when Lilly had another commitment. And, in particular, she had grown fond of Taffy. The young woman was smart, well-spoken, and friendly.

"I'd like to meet BJ," Lilly said.

"Maybe you could come over for dinner sometime," Taffy suggested. "I'm not the greatest cook, but I'm good at ordering takeout." She smiled.

"That would be great. I'm not the best cook, either. Luckily my friend Noley is a wizard in the kitchen and we mooch meals from her sometimes."

"I'll figure out a time when BJ and I are both free and we'll set it up."

"Thanks," Lilly said.

The rest of the day sped by as Taffy waited on customers and Lilly worked on a few holiday advertisements that she had scheduled to run in the days leading up to Christmas Eve. When it was time to close Taffy locked the front door and helped take down the displays and, as usual, after she left Lilly put the inventory in the vaults, locked the back door, and got in her car. She put her hands on the steering wheel and closed her eyes, taking a deep breath. She wasn't sure she was ready to meet Hassan's family, but it was as good a time as any. She looked at the address of the house he had rented and knew exactly where it was.

CHAPTER 44

The neighborhood was nestled at the foot of a small hill and backed up against a forest on the outskirts of Juniper Junction. It was an affluent area and many of the homes were owned by people who lived in other states and vacationed occasionally in Colorado. When those owners were not planning to be in town, they often rented their homes for extra income.

Lilly drove through the neighborhood slowly, looking for the address. She found it at the end of a short block of large homes. She parked out front and stood beside her car looking at the forbidding façade of the house. It was enormous and breathtaking. Mahogany cedar shakes covered the entire expanse of the home, with ivory trim accenting the windows, doors, roofline, and porch. Coach-style lamps lit the porch softly from either side of the huge double wooden front doors. Lilly couldn't wait to see the inside.

The door swung open as she climbed the steps to the porch. Hassan stood in the doorway smiling broadly.

"Welcome," he said, taking Lilly's hand and drawing her into the foyer. He helped take off her coat and hung it in a closet. "Come meet everyone." *Everyone? How many people are in there?*

He led the way into a great room where a fire roared in the fireplace and at least a dozen people sat silently in chairs and on sofas in the room. All eyes were on Lilly. She had a momentary urge to flee back to her car, but she managed a smile and ordered herself to calm down. She clasped her hands together to keep them from shaking and looked up at Hassan. He smiled down at her and put his hand in the small of her back to guide her down the two steps into the room.

He walked her over to a man and a woman seated next to each other on the sofa closest to the fireplace.

"Mum, Dad, I'd like you to meet Lilly Carlsen. Lilly, these are my parents, Amir and Basma Ashraf." Amir had a huge mane of white hair and deep wrinkles across his face, which had a pleasant and serene look to it. Basma had long black hair with gray streaks and she was tall and elegant. The stood to shake hands with Lilly then sat down again while Hassan continued introducing everyone in the room. Next was his sister, Ghada, a raven-haired beauty with large black eyes and a graceful bearing, then a roster of aunts, uncles, and cousins whom Lilly was sure she'd never be able to remember. After Hassan had completed the introductions he told everyone he would get something for Lilly to drink and asked her to accompany him into the kitchen.

"My parents and Ghada are the only ones you have to remember," he said. He seemed to sense that she was bewildered by all the names being thrown at her in such a short time. "The rest of my family will understand if you don't remember their names. Eventually you'll learn them, I'm sure."

Lilly had been pouring ginger ale into a glass when he said this; she looked up quickly to see him smiling at her. It was the first time he had mentioned anything about the future. It gave her a little thrill to hear him talk like that.

They returned to the living room. Hassan invited Lilly to sit in an empty armchair next to the fireplace while Ghada, who was sitting on the brick hearth, slid over to make room for her brother. He sat within touching distance of Lilly, which gave her some sense of comfort in the large room full of strangers.

"So, you own a jewelry store," Hassan's father said.

"Yes, I own Juniper Junction Jewels. It's right down on Main Street."

"Hassan has told us all about it." Lilly and Hassan exchanged glances and Hassan smiled.

"You should visit the shop, Dad," he said. "It looks like something out of a magazine. The Christmas display shows off the stones and metal work beautifully." Hassan's father nodded, seeming pleased with what he was hearing.

"You are divorced?" Hassan's mother asked.

"Mum," Hassan cautioned.

"I'm merely asking," she replied. She looked at Lilly expectantly.

"I am," Lilly confirmed. "And I have two children, ages sixteen and seventeen."

"And how long have you been divorced?" asked one of Hassan's aunts. Lilly glanced at Hassan's mother, who turned to her with a curious look, obviously waiting for an answer.

"Fifteen years," Lilly said. "My husband left when my children were very small."

One of the aunts leaned over and whispered something into the ear of the man sitting next to her, but said nothing aloud. Lilly thought she might throw up from the anxiety being produced by this inquisition.

"Okay, everyone, we can ask Lilly all kinds of personal questions another time," Hassan said, raising his eyebrows pointedly at his mother. "Can anyone think of something inoffensive to say?"

Lilly held her breath, wondering who would speak next and what they would want to know, but to her relief it was Ghada who spoke up.

"How did you become interested in the jewelry business?" she asked.

That was familiar territory and an easy topic for Lilly to discuss, and she warmed to the subject. As she explained how she got her start in the business, she could feel some of the stress melting away as she became aware that everyone was listening and seemed interested in what she had to say.

"We're all in the gem business," Hassan said with a sweep of his arm around the room. "Most of my uncles are gem wholesalers, but my father and I and one of his brothers are the actual hunters."

Lilly longed to hear more of the family legacy of gem hunting, and talk turned to stories of how the men had become involved in that trade. It went back a few generations to Afghanistan, where Hassan's more recent ancestors had found that a life of gem hunting was far preferable to the subsistence farming their families had been practicing for centuries.

"Gem hunting was what allowed us to see more of the world," Amir said. "It was the reason my family emigrated first to Britain and then some of us continued on to the United States."

"How often do you go back to Britain?" Lilly asked.

"Not often enough," Basma said. "I loved living there. The winters in Minnesota are dreadful."

"Then you probably don't love it here," Lilly said sympathetically.

"I like it here because there is no big city nearby. I like it because of the peace and quiet of the mountains and the forests."

"Those are the same reasons I love it here," Lilly said. Basma gave a radiant smile, the kind that made everyone who saw it smile in return.

Ghada spoke up. "It hasn't been too peaceful around town lately, it seems. We've been reading about the two murders. So you knew the people who died?"

"Yes. Everyone knows everyone in a place this small. The woman, Eden, was a store owner in town and the man, Herb, was a yoga instructor."

Everyone sat in awkward silence for a moment, waiting for someone to speak.

"It's horrible that the woman died in your store. Did she have any family?" Ghada asked.

"Yes, a husband and a son."

"Again, maybe we could think of something more pleasant to discuss?" Hassan put in.

"Hassan is right. We should not be discussing such painful topics with a guest present," said Amir. "Lilly, can you recommend good restaurants around Juniper Junction? We have been eating some meals out, but my wife and sister and daughter have been doing a lot of cooking, too. It would be nice to give them a break more often."

Lilly was relieved to talk about something other than the deaths of Eden and Herb. Taking a pad and paper from her purse, she wrote down the names of some of her favorite local restaurants and a few from places outside Juniper Junction. She suggested that Amir look for them online to get directions and take a look at the menus.

Eventually the members of Hassan's extended family began to take their leave of the Ashrafs and Lilly. Several of them were staying in the house so they just disappeared upstairs or downstairs. Others had rented houses on either side of the Ashrafs and they ventured out into the crisp, cold evening after bidding Lilly a warm goodbye.

CHAPTER 45

W hen everyone but Hassan's immediate family had
departed Amir stood up and beckoned Lilly to join him
in the dining room. Hassan joined them and Basma and Ghada
followed.

"Hassan tells me you also design jewelry," Amir said. Lilly
nodded. "He said you might like to see a particular piece of
lapis lazuli that we have in our inventory. We happened to bring
some lapis with us on this trip because on the way back to
Minnesota we are going to stop at a gem show in Ames, Iowa.
Normally we keep these pieces and all our other gems under
lock and key, but I brought some out to show you tonight."

Amir had been sifting through several boxes while he spoke.
Each box was made of plastic and had a transparent lid so the
contents could be easily identified. Finally he found the box he
was looking for and lifted it up. Setting it down in front of Lilly,
he lifted the lid with a flourish. Lilly looked into the box, which
was separated into smaller sections by plastic dividers. In each
section were nestled pieces of lapis lazuli in soft cotton, Some of
the pieces were polished and shone under the dining room
chandelier; others were matte and had a duller look to them.

Lilly had never seen so much lapis in one place before. Since it was a relatively rare stone, she didn't keep much of it in stock and she wasn't a frequent visitor to gem shows, preferring to order her gems from trusted suppliers who chose stones for her.

Hassan reached into the box and pulled out a triangular piece of lapis. "This is the one I had in mind for your design for your client's mountain pendant." He handed it to her.

Lilly turned the stone over in the palm of her hand, admiring its smooth, cool surface. Hassan had been right—this was perfect for one of the mountains in the pendant. It was a deep blue, almost purple, and it matched the color of the mountain at sunrise in the photo Lilly had seen. Tiny white veins ran through the lapis, suggesting crests of snow. Lilly would certainly be able to use this stone as the anchor piece in her pendant, surrounding it with smaller stones to add contrast. "I think this would make a beautiful piece," she said to Hassan and Amir. "How much is it?"

Hassan looked at his father, who put a hand to his chin. "I rather think Hassan would give it to you for nothing," he said with a smile, "and if it were for you I would agree. But since it is for a client who is paying you to design a piece of jewelry, suppose you tell me how much you are willing to pay and we will agree on a price." Lilly was surprised. She had expected Amir to name a price and she would either be able to purchase the stone or she wouldn't. She hadn't realized bargaining would be part of the process. She looked at Hassan uncertainly.

He grinned. "This is part of the fun for my father," he said. "You should see how bargaining is carried out in Afghanistan. It is very intricate, very complex. Sometime I will tell you about it. But for now, just tell my father how much you would normally spend for a stone that you would use in a pendant of your own design." Lilly thought for a moment, debating whether to name a price they all knew was too high in order to play along with Amir or to name a price that they all knew was too low in order to show respect to the man. She decided to go a little high.

She named a price and Amir smiled. "I see you are new at this, but you will learn." He countered with a lower price and Lilly found herself beginning to enjoy the game. She made another offer, slightly lower than the first number but not as low as the number Amir had named. Again, he suggested another number. They were both smiling by the time they had completed three rounds of bargaining and agreed on a price Lilly thought was fair and even a bit lower than she would have paid someone else. The entire exchange had taken several minutes; Lilly discovered that the most nerve-wracking part of bargaining was the silence that ran long between offers and counteroffers.

Amir wrapped the stone for her in a length of linen cloth and gave it to her.

"Thank you," she said. "My client is going to love this."

"Please take a photo of the pendant when you have finished it," Amir said. "I would like to include it in a catalogue we produce that has images of finished products jewelers have sold with our stones." Lilly agreed and thanked Amir again.

Basma and Ghada had remained silent throughout the bargaining exercise. Now Basma spoke up. "You have given my husband a great deal of enjoyment this evening," she said with a wink. "I can tell he is impressed with your skills as a businesswoman."

Ghada nodded and joined Lilly and Hassan as they made their way out of the dining room. "Dad loves that part of the business," she said. "Since he has stopped going on most gem hunting trips, he spends his days in happiness, bargaining all the time with unsuspecting people." She laughed. "He doesn't look that sly, does he?"

Lilly joined her laughter. "No, he strikes me as very mild-mannered."

"In that case, has he sucked you in!" Hassan said with a grin. He changed the subject then and suggested that he and Lilly take a short walk outside. "You should see some of the houses in this neighborhood," he told her. "I like to walk at night because they're all lit up for the holidays. Even the rentals —the owners must pay local companies to install the Christmas lights so the renters can feel like they're at home. My aunts and uncles love it."

They bundled up and Lilly said goodbye to Hassan's sister and parents. She hoped she would be able to see them again before they all returned to Minnesota.

Before setting off to see the neighbors' homes, Hassan took Lilly behind the house where he was staying. The backyard, if you could call it that, had the look of a wildlife sanctuary. There were thick stands of trees and a small stream that hadn't quite frozen yet. A quiet, soothing gurgling filled the night and the water sparkled in the moonlight as it tumbled over the rocks and around clumps of leaves leftover from the fall.

Hassan took Lilly's hand in his. "Thank you for coming to meet my family tonight. I had a feeling my father would try to bargain with you over the price of the lapis, but I didn't mention it because I wasn't sure and I didn't want you to fret or feel nervous."

"I thought it was fun," Lilly replied, looking up at him. He put his arm around her shoulders. "Was that some kind of test —the bargaining?" she asked.

"I can never be absolutely sure what is going through my father's mind, but yes, I think it was." He pulled her closer. "Look up there," he said, pointing to the sky. "We never see stars like that in Minneapolis."

"Yet another reason I love this place," she said, snuggling into his shoulder. They stared at the stars for a short while before it started getting too cold to stand still, then they went around to the front of the house and made their way to the street. There were only four other homes on the block, two of which were occupied by his own family members. Each house was decked with white fairy lights and still more lights twinkled in the trees surrounding the homes. As Lilly and Hassan walked, they paused in front of each house to admire the festive decorations. No inflatable Santa Clauses in this neighborhood, and no plastic reindeer. Everything was wrought iron and had been lit up with an elegant restraint.

"Every year our family goes away for the weeks between Thanksgiving and New Year's," Hassan said. "I think this is the best place we've visited for a lot of reasons." He stopped walking and leaned down to kiss Lilly. She felt a warmth that started in her toes and traveled up her body, into her fingertips and then her face. It was a kiss that left her flushed and breathless.

"Wow."

Hassan laughed. "Do you have time to grab dinner somewhere?"

"I really shouldn't," Lilly said, pulling up her coat sleeve and glancing at her watch. "I texted the kids before I left the store to tell them I'd be late, but that I'd have dinner with them."

"Then let's get you back to the car so you can get home."

He kissed her again when they reached her car and she pulled away from the curb with a feeling of giddy happiness. She brushed away any thought of him leaving at the end of the holiday season and treasured the time they were spending together while she could.

But it wasn't long before the happiness dissipated like a mountain fog.

CHAPTER 46

"Mom, where have you been?" Tighe asked when she came into the kitchen.

"I had to meet with someone to buy a piece of lapis lazuli," she said. "Why?"

"We've been texting you," he scolded. "Uncle Bill is looking for you. He texted you, too."

She froze. She hadn't looked at her phone all evening. "What does he want?" she asked in a rush. "Is Gran okay?"

Tighe glanced sideways at Laurel, who had been listening to the conversation. "I don't think it's about Gran," he said. "I got the feeling it was about Eden Barclay."

To Lilly, it felt like all the blood in her body solidified and stopped flowing. She didn't need to return Bill's call to know that it was bad news.

She sat down hard in one of the kitchen chairs. Laurel poured her a glass of water from the sink and set it down in front of her.

"Mom, do you want us to go upstairs while you talk to Uncle Bill?" she asked. Lilly didn't answer; she seemed not to have heard the question.

"Mom?" Laurel repeated. Lilly looked up at her daughter.

"Do you want us to go upstairs while you call him back?"

"You probably should," Lilly answered. "I'll call you down when I hang up."

Laurel and Tighe went upstairs more quietly than usual. Barney, as if sensing her stress, sat down at Lilly's feet and licked the back of her hand. She reached out absentmindedly to scratch his ears.

Taking a deep breath, she took her cell phone out of her pocket and dialed Bill's number. He answered on the first ring.

"Where have you been?" he asked, his voice rough.

"I was out buying a piece of lapis lazuli for a client," she said, her voice flat and dull. "What did you call for?"

There was a pause on the other end, then Bill spoke in a quiet voice. "Two officers are on their way to the house to question you again. Eden Barclay's first husband told them you were snooping around his auto body shop, looking for information about Eden."

"So? If anyone had a motive to kill Eden, it was Jed Horstman," Lilly replied hotly. "Of course he would say that in order to deflect suspicion from himself."

"They're questioning him again, too. The thing is, they're pretty sure one of the two of you did it. The way they figure it, the motive was money in his case, business disagreements in your case. And Jed has an alibi."

That last sentence dropped like a rock. "But, but," Lilly spluttered. "Alibis aren't always truthful, right? I mean, did his wife just say he was home when Eden was killed? Because what else would they expect her to say? Did they see him on video somewhere that would prove his alibi?"

"You watch too much television," Bill said, trying and failing to lighten the mood.

"I don't watch television. You know that," Lilly spat. It was no use getting mad at Bill—he was trying to help. She lowered her voice and spoke more slowly. "I'm sorry. I just see this coming at me like a runaway train and I don't know what to do. I didn't kill Eden."

"I know that. I'm working as hard as I can to break this open. There's someone out there who knows what happened; we just have to find that person."

"When will they be here?" Lilly asked, running a hand over her eyes.

"Won't be too long. I've been trying to get ahold of you for a few hours to give you a heads-up."

"Thanks."

"Don't worry about Mom," Bill said. "I'll stop over there on my way home from work and check on her. You've got enough to think about right now."

She called the kids downstairs and they sat down to a meal of ham sandwiches and some of Noley's leftover squash. While they ate Lilly explained what was going on.

"Bill said there are two police officers coming over here tonight. I wouldn't be surprised if they take me into the police station to ask their questions. I don't want you two worrying about anything. If you'd like, I can have Noley come over until I get home. I'm sure I won't be too late."

"Are you going to be arrested?" Tighe asked, his forehead wrinkling.

"Bill didn't say I would be arrested, so I doubt it. He would tell me if that was going to happen."

"I think I want Noley to come over," Laurel said in a small voice.

"Okay. I'm sure that's not a problem. I'll call her as soon as we're done eating."

They hadn't finished dinner, though, when the officers showed up at the front door. Barney almost lost his mind barking at them when Lilly opened the door for them to come inside; he could probably sense the tension in the air.

"I suppose Bill has told you why we're here," one of the officers said.

Lilly nodded. "You have to ask me some questions about Eden Barclay's murder?"

"Yes. We'd like you to come down to the station. We'll drive you and then bring you home when we're done. And while we're here, we have a couple questions for your kids."

Tighe and Laurel were watching the scene, their eyes wide. The officers took them separately into the living room and dining room while Lilly waited in the kitchen, fretting. She called Noley, explained what was going on, and asked her to come over. Noley agreed and said she'd be at the house as soon as possible. The kids were both back in the kitchen in just a few minutes. Neither of them looked especially perturbed, so Lilly tried to calm her own breathing. She was surprised the police hadn't talked to the kids before now.

The officers didn't wait for Noley to show up. Lilly kissed the kids goodbye, told them not to worry, and then allowed herself to be ushered out the door. She climbed into the backseat of the police cruiser and looked back toward the house, where the living room curtains twitched as the kids watched her leave.

Mrs. Laforge was watching, too. Lilly could tell by the twitching of her living room curtains. Nosey old bat.

At the police station the officers left Lilly in a small room with a table and three chairs. Lilly sat down to wait for them, wishing Bill could come in to say something reassuring, but she knew he wouldn't. He needed to separate himself from this investigation for the sake of his job; she was lucky he'd been able to call her with a heads-up about the police coming to her house.

She sat by herself for several minutes then was joined by one of the officers who had accompanied her from her house.

He took her with agonizing slowness and miniscule detail through the events of the day before Thanksgiving until the moment Lilly had found Eden's body on Black Friday. Then he switched gears to inquire about all the discussions and disagreements Lilly could remember having with Eden over business differences and issues involving the Chamber of Commerce.

As frustrating as it was to repeat everything she had already told the police about her whereabouts from the time she left the shop on the day before Thanksgiving and for the ensuing thirty hours, Lilly remained calm throughout the questioning. She didn't want to antagonize the officer and persuade him to keep her at the station any longer than necessary.

At one point, feeling the frustration and not thinking before she spoke, she blurted out, "I can't believe I forgot to lock that vault."

"Yeah, let's talk about that," the officer said, and Lilly groaned inwardly. "You say you've never forgotten to lock the vault, yet the one night you 'forget' someone is murdered in your shop," the officer said, using his fingers to make air quotes.

"I must have had a lot of things on my mind, you know, for Thanksgiving and Black Friday and the Chamber of Commerce and the holidays," Lilly said, not bothering to add *and my mother and my kids*. "And as I mentioned already, I got a call just before leaving the store on Wednesday. My mother had fallen and I was beside myself with worry. I can't believe I forgot to lock the vault," she repeated. "And the back door. I am such an idiot." She shook her head.

"No comment," the officer replied. Lilly stifled the urge to glare daggers at him.

"Are you going to arrest me?" Lilly asked. She couldn't help herself.

The officer leaned back and fixed her with a long stare. "Not yet. But don't leave town. We're not through with you yet."

"Can I go?"

He nodded and Lilly wasted no time pushing her chair back and leaving the room. She collected her purse and cell phone at the front desk and left quickly. She thought for just a moment about seeing if Bill was in, but she wanted to get out of the station and she didn't want to get Bill in trouble.

A different officer drove her home. She watched listlessly out the back window of the cruiser, lost in a fog of worry and frustration. How could she have forgotten to lock that vault? Leaving the back door unlocked was bad enough—she was lucky her entire inventory hadn't been stolen. Why was Eden in there and who had followed her? There were so many questions to be answered.

CHAPTER 47

When she got to the house she found Noley and the kids talking around the kitchen table. She plopped down in a chair and leaned her head back.

"How was it, Mom?" Laurel asked.

"Grueling. The guy asked me all the same questions they've asked before. I think they're trying to trip me up, catch me in a lie."

"Are they going to arrest you?" Tighe asked.

"Not yet, they say. I think they just don't have enough evidence to arrest me."

"Can't Bill say something?" Noley asked.

Lilly shook her head at Noley. "I suspect he already has or they would have come knocking sooner."

"How are we going to figure out who did this? That's the only way they're going to believe you had nothing to do with Mrs. Barclay's death."

"I wish I knew, Tighe," Lilly answered with a sigh.

"I'm going to get home," Noley said. "Are we still decorating your tree tomorrow night?"

"You bet," Lilly answered. "Be here at seven."

Noley bid everyone goodnight and Lilly and the kids sat at the kitchen table for a little while longer, each lost in thought.

Finally Laurel pushed her chair back and rubbed her eyes. "I'm going to bed. Do you need anything, Mom?" Lilly looked at her daughter. Laurel's tired eyes made her look younger; Lilly thought back fondly to the days when she would tuck her kids into bed. She longed for the return of those days, when everything was easier despite being a single mom. Laurel could be a handful, but she was a typical teenager and Lilly knew that despite everything, her heart was in the right place.

"No thanks, honey. I'll be up soon. Sleep tight." Laurel leaned down to kiss her mother's cheek and Lilly was reminded that she hadn't talked to her own mother all day.

After Tighe went upstairs Lilly called to Barney, who was asleep on the living room floor, for his last romp outside before bedtime. She stood in the kitchen doorway watching him play in the snow until he was ready to do his business. Snow was falling and Barney couldn't have been happier.

The town of Juniper Junction awoke the next day to eighteen inches of fresh snow on the ground. The plows were out early, so Lilly was up as soon as she heard one head down her block.

She trudged outside and brushed the snow off her car so she wouldn't be late for work, then she brushed off Tighe's truck. When she went inside he was already dressed and donning a coat and gloves.

"Are you going to shovel the walk?"

"Yeah," he grunted. He looked tired—Lilly hoped her predicament hadn't been preventing him from getting enough sleep.

"Thanks. I'll have scrambled eggs ready when you come in."

"Okay."

She called up to Laurel to take a shower so she and Tighe could leave for school early then set about making breakfast. The phone rang while she was stirring the eggs.

"I figured you'd be up early," said Noley.

"You sound way too cheerful for such an unearthly hour," Lilly replied.

"I know. I've been up working. Listen, I've been listening to the weather and it sounds like that storm will be here before evening. I'm thinking I should stay home tonight instead of coming over to help you decorate the tree."

"You're probably right. Why don't we wait to do it? We can postpone it until after the storm."

"I think you and the kids could use some time by yourselves, don't you? This has been such a stressful holiday season for all of you. You three decorate your tree just like the old days and take pictures so I can see them. I'll decorate my tree tonight, too. We'll see who does a better job." Lilly could hear the smile in Noley's voice.

"You don't want to do that alone!" Lilly exclaimed.

"Puff's here," Noley said, referring to her gigantic Angora cat. "I won't be alone."

"All right, as long as you're sure."

"I'm sure—you enjoy the kids' company tonight."

Lilly listened to the weather on her way to work. It had started to snow again just as she left the house. According to the forecast, though the sun would be out for a short time later in the morning, the calm, clear weather wouldn't last. The storm which had begun the previous night would rear its head again, this time with punishing winds and blinding snow. The meteorologist advised listeners to hunker down in their homes before the end of the afternoon because the weather was going to worsen steadily after sunset.

Lilly checked her emails as soon as she arrived at the shop. As she had suspected, she found a number of messages from her fellow business owners along Main Street and elsewhere in Juniper Junction: they were asking whether all the shops should close early.

Taking one last look at the weather app on her phone, she

composed a hasty email to all the members of the Chamber of Commerce suggesting that businesses close at two o'clock to allow shoppers, shop owners, and employees to get home in plenty of time to prepare for the coming storm. *That'll give me time to stop at Mom's house, too,* Lilly thought.

She thought about calling Taffy to tell her she could have the day off, but she decided if there were shoppers out trying to beat the storm, she would need the help. And Taffy came in early, anyway, having left her house early in case the roads were bad.

"This'll be my first Colorado blizzard," Taffy said, her eyes wide. "I'm so excited. Are they really as bad as people say?"

"I guess they can be scary if you aren't used to them," Lilly said, wondering how anyone who didn't have a snow day to look forward to could be excited about a blizzard. "But if you know enough to stay home and you've been to the grocery store for staples, you'll be fine. It's not like the towns in Colorado don't know how to handle snowstorms, so they're good about getting the roads plowed and making everything safe as soon as the snow stops."

As Lilly had hoped, there were more customers than usual that day, people who were out trying to pick up gifts before the blizzard hit.

Unfortunately, there were almost too many customers. She and Taffy bustled around the shop, waiting on people and ringing up sales. She spoke firmly to Taffy at one point about taking care to double-check the numbers on the cash register— Taffy had undercharged someone by two hundred dollars for a necklace and the customer was kind enough to point out the error to Lilly. The woman paid the extra money and the incident was forgotten.

By two o'clock the sky was beginning to darken and the wind had picked up.

CHAPTER 48

"You'd better get out of here before the snow starts, Taffy," Lilly said. "Since you live outside town, I don't want you getting stuck in blowing snow. Do you have to stop at the grocery store?"

"Yes, I need a few things."

"Then you'll need extra time, because the stores will be crazy," Lilly advised. "Everyone will be out getting last-minute stuff."

Taffy left as soon as the front door was locked. Lilly stayed a few extra minutes to lock the vault and grab her sketchbook to work on in case the blizzard lasted through the next day, then she locked the back door, double-checked it, and drove to her mother's house. The snow was starting to fall a little harder and the wind was gusty.

"Hi, Mom," she called, opening the front door. "I thought you were going to keep this door locked all the time."

"I thought it was locked," her mother answered.

"Want to come over to my house?" Lilly asked. "We're going to decorate the tree later today. We can all keep each other company."

"I don't know," her mother said. "I don't like to leave the house when the weather is supposed to be bad."

"The kids would love it if you joined us," Lilly said, knowing her mother was powerless to resist the wishes of her grandchildren.

It worked.

"All right, I'll come. Should I pack a bag to stay overnight?"

"I think you should. It's supposed to get pretty bad out there."

Lilly waited while her mother put some clothes and toiletries in a small carrying case. Then while her mother waited by the front door Lilly made sure the heat was turned down and the back door was locked.

She helped her mother down the front steps and across the snow drifts between the front walk and Lilly's car in the street.

"I hope I can get home in the morning," her mother fretted. "I don't like to leave my mail sitting in the mailbox."

"I wouldn't worry, Mom," Lilly said. "If this storm gets as bad as they're predicting, we may not get any mail for a day or two."

"They're supposed to deliver the mail through rain or sleet or snow or gloom of night," Lilly's mother said primly.

"Well, they can't deliver the mail if they can't get the trucks out on the roads."

"Humph."

Lilly closed her eyes and prayed silently, begging for patience and promising everything but her kids if God could keep her from trying to strangle her mother over the long hours to come.

The kids were already home and had made hot chocolate. They were thrilled to see their grandmother. The four sat in front of the fireplace, enjoying the warm drink and listening to the wind outside, discussing whether they should use the white lights or the colored lights on the tree that year. Every year there was a lively discussion about which lights should go on the tree, and the kids usually voted Lilly down in favor of colored lights.

This year, though, they felt sorry for their mother because of the stress she was under and they readily agreed to a tree with white lights. Lilly grinned. "Okay, I'll find the lights and you two can help me unravel them. It's not the holiday season if we don't almost come to blows over the Christmas lights." Beverly's eyes widened. "Not really, Mom."

The three of them had struggled to get the tree into the garage the weekend before Thanksgiving so it would have time to acclimate to being indoors. Now they went out to the garage again, brought it in through the kitchen, and fought with it until it stood proudly in the living room, a little lopsided but beautiful. Lilly breathed in deeply, savoring the scent of pine needles and bark.

"The needles make a mess and they hurt my feet," Laurel complained. "Why can't we get a fake tree? Nick's family has one and they can put it up the day after Thanksgiving and leave it up until they feel like taking it down."

Another strike against Nick, thought Lilly.

"Since you mention it, why don't you get a broom and dustpan and clean up the needles on the floor? While you're doing that I'll drag the ornament boxes from the closet."

"I wasn't offering to clean them up," Laurel whined.

Tighe laughed. "You ought to know better by now. Why do you think I never say anything?"

"Tighe, be nice to your sister," Beverly interjected.

Laurel heaved a dramatic sigh. "All right, I'll clean them up. I hope I get an extra Christmas gift for this."

"What are you and Nick giving each other for Christmas?" Tighe asked.

Dear God, please don't let it be offensive, Lilly thought.

Laurel brightened immediately. "We're getting each other matching ski hats. We're having them monogrammed."

That's not bad at all.

"Cool," said Tighe.

Lilly found the lights for the tree and the ornaments in the downstairs closet. She dragged out the boxes and piled them in the middle of the living room. She reached for the tangle of lights and gave one of the ends—the only one she could locate —to Tighe.

"You hold this while I try to unravel the rest of the lights," she instructed. For the next half hour she unknotted and untangled, twisting and pulling and coaxing and teasing the strings of lights into a relatively straight line. By the time she finished she was furious.

"It's like a rat's nest," Tighe said. "Why don't we just get new lights every year and throw them away when Christmas is over?"

"Because this is part of the fun," Lilly grunted, bending down to find the outlet under and behind the tree. "And your way is expensive and wasteful." She plugged in the lights and turned with the unreasonable hope that they would all light up like magic.

Two strings of lights didn't light.

"Nick's family has a pre-lit tree," Laurel offered. "They don't have to deal with this every year."

"Good for Nick's family," Lilly mumbled, only half under her breath. She stood up. "Tighe, let's unplug the strands that don't work and I'll replace them with new ones I have in the closet." She retreated to the closet again and came back holding two boxes of lights.

"I can only find colored lights. I thought I had boxes of white ones."

"That's okay, Mom," said Tighe. "We can use the white ones and the colored ones. It'll be sort of a compromise."

Lilly thought of the perfect tree Noley was no doubt putting up at her house and grimaced. "Okay. It's either that or have a tree that looks anemic. Let's plug them in and see how they look."

They looked terrible.

But the kids had no problem with using both colored and

white lights, so Lilly bit her tongue and kept quiet about how bad it looked.

"Let me get these lights up while you two get out stuff for sandwiches," Lilly said. Barney was lying on the floor watching everything but suddenly he sat up straight, his ears cocked.

"Yes, I said 'sandwiches,'" Lilly said with a laugh. "Don't give him too much sandwich meat, you two." Tighe and Laurel went into the kitchen, followed by Barney.

Lilly had been hunched over the lights for too long, and her back was starting to hurt. She stood up to stretch and walk around the living room for a few moments. She stood at the living room window and pulled aside the curtains to a world of swirling, blowing white flakes. She couldn't even see the house across the street.

"How does it look out there?" her mother asked.

"Pretty bad," Lilly answered, stretching backward.

"I hope the power doesn't go out."

"Don't worry. If it does, we have flashlights and candles. The kids actually like it when the power goes out."

"For heaven's sake, why?"

Lilly shrugged. "I guess it's because it seems cozier in the dark. More like the dark of winter. They just love it—they always have."

"Tighe used to be afraid of the dark when he was very small," Beverly remarked.

Now why can she remember that but not remember what a jerk Beau was?

"I remember," Lilly said with a chuckle. "Luckily he's grown out of that."

"Time to eat!" Laurel called from the kitchen.

"Come on, Mom. I hope you're hungry," Lilly said.

The kids had set out everything buffet-style so everyone could help themselves. They all made thick sandwiches and loaded their plates with potato chips, pickles, and three-bean salad that Noley had brought over the last time she visited.

Bill phoned as they were sitting down in the living room in front of the fireplace.

"How's everyone over there?"

"Good. I brought Mom over to ride out the storm with us. Want to come? We've got food."

Bill paused. "Actually, I thought I might go over and spend some time at Noley's house."

Lilly let out a little squeal. "Have fun and tell me all about it tomorrow!"

"I have to come back into work later, so don't expect much of a story. She said she was going to decorate her tree. I might be in time to help her with that."

"Well, have fun anyway. And be careful."

"I always am."

After everyone had eaten and the dishes were done, it was time to decorate the tree. The mismatched lights were on and shining brightly. The boxes of ornaments were strewn across the living room floor and it was the annual free-for-all as Lilly, her mother, and the kids each put their favorite ornaments on the tree. It was light-hearted, without so much as a snarky word from anyone, and by the time the ornaments were hanging on the tree Lilly had been able to relax enough to feel the spirit of the season beginning to seep into her soul.

"Mom, why don't we watch a movie?" Laurel asked.

"Good idea. You guys and Gran decide on one while I put these boxes away and let the dog out." When the weather was especially bad, Lilly attached one end of a long rope to Barney's collar and the other end to a hook beside the back door. That way Barney didn't get lost in the whiteout conditions and Lilly could pull on the rope until he made his way back to the kitchen door.

She put the ornament boxes back in the closet and called Barney. He loved the snow and was even more excited than usual to go out. She attached the blizzard rope, as she called it, to his collar and let him run. She didn't want to stand in the doorway and let the snow fall into the kitchen, so she closed the door to wait for him.

"Mom, the DVD player isn't working," Tighe called from the living room.

"I'm coming," she answered.

She went into the living room and tinkered with the aging DVD player until the movie came on. The kids had somehow persuaded their grandmother to watch "The Nightmare Before Christmas."

"Tighe and Laurel, really?" Lilly asked. "Gran isn't going to like this movie."

"I think I'll be the judge of that," Beverly said.

Lilly stood up in the middle of the living room and waited to make sure the DVD was going to play properly. When the opening credits started to roll, she nodded to herself and turned around to fetch Barney from his snowy playground.

She had only gone a few steps when the house was plunged into darkness. The sound coming from the television set stopped and she could hear gasps of surprise from the living room.

CHAPTER 49

"Mom, the power went out," Laurel called.

"I see that," Lilly said. "Hold on a minute while I get a flashlight and the candles. I have a feeling the power may not come back on for a while." She kept all the emergency supplies in a narrow cupboard in the pantry and she made her way toward it, feeling for the table and chairs so she wouldn't trip.

She hadn't gotten to the pantry when there was a loud crash accompanied by the sound of breaking glass from the living room. Laurel and her grandmother let out screams.

"What happened?" Lilly called, turning toward the living room and feeling her way in the dark.

"I don't know!" Laurel shrieked. "It's freezing in here!"

Indeed, snow was flying sideways into the living room from a broken window. "Tighe, help me cover this window with something," Lilly ordered.

"With what?" he asked, his voice tense. Laurel was crying and her grandmother was trying to comfort her. Lilly knew her mother must be afraid, too. She had always hated storms.

"Let me grab a tablecloth from the closet," Lilly said. "We can put that over the window and at least keep out the snow until we find some plastic in the garage. The wind must have cracked the window."

"Hurry, Mom," Laurel urged.

"I am, honey. Just give me a second." Lilly made her way through the darkness to the closet and reached up to the top shelf, feeling for the stack of tablecloths she kept in there. The noise from the rushing wind outside made it hard to hear anything except the sound of Laurel's cries.

"Here," Lilly said, grabbing two tablecloths. She stumbled back toward Tighe and handed him one of the cloths.

"What am I supposed to do with it?" he asked, the frustration in his voice obvious.

"Tuck it around the curtain rod," Lilly directed. "It's only for a few minutes, until we can find the plastic sheets." She climbed onto the couch under the window and held up her tablecloth, working clumsily with hands that were growing more cold and numb by the second. She hung it up on the curtain rod and stepped down.

"Let me get the flashlight and candles," she said. "Then I'll go out and get Barney."

She went back out to the kitchen and found the emergency supplies in the pantry in short order. She turned on the flashlight and returned to the living room, shining it around to make sure everyone was okay.

She was shining the beam of light toward the fireplace and she didn't see the thing on the floor that made her trip.

"Ouch!" she exclaimed. "What the heck was that?" She shined the beam toward the floor where she had stubbed her toe.

Laurel let out a scream. A large brick lay on the floor.

Lilly's blood ran cold.

"How did that get there?" Beverly asked in a shaky voice.

"I don't know. Don't worry, Mom. I'll take care of it." Lilly's heart was pounding double-time.

"Don't touch it!" Tighe told her. "I'll call Uncle Bill and have him come over. He needs to see that."

Laurel was sobbing; her grandmother was stroking her hair, but it wasn't working. "Mom, why would someone do that?" she cried through her tears.

"I don't know, Laurel. But I'll call Bill and we'll get it cleared up right away." Lilly fumbled through her purse, holding the flashlight between her chin and neck, until she found her cell phone. She dialed Bill, her hands shaking. But not from the cold.

When he answered she launched into a babbling account of what had just taken place.

"Wait a minute! Slow down," he said. "What are you trying to say?"

"Someone just threw a brick through the front window. The kids and Mom are terrified. Can you come over?"

"I'll be over as soon as I can get there." He hung up.

Lilly went back to the living room. "Kids, take Gran upstairs. It'll be warmer up there. Bill will be here soon."

Tighe and Laurel helped Beverly up the stairs and the sounds of their footsteps disappeared into the howling wind that was barreling into the living room. Lilly shivered. She wanted to take the brick and hurl it back outside, but she dared not touch it until Bill could see it. Instead, she took a picture of it with the camera on her cell phone and emailed a copy of it to herself. She didn't plan to open the email as long as she lived, but she wanted to have it just in case.

Then she remembered that Barney was still outside. If he was barking to get in, she wouldn't be able to hear the sound over the wind. She felt terrible. How many minutes had he been outside, freezing, while she dealt with the situation inside?

She ran through the kitchen and opened the door to wind

that screamed in her ear and snow that swept into the kitchen like a dervish. She reached for the hook next to the door so she could pull Barney in using the rope.

But the rope hung in her hand limply—Barney wasn't on the other end.

CHAPTER 50

Lilly's heart began to hammer a staccato beat. "Barney!" she yelled into the wind. "Barney! Come here, boy!"

There was no answer—at least, not one she could hear. She wasn't sure if Barney would be able to hear her voice above the keening wind. She closed the door just long enough to call for Tighe to come downstairs and to grab a coat and hat and mittens.

"What do you need, Mom?" he asked, hurrying into the kitchen.

"Barney isn't attached to the blizzard rope. I clipped it to his collar when I let him out to go to the bathroom, but it's come off somehow. I need to go out and look for him."

"I'll help you," he offered, already taking long strides toward the closet to get his outdoor things.

"Don't tell your sister or Gran what's going on," Lilly said in a low voice. "There's no sense in worrying them."

"Do you think the same person who threw the brick unhooked the rope from Barney's collar?"

"I don't know. All I care about right now is getting Barney back inside." They shut the door behind them. Lilly handed the blizzard rope to Tighe and told him to use it while he was trying to find Barney.

"What are you going to use?" he yelled over the wind.

"My sense of direction."

He gave her a look of disbelief, rolled his eyes, handed her the rope, then started down the steps. Lilly could hear him yelling for Barney, so she hoped Barney could hear him, too. Grasping the rope and twisting it around her wrist so she wouldn't drop it, she imagined the backyard as a grid and stepped off the steps and to the left, where she knew Barney usually headed as soon as he went outside. The flying snow made it impossible to see more than a few inches from her face, but she peered ahead as best she could.

"Barney!" she yelled.

She strained her ears to hear a bark, a whimper, anything, but there was nothing but the wind rushing around her ears. She walked slowly, trying to keep her balance, feeling in front of her for any object.

It wasn't long before her foot hit something. Reaching out her hand, she felt it to see if she could identify it—it was one of the patio chairs. It had evidently been knocked over and blown around by the wind. Stepping carefully over it, she continued her slow walk forward. Eventually her hand whacked something and she knew she had found the table. She placed both hands on the edge of the table and felt her way around it to the other side.

The fence separating her property from Mrs. Laforge's property wasn't far. Between Lilly and the fence were several feet of mulched beds containing Lilly's hosta garden. She stood next to the table, breathless from the wind and cold, wondering what to do next. Should she head back to the house or make her way to the right and try the same search again?

She opted to go to the right and search again using the grid layout in her mind's eye. She felt in front of her and moved, she thought, in a straight line to the mulched beds. Then she moved farther to the right and did it again.

She could hear Tighe yelling Barney's name as he made his way toward her in the snow. Her breath caught in her throat—he obviously hadn't found Barney and she was having no luck.

"Mom, I think he's gone!" Tighe shouted above the wind.

"Let's go inside," she yelled.

They held hands and made their way slowly across the yard to the back steps. Tighe started to go up and Lilly turned around. "What are you doing?" he shouted.

"I'm going to make sure the gate is closed! Stay here!"

With her hands outstretched in front of her, Lilly moved slowly in the direction of the gate. She stumbled as she made her way through the snow drifts, but eventually reached the gate. Feeling her way along the wooden slats, she came to the latch.

It was open. Her reaction was swift and visceral. Her vision began to swim and she bent down to catch her breath. Reaching out to grab the nearest slat, she held onto it so she wouldn't faint.

Barney was gone. He was somewhere out in the snowstorm and she had no way of finding him.

By the time she got back to the house the tears were coursing down her cheeks and she couldn't catch her breath. Tighe was making his way up the back steps.

"I checked under the back deck—he's not there, either!" Tighe shouted. He leaned forward toward Lilly so she could hear him better.

"Mom! What's wrong?" He was still yelling to be heard over the wind.

She motioned for him to go inside. When he had shut the door behind them, she slid down to the floor and covered her face with her hands. Her chest heaved from the sobs which were wracking her body. Laurel came crashing down the stairs in the dark.

"What's wrong? Why is Mom crying?"

"I don't know," Tighe said.

"The gate is open," Lilly croaked.

"So what?" Laurel asked.

"Barney's out there. I'm afraid he got unhooked from the blizzard rope somehow," Lilly said in clipped tones through her cries.

"No!" Laurel cried. "How do you know? Where did he go?"

"I don't know for sure, but Tighe and I have been out looking for him in the backyard. We've checked everywhere. I just have a terrible feeling about this."

Laurel's sobs matched those of her mother. Lilly couldn't see Tighe in the dark, but she suspected he was shedding tears, too. She wanted to be strong for her kids, but she couldn't summon the courage right now. She missed her dog and she couldn't stand the thought of him lost out in the snowstorm.

"I'm going to go back out there," Tighe said, his voice was nasally and clogged.

"No, Tighe. You can't do that. It's not safe out there," she said.

"But how are we going to find Barney?" he asked, his voice rising in panic.

"What's going on down there?" Beverly called.

"Nothing, Mom. I'll be up in a sec," Lilly answered.

"If Tighe goes out, I'm going with him," Laurel said. She started crying again. "I miss Barney already." Her weeping made Lilly's heart break.

"At least wait until Uncle Bill gets here," Lilly said. "If he'll go out with you while I stay here and keep looking in the back-yard, then it's okay."

She dried her tears and went upstairs to check on her mother, who was lying down on Laurel's bed.

"Why don't you rest for now, Mom, and I'll come get you later when we've got the window fixed."

"All right."

Lilly went back downstairs to find both Laurel and Tighe peering out the windows, searching for any sign of the dog. Tighe was still wearing his coat but Laurel had on a flannel shirt and was shivering. She didn't even seem to notice.

A moment later all three of them jumped when there was a loud pounding on the front door, then the door handle started rattling. "Stay here," Lilly ordered the kids. "I'll see who it is."

It was Bill. He swept into the house on a gust of wind and slammed the door shut with an effort.

"How did you get here?" Lilly asked.

"Very slowly."

He had a flashlight; he walked over to the window and examined the makeshift curtain. "First things first. We need to get a sheet of plastic put up here so you guys don't freeze. Where's Mom?"

"Upstairs resting," Lilly replied.

"Good. Tighe, will you come out to the garage with me to get plastic sheets to put up over this window?"

"Wait a minute, Bill," Lilly said. "Barney's gone. We need to find him first."

"What do you mean, Barney's gone?"

"I let him out and he wasn't attached to the blizzard rope when I went to bring him back in. The gate's open. Tighe and I looked everywhere for him in the backyard. He's not there."

"Oh my God. I'll go out to look for him," Bill asked.

"I'll go with you," Tighe offered.

"Me, too," Laurel said.

"Wait. Let's get the window fixed. We can do that in just a few minutes. Then we'll go out and look for Barney. I don't want you guys and Mom to freeze."

"The kids and I can do that, Bill," Lilly said. "It would be better if you could just go look for Barney."

"All right. I'll take a look at that brick when I get back, too."

He pulled his gloves on and clicked his flashlight on, then

stood at the back door waiting for Laurel to get her coat on. "Hurry up, Laur."

"I'm hurrying," Laurel said, pulling a hat down over her ears.

"Let's go," said Tighe. Bill opened the door and the three of them pushed their way outside into the wind. Anything they may have said to Lilly as they left was whipped away into the sky.

Lilly was beside herself with worry. She paced the downstairs, looking out every window as she passed, trying to catch a glimpse of the kids or Bill or Barney. She went down to the basement to bring wood up to the living room, even though there was plenty stacked next to the hearth. She went upstairs to check on her mother, resting peacefully and blessedly unaware of the missing dog. She went back downstairs and sat at the kitchen table, trying to scroll through messages on her phone, but her eyes wouldn't focus and the tears started to fall again.

Over an hour had passed before she heard a noise at the back door. Leaping up from her chair, she ran to open it.

Mrs. Laforge stood there. And Barney was next to her, sitting on his haunches as if nothing was wrong.

CHAPTER 51

"Edna! Barney! Come in, come in," she cried, drawing Mrs. Laforge into the kitchen. "What on earth is going on? How did you find Barney?"

"I don't know how he got loose, but somehow it happened and I heard him scratching out on my porch."

"I can't thank you enough for bringing him back," Lilly said. She dropped to her knees and examined Barney while he licked her face, seemingly no worse for wear after his bitterly cold and frightening experience.

"Didn't really have much choice, did I?" Mrs. Laforge asked. "He smells terrible and I couldn't very well let him stay at my house."

Lilly wanted to laugh. On any other day a comment like that would have enraged her, but she was so happy to have Barney home that she was only capable of feeling joy for the time being.

"Well, thank you for not letting him freeze. I hope you'll stay here until the storm stops."

"And smell this dog all night? No, thank you. I'll go back to my own house. He scratched my front door, by the way. I assume you'll pay to have it repainted."

"Of course I will. As soon as this storm is over. Please let me make you some hot chocolate and when my brother comes back he'll walk you home."

"Might as well," Mrs. Laforge grumbled.

Barney sat next to Lilly on the floor, wagging his tail and panting. His coat was wet from the snow and Lilly was worried that he might be lame from being out in the cold.

"Good Lord! It's cold in here! What's wrong with you, not keeping the heat on in a blizzard?" Mrs. Laforge asked with a scowl.

It was a good thing Mrs. Laforge had saved Barney's life. Lilly took a deep breath. "Our front window broke. I was waiting until Bill and the kids got home to put up plastic. I wanted to look for the dog first."

"It's miserable in here." *It's probably miserable wherever you go,* Lilly thought with a grimace. But one look at Barney and she softened. She owed Edna Laforge a huge debt of gratitude.

There was a rush of sound from the kitchen and Bill and the kids slammed the door shut behind them. Lilly could hear Laurel crying.

"Barney's home!" Lilly called out. Barney stayed by her side while Laurel and Tighe came rushing over, each of them holding a flashlight, tripping over each other in their happiness that Barney was home.

"How did you find him?" Laurel cried.

"I didn't. Mrs. Laforge did," Lilly said.

"You're darn right. That dog has caused no end of trouble for me today," Mrs. Laforge said. Neither Tighe nor Laurel had seen her sitting at the table.

"Mrs. Laforge! Thank you!" Laurel walked over to her and put her arms around the elderly woman's neck.

"That's enough of that," Mrs. Laforge said gruffly. "I'm just glad he's all right."

Tighe and Laurel sat down next to Barney; he shifted so they could pet him. They stroked his fur, murmuring to him in low voices. Laurel went to the closet and returned just a moment later with an armful of blankets. She knelt on the floor next to Barney and folded a blanket into a pillow for him. Then she covered him with another thin blanket while she massaged his legs and paws. Tighe rubbed Barney's side. Bill had moved closer to the group and he knelt down to pat Barney, too.

"Someone unhooked that blizzard rope. Who would do that to an animal?" Tighe asked half-aloud. Lilly knew he didn't expect an answer.

"Can you take me home, Bill?" Mrs. Laforge asked.

"Sure, I'd be happy to take you home. Tighe, want to go with me?"

Tighe hadn't even taken off his coat since coming in the house. He stood up and offered his hand to their neighbor. "Sure. Come on, Mrs. Laforge."

"You're not going to swear at me, are you?" she asked.

"Of course not," he answered.

"That mouth of yours…"

He wisely ignored her. He and Bill left with Mrs. Laforge; because of the blizzard a trek that normally would have taken five minutes took twenty.

"She's an old witch," Tighe said when they were back in the house.

"I have to agree," Bill said.

"I know, but there are times I feel sorry for her. And we wouldn't have Barney right now if it weren't for her," Lilly reminded them.

"Okay. Now show me the brick." He withdrew a pair of plastic gloves from his coat pocket.

Lilly shone the flashlight on the brick, still on the living room floor where it had landed. Bill crouched down to look at it. He took several photos with his cell phone camera before touching it. He picked it up in both hands, hefting it as if to determine its weight.

"It's too bad any footprints or even tire tracks are long covered up by now. You didn't see anyone?"

"I couldn't see a foot in front of my face out there. That brick came out of nowhere and scared the heck out of all of us."

"How's Mom doing?"

"She was scared. And she doesn't even know about the dog."

"That's probably best."

"So Barney was unhooked from the blizzard rope and the gate was open?" Bill asked.

"Yes—it was the same person who threw the brick. I'm sure of it. I hooked that blizzard rope to Barney's collar myself and I know it was secure because I tested it."

"Okay. Can I see the hook?"

Lilly led him through the kitchen to the back door. He opened the door and bent down to examine the hook where the blizzard rope had been attached.

"Bill, this must have something to do with everything else that's been going on around here. People just don't go out and do stuff like this randomly."

"I'm sure you're right. Unfortunately, I doubt there's going to be much evidence for us to go on because of the weather. Everything's been destroyed."

"Do you think you could get fingerprints from that hook?"

"We might be able to, but I'm guessing in this storm whoever did it wore gloves."

Lilly sat down hard on one of the kitchen chairs. "What can I do? The kids are scared, Mom's scared, I'm scared. And who does something like this to a dog? It's sick!"

"Easy does it, Lil. Let's take one thing at a time. First, as soon as this storm stops you need to call someone to come and replace your window. Second, I think you should get Barney checked out to make sure he's okay. And third, I hope you're all going to hunker down in the same room to conserve warmth."

"But what am I going to do until the storm stops? What if that person comes back?"

"I'm sure the person or persons who did this sought shelter immediately and aren't leaving until the storm stops. I doubt you need to worry about them right now."

"They were lucky the power went out just before they did this."

"It probably wouldn't have mattered. By the time you could have gotten outside after the brick was thrown, the footprints would have been covered up already and the person would be gone. Or hiding. You wouldn't be able to find them in this storm."

"I feel like I'm losing my mind." Lilly ran her hands through her hair.

"We'll get to the bottom of this, I'm sure. It's just going to take some time. Sooner or later everyone makes a mistake. And if the same person is behind these pranks and the deaths of Eden and Herb, they're bound to make one soon."

"So why did I have to be questioned again?"

"They're just going back over the evidence they have to see if they've missed anything. And, like I've said, you have as much motive as anyone else right now. But those two officers don't think you did it, if that makes you feel any better."

"I guess that makes me feel a little better."

"Got anything to eat?"

"Didn't you eat at Noley's?"

"Didn't get a chance before you called. I'm starving."

Lilly made him a sandwich and sat down with him. While he was eating Beverly came into the kitchen.

"Thank you for coming over, Bill. It's just been harrowing." She glanced at Lilly. "I don't know how Lilly gets herself into these scrapes."

"I wouldn't call this a 'scrape,' Mom. If anyone had been standing in the wrong place when that brick came through the window, we could be dealing with something much more serious here," Bill replied. Lilly shivered and Beverly had the grace to look chagrined.

"Mom, we're all going to sleep in my room tonight to stay warm, if that's okay with you," Lilly said.

Laurel joined the group in the kitchen. "Gran, want to watch a movie on my tablet? It's all charged up." The two of them went upstairs to Lilly's room.

"Can you think of anything that might help that you may not have thought to tell the guys who brought you in for questioning?"

Lilly shook her head. "Not that I can think of. If only I hadn't left that door unlocked on the day before Thanksgiving, maybe none of this would have happened. Or at least it wouldn't have happened in my store."

"That's what we've got to figure out—what was Eden doing in your store? The only person who knows that, besides Eden, is the person who killed her. And maybe Herb, but he's no use to us now." Bill paused for a long moment while he ate his sandwich, then spoke again.

"Do you remember the last time you and Eden talked before she died? Do you remember what you talked about?"

Lilly sat deep in thought, trying to remember the last time she and Eden had spoken.

"It was the week before Thanksgiving. We had our monthly Chamber of Commerce cocktail party and she was there with Herb."

"She was? Did you tell us this before?"

Lilly shrugged. "I thought I did, but maybe I didn't. I'm so confused."

"Okay, don't worry about it. So she was there with Herb. Did they both talk to you?"

"Yes. I remember—the three of us were standing by the bar. I had been talking to someone else and Eden and Herb came up together."

"What did they want?"

Lilly cocked her head, her eyes narrowing, as she thought back to that night. "I wish I could remember. I think I was on my second glass of wine."

Bill grimaced. "Try to remember, but don't force it. It'll come to you when you least expect it."

"Are you going to stay here tonight?"

"I'm supposed to be at work, but the radio is working and I haven't had any calls. Do you mind if I crash here?"

"Not at all. You can sleep with all of us upstairs if you want."

"Nah. I'll stay down here. Got a sleeping bag I can use?"

"Sure. It's in Tighe's room. I'll get it for you." Lilly went upstairs to get the sleeping bag. When she came down she brought Tighe with her. He got a hammer, nails, and a sheet of plastic from the garage and while Lilly held the flashlight, Tighe held the plastic over the window and Bill hammered the nails into place. When they were finished, Tighe held the flashlight while Lilly nailed the two tablecloths over the plastic to insulate the room a little bit. Then Tighe went upstairs, exhausted.

When Lilly went upstairs a few minutes later to get Bill a pillow, Tighe was under his own comforter on her floor. She pulled the comforter up to his chin; he groaned and turned over. She smiled in the darkness, remembering all the times she would check on him before she went to bed. Her mother and Laurel were both nodding off as they watched a movie on the small screen of Laurel's tablet. They were snuggled up together in Lilly's bed, so Lilly tiptoed over to the bed, closed the tablet, and made sure both her favorite girls had plenty of blankets.

She grabbed a pillow from her closet and took it downstairs for Bill, along with an extra blanket she had gotten. The living room was uncomfortably cold.

After she gave Bill his supplies for the night, she went into the kitchen and called Hassan to check on him and make sure his family was safe. They didn't talk for long because she wanted to conserve her cell phone battery, but she was relieved to hear that his family was safe and warm.

She hugged Bill before she went upstairs—she couldn't believe how lucky she was to have a brother like him. If Tighe turned out half as good as Bill, she would have done her job. She climbed the stairs slowly, exhausted from the stress of the afternoon, and fell asleep almost immediately on the loveseat in her room.

CHAPTER 52

T he storm continued unabated all through the night and through the long day that followed. Everyone in the house was grumpy from being cooped up, from the cold, and from stress. Bill's radio remained silent except for a few squawks that were answered by other officers already at the station, so he stayed most of the day. He was able to reach Noley on her cell phone, which was a good sign that the cell phone towers nearby were still standing. He passed the phone to Lilly so she could talk to her friend and satisfy herself that Noley was all right.

Finally, around dinnertime the wind began to die down a little bit and when Lilly peered out the back door she was able to make out the faint roofline of Mrs. Laforge's house. She had let Barney out several times during the day, attaching the blizzard rope to his collar and making sure to stay out there with him each time. He didn't seem to want to play in the snow as he normally did during a storm—Lilly surmised that the experience of being lost and disoriented in the blizzard contributed to his urge to get right back into the house each time he went out.

It was a welcome sound when the first plow made its way up the street a short while later, and not long after that the lights flickered back to life. Bill left on foot to pick up his car at Noley's house and get to work.

"Lilly, do you think you'll be able to take me home in the morning?" her mother asked, coming into the kitchen. She was wearing a parka because it was so cold in the house. Lilly looked at her mom with a pang of sympathy. Poor woman—she shouldn't have to endure such discomfort.

As so often happened immediately following a blizzard, the temperature was plummeting. Lilly had told everyone that they would all sleep in the same room upstairs again that night. She could hardly wait until the next day, when the man she had called to install another window would be able to come out to the house.

"Sure. I'll take you home first thing in the morning. Tonight we have to snowblow the driveway and get the snow off the cars." She called the kids downstairs and told them to get busy clearing snow outside while she shoveled the back porch. She asked her mom to keep an eye on Barney.

"Barney gets an awful lot of attention for a dog," Beverly grumbled. "My dog is just a dog."

"Mom, you don't—never mind," Lilly said with a sigh. "Barney is part of the family. He deserves all the attention he gets."

"Hmph."

Lilly rolled her eyes, not feeling quite so sorry for her mother anymore.

Tighe and Laurel came in about an hour later, ruddy-cheeked and tired. "Do you think there'll be school tomorrow?" Laurel asked.

"Definitely," Lilly answered with a smile. "That's why we're all going to bed early. You guys haven't gotten much sleep for a couple of teenagers who've had nothing to do for two days."

As promised, Lilly took her mother home first thing in the morning. She had called Taffy and asked her to open the shop so she could get her mother inside safely and shovel the walk, then wait for the window man at her own house. By the time Lilly left Beverly's house she was exhausted from shoveling.

The window man was right on time. When Lilly showed him the damage he let out a low whistle.

"What happened here?"

"The window broke."

"I can see that. How'd it happen?" he asked, glancing at her from under bushy eyebrows.

"A branch came sailing through it," she lied.

"Are you sure? Must've been a pretty big branch."

"It was," Lilly answered with a hint of impatience. "How long will it take to get a replacement?"

"I've got one in stock," he said. "I can come back here this afternoon with my assistant and put it in."

"Thank you." Lilly breathed a sigh of relief. They agreed on a time for him to return so Lilly would be able to go into the store for a while. After he left she gathered her sketchbooks and left for work. Because the power had gone out she hadn't been able to do any design work at home.

There were a few customers in the store when Lilly arrived and she was pleased to see that Taffy was handling everyone with professionalism and patience. Lilly hurried to put her books away in the office and went out to the front of the store to help.

It wasn't long before Hassan came into the store. Taffy greeted him and turned back to help another customer and he headed right for Lilly.

"What an incredible storm!" he said, his eyes bright. "I've experienced my first Rocky Mountain blizzard and I loved it!"

Lilly laughed. "I don't hear that very often."

"I wish you and the kids could have come to my house." He leaned over to kiss her on the cheek after making sure no customers were watching.

"I had my mother, my brother, and the dog, too. Believe me, you wouldn't have wanted all of us."

He laughed. "What are you doing for lunch?" he asked.

"I was planning on eating here since I came in late and I have to leave early."

"How about I pick up some stuff from the diner and we eat together?" he asked.

"Sounds good," she said with a wide smile. She gave him her order and he left. He was gone quite a while before he came back bearing a brown paper bag and two bottles of sparkling water.

"Shall we eat in my office?" she asked. "Taffy, could you mind things out here while we eat, then I'll take over and you can grab lunch?"

"Sure."

Lilly's office was warm thanks to a space heater that she kept back there. She and Hassan slid up to the desk across from each other and opened the bag from the diner.

"So why do you have to leave early?" he asked.

Lilly hadn't told him about the brick incident during the storm because she didn't want him to worry and because she didn't want to discuss it at home where her mother or the kids could overhear.

His eyes grew wider and he stopped eating as she related the story.

"I can't believe it," he said, covering her hand with his own. "You must have been terrified."

"And freezing," she added, attempting to make light of the situation.

"And freezing," he repeated. "I am so sorry I wasn't able to help you."

"There's nothing you could have done. My brother walked to the house and stayed overnight, so I felt safer with him there."

"But the brick wasn't the only thing," she continued. "Someone, probably the same person, unhooked Barney's rope from the wall by the back door and he got disoriented in the storm. Our neighbor found him and brought him home."

Hassan covered his mouth with his hand. "Oh, my God. How is he now?"

"Okay, but I need to make an appointment with the vet to have him checked out. He doesn't want to spend much time outside right now. I imagine he'll get braver as time goes on and he'll eventually want to go out and play again."

"Whoever did that should be put away for good."

"I agree, but it's not going to be easy to figure out who did it. No fingerprints, no footprints, no tire tracks. The snow obliterated all the evidence."

Hassan shook his head. "I cannot forgive myself for not inviting you and your family over to my house."

"Even if you had asked, we couldn't have come. Especially after the window broke, I needed to stay in my own house to keep an eye on everything and everyone."

Hassan stared at her.

"What?" she asked.

"You are an incredibly brave woman," he said. She laughed.

"I am about the least brave person there is," she said. "I was scared to death."

"You can be brave and scared at the same time," he said, fixing her with an intent look. "You did what you needed to do throughout the storm while taking care of your family and facing your fear. I'm very impressed."

"Thank you. Now before my ego gets the better of me, I'm going to go relieve Taffy so she can have lunch." She stood up to go, but he reached for her arm and pulled her toward him and kissed her.

"You know how much I will miss you when I go back to Minnesota," he said.

She smiled and nodded, suddenly feeling empty and sad. "You finish your lunch," she said.

CHAPTER 53

S he went back to the front of the store and left Hassan at her
desk finishing his lunch. She was sorry she had eaten hers
because now she felt sick to her stomach. She had known
Hassan would be leaving, but she didn't want him to talk
about it.

Taffy went over to the diner and returned quickly with a
container of soup and a soda. She took it back to the office and
shortly Hassan came out, holding the remnants of his lunch in
the bag.

"Would you like to go out to dinner tonight?" he asked.

"I don't think I should," Lilly replied. She was about to lie
and explain that she had too much work to do when he spoke.

"Is something wrong?"

"No, no," she hastened to assure him. "I just have a lot of
work to do," she finished lamely.

"All right. If you change your mind, let me know. I'll come
by tomorrow to see you."

She wanted to tell him to stay away, that it would be too
painful to keep seeing him when he was going away after the
holidays, but she couldn't bring herself to say it.

She was struck by a feeling of embarrassment and despair usually reserved for teenagers in the throes of puppy love. *What if I like him more than he likes me? What if I don't mean anything and this has been nothing more than a fun vacation fling for him? I should break up with him now before he can break up with me.*

When Taffy came out of the office after eating her lunch she took one look at Lilly and exclaimed, "What's wrong with you? You look terrible!"

"Is it that bad?"

"I'm afraid so. Why don't you take off early and do something for yourself while you wait for your window guy to come? Go get a facial or a manicure or something."

"Maybe you're right," Lilly said with a sigh. "Are you sure you don't mind? I hate to leave you in the lurch like this."

"This is why you hired me, remember? Now go so you have some time before you have to be home."

Lilly grabbed her purse and, thanking Taffy, went out onto Main Street, where the snow sparkled in the sunshine and the Christmas decorations creaked and swayed in the winter wind. She headed straight for the day spa right up the block, where she knew her friend Leslie would squeeze her in for a quick facial.

An hour later she emerged into the blinding white of Main Street feeling fresh, scrubbed, and hopeful. Taffy had been right —an hour-long facial had done wonders for her mood and her outlook. Walking behind the Main Street shops she was headed toward her car when she saw Hassan exit through the rear of the jewelry store. He held a folder and he strode off in the opposite direction.

What is he doing now? She opened her mouth to call out to him, but thought the better of it and said nothing. If she was going to stop seeing him she needed to have the willpower to keep quiet when she saw him from a distance, for God's sake.

At home she waited for the window man in her winter coat and mittens. Barney sat beside her in the den and their body warmth kept each other from freezing. The man was right on time. He and his assistant got right to work and by the time the kids got home from school there was a new window in place of the broken one and Lilly had the heat cranked up.

"Finally! It feels good in here," Laurel exclaimed when she came through the door. Tighe voiced his agreement and the small family ate a quiet dinner in the cozy kitchen.

That evening Lilly's cell phone buzzed several times. Each time she looked at it, she saw that Hassan was calling and declined to answer. When she went upstairs she called Noley.

"I feel like I haven't seen you in weeks!" her friend said. "How's everything?"

"Everything stinks." Lilly proceeded to tell Noley about Hassan. "He's going to go back to Minnesota after New Year's and I just don't think I can see him again. It's going to be too hard when he leaves."

"I wish I could help," Noley said, her voice sympathetic. "If you want my two cents, keep going out with him. You enjoy his company and he obviously enjoys yours. So have fun while you can."

"Easy for you to say," Lilly grumbled. "Bill's not going anywhere."

"Maybe he can find you a good cop down at the station and we can double-date."

"That would be a great idea if cops could fraternize with suspects," Lilly said grimly.

"You're not a suspect."

"It sure feels like I am."

"Listen—you're grouchy. Get some sleep and we can talk tomorrow. I think everything is going to work out just fine, but you're too miserable to hear that right now."

"Okay. Goodnight." Lilly lay back against her pillows. She was grateful for a friend that would tell her the truth, even when it wasn't pleasant.

Lilly got to work early the next morning to make up for

being out of the shop for so many hours the previous day. After hanging up her coat, the first thing she did was turn on the space heater so the office would be toasty warm in no time. She went through the receipts from the day before, noting that Taffy had made some substantial sales.

Once the office was cozy and comfortable, she turned to her bookcase. This would be the perfect time to get some design work done. Reaching for the sketchbooks she kept at the far end of the top shelf, she was surprised to see they weren't there.

She ran her finger across all the titles on the top shelf, but the sketchbooks weren't there. Then she knelt down to examine the other shelves, but the books weren't there, either. She stood up and brushed off her knees, then turned to look around the office.

Thinking she had probably left the books on the desk yesterday, she rifled through the contents of the desktop, but the books weren't there. Her heart was beating a bit faster now and it felt hot in the office. She switched off the heater and wiped her forehead, which felt damp.

Stop it, she chided herself. *They have to be here somewhere.* But the ensuing thorough, if rather frantic, search of the small office turned up no sketchbooks.

That's when she remembered seeing Hassan leave the jewelry shop through the back door the previous day. He had been holding a folder.

Could Hassan have taken the sketchbooks? He had seen her work and commented on the quality of her designs.

She swallowed hard. His family was in the business of selling gems. Could it be that they were looking to branch into jewelry design and had decided to use her ideas?

It seemed impossible, but she was growing more sure every passing minute—Hassan had taken the sketchbooks. Everything pointed to his hand in stealing the designs for his own family's gain. She reached for her cell phone and called Bill. It seemed like she was calling him with every little thing, but then again, nothing had been little lately.

CHAPTER 54

"Bill, I think Hassan stole my sketchbooks. They had all my jewelry designs in them. I saw him leaving here with a notebook in his hand yesterday. I'm sure he was using it to hide the sketchbooks." She finally drew in a long breath.

"Whoa. Slow down. Tell me exactly what happened."

Lilly told her brother how she discovered her sketchbooks missing. She told him that she had seen Hassan leaving the shop through the back door the day before, something he hadn't done before.

"Did you talk to him?"

"No. It's a long story. I was going to, but I didn't because I've decided not to see him anymore."

"Why?"

"He's going back to Minnesota after the holidays and I just don't want to see him anymore, that's all."

"I'll never understand women," he said.

"Stop it. Now tell me what I should do about the sketchbooks."

"I'll send someone over to the shop right now and you can file a complaint."

"Thanks." After she hung up she tried replying to some of her emails, but she couldn't concentrate long enough to craft a coherent sentence. She gave up and went to the front of the shop to wait for the officer to show up.

She didn't have to wait long—it must have been a slow morning at the police station. She admitted the officer then locked the front door again behind him. She took him back into the office and showed him where the sketchbooks were supposed to be and told him how she had come to find them missing.

She filled out a complaint and he told her he would do some investigating to see if he could find some answers. He also said he could take a look at some of the security cameras along Main Street to see if he found anything unusual or suspicious.

"But I think I know who did it," she said. "His name is Hassan Ashraf and he's renting a house over in the Aspenwoods section of Juniper Junction."

The officer took down the information she was able to provide about Hassan and the rest of the Ashraf family and promised to look into it.

When Taffy got to work Lilly told her what had happened. Taffy listened to her, wide-eyed and mouth agape.

"I can't believe he would do such a thing," Taffy said. "What makes you think it was him?"

"I saw him leaving the back of the store yesterday with a folder under his arm. I think he took the sketchbooks and hid them in the folder. Did you see him after I left the shop yesterday?"

Taffy's eyes narrowed as she thought back to the previous day. "Come to think of it, I did see him after you left. He came into the shop and I remember he was holding the folder. He didn't tell me what it was for, but I guess now we know."

"And what did he say? What did he do?"

"He asked if you were still here and I told him you had left. He asked if it was okay for him to leave through the back door because he had parked in the lot back there. I told him it was okay. I'm so sorry. I had no idea what he had in mind."

"Don't worry about it, Taffy. You couldn't have known. None of us had any reason to suspect him."

"Are you okay?"

Lilly smiled ruefully, trying to imagine if there was a worse judge of character anywhere on earth. "My pride is hurt, but otherwise I'm okay. I've filed a report about the missing sketchbooks. The police officer said he would check out Hassan and his family."

"Do you want to go home or take some time for yourself?"

"Actually, that's probably the last thing I should do right now. All I'll end up doing is feeling sorry for myself. Working is the best thing for me right now, so I can keep my mind off everything."

"Whatever you say. If you need some time to yourself, you know I'm happy to take over here."

"Thanks, Taffy," Lilly said with a wan smile.

CHAPTER 55

C hristmas was now only a week away, and shoppers were out in force buying last-minute gifts. It seemed jewelry was an especially popular choice for gifts this year; Lilly could always gauge the health of the economy based on her sales. People liked to give jewelry for Christmas every year, but in certain years she sold more precious stones. Diamonds and sapphires were selling like hotcakes this year, so Lilly knew the local economy was booming.

Lilly helped one customer after another all morning and into the afternoon. Despair was never far from her mind and heart, but she kept it at bay as long as she had new and old clients to engage. Hassan didn't stop by as he had said he would; Lilly wondered if he had been contacted by the police yet. He was probably furious that his twisted plan had been unearthed.

She got two calls that afternoon: Tighe phoned to ask permission to have dinner at the Main Street Diner with a friend and Laurel called to say she had been invited to have dinner with Nick's family.

Lilly was faced with the prospect of eating dinner alone. Well, Barney would be there, but he wasn't much of a conversationalist and she needed conversation tonight to keep her mind busy.

"I couldn't help overhearing those calls," Taffy said a little while later. "I feel so bad that you'll be eating alone tonight. Why don't you come for dinner at my house? You could probably use some company."

Lilly sighed with relief. "That would be great, Taffy. Thanks so much. I didn't know how I was going to handle being alone this evening."

"I'll help close up tonight and you can follow me to my house," Taffy said.

"Great."

The rest of the afternoon sped by as Lilly and Taffy waited on more clients and Lilly began the laborious process of trying to recall and sketch some of her lost designs. She left Taffy to wait on people in the front of the store and put on headphones in her office while she tried to concentrate on the fledgling pencil drawings in front of her.

Six o'clock came and Taffy poked her head into Lilly's office. "Ready to lock up?"

Lilly took off the headphones and pushed her chair back from her desk. "I'm ready. If you could help me put away the displays, I would appreciate it. Then we can head out. You're sure it's not a problem for me to come home with you?"

"Not a bit."

They put away the display pieces and made sure the vault was locked, then left through the back door. Taffy got in her car and waited at the end of the alley for Lilly to catch up, then she drove up Main Street and headed out of town.

Not far from Juniper Junction Taffy turned her car into the parking lot of a condominium complex. Lilly had seen the complex many times: it was one of the older developments outside town, but it was still in nice shape. The parking lot had been plowed and Lilly could recall the beautiful landscaping that surrounded the units in the springtime.

Taffy pulled to a stop in front of an end unit that was attached to another, larger unit. There was another large building next door, but it didn't look like another condo. She got out of the car and waited for Lilly to join her. Together they walked up the steps that led to the front door.

Taffy unlocked the door and stood aside to let Lilly pass. "Take off your stuff and have a seat," she said. "I don't cook, so I sent BJ to the diner for take-out. He should be here before too long."

"Sounds good to me," Lilly said. "I hope roast beef is okay," Taffy said. "That's what we usually order. I do have a killer chocolate fondue I make for dessert, though."

"Perfect."

"Can I get you a glass of wine? Beer?"

"I could use a glass of wine, thank you."

While Taffy went to the kitchen to pour two glasses of wine, Lilly stood up and walked around the spacious living room, glancing at mementos and knick-knacks that were placed about on tables and shelves. She was surprised there were no photos of Taffy or BJ. Most of the photos were of flat and rather plain landscapes, though a few were of snow-capped mountains, taken from a distance. Lilly recalled that Taffy was from Missouri and so assumed some of the photos were of Taffy's home. The others were probably from Colorado—the mountains looked like the Rockies, but who could tell?

Taffy returned with the wine.

"I'm eager to meet BJ."

"Come on, I'll show you around," Taffy said. Lilly followed her through the first floor rooms, including the kitchen, the dining room, and a small den. "Do you want to see the upstairs?" she asked.

"No, that's private," Lilly said. She had no interest in seeing Taffy and BJ's personal living quarters.

"Why don't we wait in the dining room?" Taffy asked, looking at her watch. "He shouldn't be long."

Lilly followed Taffy to the dining room, which was decorated with a nod to mid-century furnishings and artwork. It reminded Lilly a bit of some of the old television shows she had watched as a kid.

"Have a seat," Taffy directed, pulling out a chair for Lilly. "I'll get the placemats and utensils and everything."

She left the room and returned a moment later with the things she needed to set the table for dinner. Then she sat down next to Lilly and smiled. Lilly was going to ask more about BJ when there was a quick knock on the front door, followed by the sound of a knob turning.

"Time for dinner!" rang out a voice.

Lilly froze. She knew that voice.

CHAPTER 56

S he looked toward the dining room doorway and Beau stood there.

"What ... what's going on?" she asked, stammering.

"This is BJ," Taffy said, her smile just a little off and her eyes just a little narrower than usual.

Beau Jonathan. BJ. Lilly's ex-husband was her employee's boyfriend.

"Hi, Lil," Beau said, smiling. "What do you think of our little prank?"

"What do you mean, prank?" Lilly asked. She could feel her cheeks growing hot from embarrassment and confusion.

"Taffy didn't want you to know we were dating. She wanted you to find out in this dramatic way," he explained. He grinned, a sickening, ear-to-ear manifestation of a perverse sense of humor.

"I'm leaving," Lilly said. "Taffy, this wasn't funny. I'm afraid I'm going to have to let you go from the jewelry shop, too."

Taffy tossed her blond locks. "That's okay. I don't even care."

"Whoa!" Beau interjected. "You're firing her just because we're dating?"

"Not just that, of course, but also because she deceived me and because I don't trust her anymore. A jewelry store is not a place where you can have untrustworthy employees."

"It was just a joke!" Beau exclaimed. "Taf, tell her it was just a joke!"

"Sit down, both of you," Taffy ordered. "You've brought home a perfectly good roast beef dinner and we're going to eat it."

"I'm not eating with either of you," Lilly said, looking around for her purse. Where had she left it?

"Your purse and your car keys are hidden," Taffy said, her lips curling into a malicious smile. "So you might as well sit down and eat dinner."

"I'm calling the police," Lilly said, a sudden fear beginning to grip her throat. "You can't keep me here—that's false imprisonment."

"I also have your cell phone," Taffy said, popping a piece of roast beef into her mouth as she unpacked the takeout containers from the diner bag.

Something wasn't right.

Lilly's hands were shaking, whether from anger or frustration or her growing sense of unease, she didn't know. Her breathing was fast and irregular. She had never been so humiliated.

She sat down hard, refusing to look at either of them.

"Here," Taffy said, handing a plate laden with beef and potatoes to Beau. He accepted it without a word, giving Lilly a sidelong glance.

Taffy helped herself to a heap of meat and vegetables and sat down. She took a big gulp of wine. "Hurry and eat because dessert is going to be delicious," she said brightly. "I got it started when I got the wine. It's heating right now."

She and Beau ate quietly, though she mentioned now and

then how good dinner was and that Lilly didn't know what she was missing. Lilly felt so sick to her stomach that just the thought of eating prompted waves of nausea to wash over her.

After what seemed like hours, but was probably only about fifteen minutes, both Beau and Taffy were finished eating. Taffy pushed her chair back and gathered the plates from the table.

"I'll help you," Beau offered, pushing his chair back and standing.

"Sit still," Taffy commanded. "I'll do it." Beau did as Taffy directed, wrinkling his brow. When Taffy left the room he looked at Lilly and shrugged, though she pretended not to see him.

Taffy had been gone for a couple minutes when Lilly decided to enlist Beau's help to leave.

"Beau, can you go get my purse?" she asked in an urgent whisper.

"I'd rather not. She's not acting like herself tonight and I don't want to make her angrier."

"Something's wrong, Beau. I know her, or at least I thought I did, and something is wrong."

"All the more reason not to piss her off," he whispered loudly.

CHAPTER 57

"What was that?" Taffy asked, coming into the room carrying a tray. "Secrets, secrets are no fun unless they're shared with everyone!" She let out a cackle that sent shivers up Lilly's spine.

"Taf, are you all right?" Beau asked.

"Of course! Now it's time for dessert. Lilly, I shouldn't let you have any because you didn't eat your dinner, but I'm going to let you because I'm nice like that." She set the tray down on the table. A small pot sat on the tray, surrounded by small plates of fruit and cubes of cake.

"This chocolate fondue is my specialty!" Taffy cried. "You're going to love it, Lilly. It's BJ's favorite, but you probably knew that. Now, let me pass the forks around and we'll dig in!"

She handed a fork to Beau and placed a fork on her own placemat. She tried handing Lilly one, too, but Lilly refused to take it.

"Lilly, I must say you're not being a very gracious guest," Taffy said, her eyes glittering.

"I'm not hungry."

"That may be true, but it's rude to refuse to eat when you've been invited to someone's house for dinner. Didn't your parents ever teach you that?"

"Leave my parents out of this."

"Your mom is pretty cool," Beau said. If looks could kill, Beau would have been stiff and cold after the glance Lilly bestowed on him.

"Be quiet, BJ," Taffy said in an imperious voice. "I'm trying to talk to Lilly."

Beau held up both hands and stared at Taffy, bewildered. Taffy stood up and walked over to Lilly's chair.

"You'd better take this fork right now, Lilly."

Something in the tone of Taffy's voice warned Lilly that she should take the fork. She reached for it, but Taffy pulled it out of her reach.

"On second thought, maybe I'll use this fork," Taffy said, leaning down close to Lilly's ear, running the tines of the fork lightly across Lilly's neck as she spoke. A current of fear raced up Lilly's spine and the hair on the back of her neck stood on end. Her gaze darted around the dining room, looking for anything she could use as a weapon or anything that would help her escape. Her mind was racing so frantically that she couldn't think clearly. There were the other fondue forks, of course, but she knew the moment she reached for one Taffy wouldn't hesitate to attack her.

"Taffy, take it easy," Lilly said. She was out of breath even though she had been sitting motionless. "You don't have to do anything violent. We can work this out."

"There's nothing to work out," Taffy replied. She shifted the fork in her hand so she was holding it like a spear, then proceeded to poke the tines into Lilly's arm ever so lightly. "It's a shame you won't be able to leave here tonight."

"That's insane. Of course I'm leaving," Lilly scoffed. Too late, she regretted those words.

Taffy stuck Lilly's arm with the fork. Hard. Lilly could feel blood seeping from the puncture holes, though it was a second or two before she felt the pain.

"Insane? *Insane?*" Taffy screeched.

"I'm sorry, Taffy, I didn't mean that. What I meant was, why are you doing this? I haven't done anything to you."

"Wrong. You just fired me."

"You deceived me."

"And *you* were just waiting for a chance to accuse me of Eden's murder!" Taffy was yelling. Lilly could only hope the neighbors in the attached unit would hear the shouting and call the police.

"Taf, what are you talking about?" Beau asked.

"Would you *shut up?*" she screeched. "This is between me and Lilly!"

"What *are* you talking about?" Lilly asked. Her mind was reeling—why would she accuse Taffy of killing Eden? All her senses were on high alert, focused on the fondue-fork-wielding woman standing over her. She knew the minute she tried to get up from the table Taffy would stab her again, and perhaps not in the arm.

"I'm talking about killing Eden! I had to! I had to stop her from telling you she had fired me because I never would have found another job!"

Lilly's breath froze in her throat. Just as Bill had promised, she suddenly remembered the conversation she had had with Eden and Herb the week before Thanksgiving. Eden had mentioned that she suspected an employee of hers was stealing from her. She was going to watch the employee carefully and planned to fire the person if she saw any suspicious behavior. She had told Herb about it and he had suggested mentioning it to Lilly. She could get the word out to other Juniper Junction merchants not to hire that employee. That employee must have been Taffy.

CHAPTER 58

"Taffy, I had no idea you were the one she had fired," Lilly said, trying to keep her voice even.

"Of course it was me! I was the only employee—Eden didn't have enough money to hire anyone else."

"What makes you think you're going to get away with keeping me here?"

"I'm only going to keep you here long enough to kill you."

"That's ridiculous. Beau will know what you did."

"If Beau doesn't want me to kill him, too, he won't tell anyone." Her logic was frightening. She snapped her fingers. "I just had a thought. Maybe I can buy your store when you're dead! You know, the grieving employee who misses her boss and buys the store to carry on the boss's legacy. It'll be great."

"You went bankrupt trying to run a store in Missouri," Beau said, finally finding his voice.

"I didn't ask you! Would you just keep your big mouth shut?" Taffy seethed through clenched teeth.

"Taffy, running a business is hard work," Lilly said. She wanted to keep Taffy talking until she could figure out how to get out of the condo. It was becoming clear that Beau wasn't going to be much help.

"A-ha, but I have the money from selling your sketchbooks, so that will give me a little cushion," Taffy said matter-of-factly. Lilly couldn't believe her ears.

"*You* stole the sketchbooks?" she asked.

Taffy laughed. "How lucky was it that Hassan came in with a folder that day? I still can't believe you thought that lovesick sap would steal anything from you. But it worked for to my advantage, so I'm not complaining."

I can't believe I told the police Hassan stole the sketchbooks, Lilly thought. She lost her focus for a moment in her dismay. Taffy noticed and yanked Lilly's injured arm. Lilly stumbled to her feet. Taffy raised the fork again.

"Don't do this, Taffy. Beau, do something! What's the matter with you?"

"Taffy, let Lilly go. We can get you some help." Beau was still seated at the table. It was as if he had lost the power of movement.

"Ha! The only help you're going to give me is to hide the body. Now stand up!"

Beau did as he was told; Lilly stared at him, incredulous. The fear in his eyes told the story—he couldn't help because he was afraid of Taffy. Afraid of what she was going to do to him once she was finished with Lilly.

"When did you steal my sketches?" Lilly asked, frantic to keep the conversation moving.

"The day Hassan came into the store, when you two ate in your office, I ate in there by myself afterward. It only took a second to take the books." She shook her head and barked out a harsh laugh. "Hassan is probably in custody right now, being tortured by your brother into giving up the hiding place of the books. And he has no idea where they are!" She kept laughing.

"How much did you get for them?" Lilly asked.

"Fifteen thousand dollars."

Lilly was shocked. "That's not enough of a cushion at all, Taffy." *No wonder she bankrupted her store back in Missouri.* But the statement must have unnerved Taffy for just a moment. Perhaps she was thinking that she should have sold the sketches for more, perhaps she was furious that Lilly had insulted her business sense. Whatever the reason, her eyes lost focus for a split second.

Lilly seized her chance. Bolting out of her seat, she ran toward the front door. Taffy let out a shriek as soon as she realized what had happened. Lilly didn't turn around to see where her pursuer was, but she heard a *thump* and assumed Taffy had tripped. She was only a few steps from the front door when Taffy grabbed her by the arm and yanked her around to face her.

"Taffy, please. I won't tell the police anything. Just let me go and I'll give you the sketches, I promise."

Taffy's face was flushed and red. "I told you I already sold the sketches! Don't you even listen? What good is your promise?" she seethed. She raised her arm; the fondue fork glinted in the light of the foyer.

As she brought the fork down, Taffy let out a yelp. Lilly hadn't seen Beau sneaking up behind her; he had grabbed her arm and wrenched it backward. Taffy, rage glinting in her eyes, spun around to face Beau and plunged the fork into his shoulder. His eyes registered the pain from the stabbing before he could say anything; he dropped her arm to stem the blood flowing from his own.

Lilly felt a buzz of urgency. Taffy would be after her next.

As Taffy was turning back toward Lilly and raising the fork again, Lilly yanked the front door open and tumbled out onto the stoop, slipping in the snow and falling headlong down the front steps.

Two people, bundled up and walking briskly, were out front. They looked up in amazement when Lilly crashed through the door and down the steps.

CHAPTER 59

"M om?" came a questioning voice. *Laurel?*
"Laurel? Run! Get out of here!"

"Nick, do something!" Laurel yelled. Nick disengaged himself from Laurel's mittened hand and ran up the steps. Taffy, who had started down the steps after Lilly when she realized there were other people outdoors, turned around to head back inside, but Nick grabbed her by the arm and yanked her around. Beau came running from the direction of the dining room and pulled both Taffy and Nick to the ground underneath him. Blood from his injury seeped into the pristine white snow around them.

"Dude! What's wrong with you?" Nick sputtered, trying to get up. "I can't breathe!"

Beau was speechless with confusion. He knelt in the snow and let Nick get up. He kept his elbow in Taffy's back, making it impossible for her to move.

"Call Bill," Lilly directed Laurel breathlessly. Laurel pulled her cell phone from her pocket, whipped off her mittens, and punched a few numbers.

"Uncle Bill, I'm with Mom. I don't know what's going on,

but she's here at Deer Run Condos and Nick just saved her from being attacked by a crazy woman. Hurry and get here and call an ambulance. The woman is on the ground and..." She looked up. The expression on her face changed from grim and confused to shock. "And my father is making sure she doesn't get up. Yeah, my father. He's bleeding. A lot. I have no idea what's going on. Please, just get over here." She put the phone back in her pocket. "He'll be here in just a few minutes."

The adrenaline finally hit Lilly and she started to cry. She stood up and bent over with her hands on her knees, sobbing. Laurel put her arm around her mother's shoulders and whispered again and again that Lilly was safe, that Beau and Nick weren't going to let anything happen to her. She led Lilly around Taffy's still-struggling form in the snow and they sat down on the steps of Taffy's condo. Lilly continued to cry, but as the sobs began to subside, she was able to explain to her daughter what had happened.

"What are you doing here?" Lilly finally asked Laurel.

"Nick's parents went out for dessert after dinner. Nick and I were watching television in his condo, which is the one attached to this one. The noise got so bad coming from next door that we decided to go out for a walk until the fight was over."

Lilly couldn't help but smile over the happy serendipity. She had a feeling she wouldn't mind Nick so much in the future.

Bill and another officer were on the scene in a matter of minutes. His partner quickly handcuffed Taffy and put her into the cruiser while Bill listened to the story from Lilly. All he could do was shake his head.

The ambulance driver walked over to Bill. "I'm taking Mr. Carlsen over to the hospital now," he said.

"Wait. Can I talk to him for a second?" Lilly asked.

The driver shrugged and nodded his head toward the ambulance. Lilly walked to the back doors, which were still open.

"Beau, I wanted to thank you for helping me tonight."

"I'm sorry for everything that happened. I'm just glad you

didn't get hurt," he replied in a quiet voice. She looked at him sadly and turned away.

She went to stand beside Bill, who was giving an order to secure the scene. "Has anyone talked to Hassan about the sketchbooks?" she asked. She was sick thinking of how she had wrongly accused him.

"Yeah. Two guys went over there today. They didn't find anything and naturally Hassan and his family claim to know nothing about where the sketchbooks are."

"Taffy stole them, Bill. Then she sold them. I'm so sorry I was wrong about Hassan."

"Don't worry about it right now. Go home, get warm, and we'll talk about this tomorrow."

"Will you stop at Mom's to check on her when you get off work? I just can't do it tonight," she said.

"Sure."

After retrieving Lilly's purse, cell phone, and car keys from inside the condo, Bill and his partner left with Taffy in the back of the police car. Lilly turned to Nick before getting in her own car and opened her arms. He stepped into them and she hugged him as if he were one of her own children.

"I can't thank you enough for helping me tonight, Nick."

"Does this mean you don't hate me anymore?"

She held him away from her. "I never hated you, Nick. I just didn't know what to make of you."

"Did I pass the test?"

Lilly laughed for the first time in many hours. "With flying colors." She got into the car and Laurel kissed Nick goodbye before joining her mother. They drove home in silence, each lost in her own harried thoughts, but thankful to be together and safe.

CHAPTER 60

Tighe couldn't believe what had transpired while he was at the Main Street Diner. "I wish I'd been there," he said. "I would have let her have it!"

"Well, I'm just glad it's over," Lilly said. "Laurel and I have to go down to the police station in the morning, then I owe Hassan an apology."

When mother and daughter arrived at the police station the next morning, they found Beau and Nick already there. Beau, his arm and shoulder bandaged heavily and in a sling, pulled Lilly aside before she was called to give her statement. "I hate to tell you this, but I found two envelopes stuffed with money in the credenza last night after you left. Fifteen thousand dollars, to be exact. It looks like Taffy really did sell your designs. I was hoping she was bluffing last night, but obviously she wasn't. I'm sorry about that. I guess I didn't know her as well as I thought I did."

"Thanks for telling me." Lilly's shoulders slumped as she walked to the back of the station when she was called to give her statement. The one time Taffy told the truth, and it had to be *this* time. She had worked so hard on those designs.

Once she and Laurel had given their statements and Laurel

had gone to school, Lilly got in her car and drove straight to the house Hassan and his family were renting. She took a deep breath and rang the doorbell.

Hassan answered after a long moment. He didn't say anything at first, but gestured with his hand for her to come inside.

Once she was standing in the foyer her words tumbled out in a torrent. "Hassan, I owe you an apology. And your family. I'm so sorry. I saw you leaving my shop from the back door the other day. You had a notebook or folder or something in your hand. I didn't call to you because I had decided that we shouldn't see each other anymore because you're leaving and I'm going to miss you too much. Then when I found the sketchbooks missing, I assumed you had taken them and I hope you can forgive me." She finally inhaled, then let out her breath in a noisy exhale. Hassan continued staring at her.

"Say something, will you? Yell or something," Lilly said.

When he still didn't say anything, she turned to leave. She was stepping out onto the stone porch when he finally spoke.

"What do you suppose was in the folder I was holding?" he asked.

Lilly shook her head and turned to look at him. "I have no idea."

"The folder contained some pages that I printed from the computer. A real estate listing for this house. It's for sale and I was thinking about buying it. I had stopped by to ask your opinion and when you weren't there I left because I had parked behind your store."

Lilly stood still, the freezing air creeping up her pantlegs. "I'm so sorry," she said in a whisper. "I should have known you'd never steal anything from me." *Except my heart, that is.*

"It sounds like you and I were not on the same page as far as our relationship," Hassan said.

"How could we be on the same page?" Lilly asked. "You've mentioned several times that you'll be going back to Minnesota after the holidays. How was I supposed to know that you were thinking of buying a home here?" She swallowed hard, blinking back tears that burned the backs of her eyes.

"Come inside," he said, taking her arm gently and drawing her back into the house. "I am the one who should be apologizing. I wanted to surprise you, but I fear I pushed you away instead. I can understand why you felt you didn't want to see me anymore, and I can even see why you thought I had taken your sketchbooks."

Lilly sniffled. "Thank you. I ... I don't know what to say anymore. It seems I've misjudged almost everyone I know in the last few weeks."

"Are you still unsure about me?"

"No, of course not. I'm just sad for what could have been."

"Who says it can't still be that way?"

Lilly looked up at him in confusion. "Do you mean you're still thinking about buying this house? After all I've put you through?"

Hassan chuckled. "I guess that's exactly what I mean. I am a glutton for punishment, aren't I?"

The tears were coursing down Lilly's cheeks. She could only nod and hang her head. He lifted her chin with his finger.

"Don't cry, Lilly. I want you to be happy."

"I am happy." She was sobbing now.

"I've seen happier people at a funeral." She was sobbing and laughing now.

"Can I take you to breakfast?" she asked. "I know a good place. But I have to stop at the store first."

CHAPTER 61

From their booth at the Main Street Diner they could see the people walking by Juniper Junction Jewels and reading the sign on the door: Closed Until January 2nd. The note gave Lilly's cell phone number for anyone needing to pick up a special order.

"I need a break," Lilly told him between bites of rye toast. She had related the events of the previous evening and Hassan was speechless. "It's Christmas time. I've never taken a vacation before Christmas because I've always been working, but it's time. My kids, my mom, my brother and Noley, they've barely seen me lately except for when we were cooped up during the blizzard, and that was so stressful it didn't count. And you, of course. Maybe you and I could spend some time together before you go back to Minnesota?"

"You know I would love that," Hassan said with a broad smile. He put his hand over hers. "I have a special Christmas gift for you."

"I didn't think you celebrated Christmas."

"I don't. But you do, and I want to give you something. But you have to wait until Christmas Day."

There was so much to look forward to.

Bill stopped by her house that afternoon. "Taffy spilled her guts," he said.

"What was there to spill? She killed Eden Barclay, stole my sketchbooks, and wanted to kill me."

"She may not have killed you, but after she killed Eden Barclay, she killed Herb Knight."

His words hit her like a popping chestnut. "You're kidding. Why?"

"Apparently Eden found more evidence that Taffy was stealing from her. She went to your store to talk to you the day before Thanksgiving. You had already left for the day, but since you forgot to lock the back door she opened it thinking you were inside."

"I still can't believe I did that."

"I can't either. Anyway, according to Taffy, Eden had just fired her and wanted to talk to you about it."

"Why did she have to talk to me about it?" Lilly was confused.

"She figured Taffy would be looking for another job and she knew you were the best person to get the word out to other merchants that they shouldn't hire her."

"So Taffy followed her into my store?"

"Yeah. I don't think she planned to kill Eden, but the opportunity presented itself when she saw the vault was open. She grabbed the closest thing, which happened to be a pearl necklace. She was crazy with anger over being fired."

"I never could understand why she would risk leaving the necklace behind."

"I think it simply landed under Eden and she didn't want to stick around to try to grab it." Bill rolled his eyes. "She admitted to throwing the brick through your front window during the blizzard and taking Barney off his rope, too."

"I knew it had to be a crazy person out in that blizzard. Either that, or someone who didn't know what it was like to be in a blizzard. And I knew the person was a monster, too, for doing that to an animal."

"She said she just wanted to scare you."

"It worked. But what did I do to deserve that? She had no reason to want to scare me."

"She said she was mad at you over some incident at the store. Did she overcharge someone? Something like that."

Lilly knew exactly what Bill was talking about. She thought back to the day of the blizzard, when Taffy had undercharged someone for a necklace. She had spoken to Taffy in a harried tone because the store had been so hectic.

"She was mad over *that*? And she thought freezing my family to death and almost killing my dog would be a good way to deal with it?" She shook her head and changed the subject. "So what about Herb?"

"We knew that someone had *seen* Eden talking to Herb just before her death. But Taffy had actually overheard them. Eden had told him she had concrete proof that Taffy was stealing from her. Once Eden was dead, she assumed Herb would figure out she did it because he knew Eden had just fired her, so she killed him, too."

"And here I thought both Eden and Herb died because of some reason to do with the big chain stores. Taffy certainly had everyone fooled."

"Including Beau. He was blindsided by all of this," Bill said solemnly.

"I almost feel sorry for him. Almost."

"He really thought it would be fun to surprise you with the news that he and Taffy were a couple."

"I can't believe anyone would think that's a fun surprise. That's part of the reason I can't quite bring myself to feel sorry for him. That, and the fact that he kept showing up at Mom's house."

"I asked him about that. He knew you'd want nothing to do

with him, so he thought he could get to the kids through Mom."
He shook his head.

"But she couldn't stand him for years."

"I know, but he thought his chances were better with her
than with you. He really does seem to want a relationship with
the kids." Bill gave Lilly a questioning look, then continued.
"There's something else you need to know, though."

"What is it?"

"It has to do with the broken doorknob. Beau admitted
knocking on the back door the day the doorknob broke. He
wanted to talk to you. But only Barney was there, and Beau
swears Barney went so nuts that he broke the doorknob by
scratching at it ferociously with his paws. So there never was an
intruder, though Beau was there that day."

Lilly gave her brother a skeptical look. "And you believe
him?"

"Actually, I think I do. He seemed terrified of Barney." Bill
laughed. "Imagine being terrified of that ball of fur." Lilly felt a
cautious sense of relief creep over her.

"Intruder or no intruder, Beau is not someone I'm ready to
deal with right now," she replied. "Too much has happened.
Maybe at some point, but not now. Have you talked to Mom?"

"I swung by her house last night. I haven't told her about
any of this. All she could talk about was her dog."

Lilly shook her head. "What are we going to do with her?"

"Right now her delusions are pretty harmless, but I'm afraid
they're only going to get worse."

Lilly was thoughtful for a moment, then she smiled. "I think
I have an idea that might help."

"What?"

"You'll see. It's a surprise."

CHAPTER 62

That night Lilly hosted an impromptu dinner. Noley came and brought Bill, Hassan came and brought his sister and parents, and Lilly let Laurel invite Nick, who came bearing a gift of fudge his mother had made. Beverly came and Tighe invited one of his friends, too. Lilly even invited Mrs. Laforge, who brought dozens of Christmas cookies. The only uninvited person who might have appreciated an invitation was Beau—Lilly wasn't ready to be around him yet and she needed to talk to the kids in private about their wishes regarding their father.

Dinner was simple—buffet-style make-your-own sandwiches, chips, eggnog, hot cider, and lefse, a traditional food unique to Minnesota, that Hassan's mother and the other women in the family had made. Barney loved it.

The noisy house was warm and the scent of the Christmas tree, the snow falling outside the new window, the twinkly lights, and the carols playing in the background filled Lilly with a sense of peace and cheer. *This is the way the holidays were meant to be.*

Lilly spent the following days sleeping in, baking, finishing up a few custom designs for clients, and continuing to recreate the sketches Taffy had stolen. On Christmas Eve morning, Bill called with good news.

"Taffy gave up the name of the guy who bought the sketches," he said.

"Did he know he was buying stolen property?"

"I don't know. He lives out of state, but we'll have his local police talk to him. You know Beau found the money—we have it here at the station, so the guy can get his money back if he's willing to return the drawings."

He was willing, especially after being reminded that Lilly's customers could vouch for her ownership of the sketches. Though Lilly had known, somewhere in the back of her mind, that he had no choice but to return the stolen drawings, tears sprang to her eyes when she heard she would be getting her sketches back.

That evening Hassan dropped by with a small package. "Put this under the tree and unwrap it in the morning," he said. "It's just a little something I thought you'd like."

"Wait, I got you something, too," she said. He sat down in front of the fire while she sorted through the gifts already under the tree. She drew out one with his name on it. "Take this back to your house and don't open it until tomorrow morning," she said. He set it aside on the couch and she joined him, nestling her head against his shoulder.

"What are you doing New Year's Eve?" he asked. The song lyrics popped into Lilly's head.

"I don't like to go out," she said. "I thought I'd stay in and have a little party for everyone here. Can you come?"

"I wouldn't miss it."

Christmas morning dawned snowy and gray. Beverly had spent the night at Lilly's house, so they waited for Bill and Noley to arrive before having breakfast and opening their gifts. They arrived bearing sticky buns Noley had made. Between those and the hash brown casserole Lilly had prepared the night before and popped into the oven first thing Christmas morning, everyone was stuffed and happy by the time they all adjourned to the living room to open gifts.

The kids loved the gifts Lilly had picked out for them. Laurel was thrilled with her dress and Tighe loved the camping gear. Noley was delighted when she saw Lilly had bought the hand-thrown tray from the cooking shop. Lilly had chosen a gorgeous cashmere sweater for Bill.

Barney wouldn't stop barking. Bill had just opened his sweater when he set it aside and snorted. "Lilly, can't you make him be quiet?"

"I don't know about that," she answered, glancing toward her mother. "But I can get him focused on something else."

She went to the kitchen; Barney followed her, his tail wagging. Everyone in the living room could hear the door to the garage opening, then a scuffling, scraping sound. Seconds later a Cocker Spaniel puppy ran into the living room, a red bow tied around his neck.

"Mom, I thought you might like a puppy for Christmas," Lilly said. Laurel gasped. The puppy ran straight for Tighe and began licking his face. He laughed until the tears ran down his face. Lilly picked up the puppy and placed him at her mother's feet.

The smile on Beverly's face brought tears to Lilly's eyes. Even Bill was blinking furiously and wiping his nose. Noley sat on the floor, mouth agape. Beverly nuzzled the puppy's face and he licked her in return.

"This is my puppy?" she asked.

"Yes, Mom. I thought we could keep him here but bring him to your house every day to spend time with you. What do you think?"

"I love him," she said in a quiet voice. "Thank you."

Lilly supposed the idea for a pet for her mother had been planted by Tighe the day he suggested getting a kitten for Gran. Though Lilly had initially thought a pet would be too much of a responsibility, she had been rethinking that. She had done quite a bit of reading about the benefits animals could have on the well-being of elderly people with dementia and had eventually decided that a puppy might be just the thing for her mother. She knew she would be the one responsible for cleaning up the puppy's accidents, walking him, taking him over to her mother's house every day, and getting up with him in the middle of the night until he was a little older, but one look at her mother's face and she knew all that work would be worth it.

While everyone was fawning over the puppy, Lilly slipped her hand under the tree and brought out the gift Hassan had left for her. She unwrapped it and opened the box.

Nestled inside a piece of white velvet lay a pendant of lapis lazuli. It had been polished to a high sheen, but looked uncut. Tiny rivulets of white ran through the brilliant blue stone. Lilly held it in her hand, wishing Hassan had seen her open it.

When the phone rang, Lilly ran to answer it—it could only be Hassan, and she wanted to thank him for such a breathtaking gift.

But it wasn't Hassan. It was Beau; he was calling to wish the family a merry Christmas. Lilly put each of the kids on and they talked to their father for a few minutes, telling him what they got for Christmas and asking about Taffy.

Tighe talked to him first, then it was Laurel's turn. When Laurel was done, she handed the phone back to Lilly.

"Beau, why don't you come over for a little while? We're finished opening gifts and we're just going to hang out here, maybe play some games or go sledding. You're welcome to join us."

There was silence on the other end, and finally Beau spoke. "Are you sure?"

"I'm sure."

"Thanks, Lil."

He hung up; Lilly had replaced the receiver on the hook when it rang again.

"Hello?"

"Thank you for the book," Hassan said. "I love it." She could hear the smile in his voice. She had chosen the coffee table book, filled with photos of Colorado and the Rocky Mountains, after he told her he was buying the house in Juniper Junction.

"It pales in comparison to the one you gave me," she said. "The pendant is just beautiful. Thank you."

"You like it?" he asked.

"It's perfect."

What had started on Black Friday as the worst holiday season ever had turned out to be one of the best for the Carlsen family, which now included a Cocker Spaniel puppy that Beverly had decided to name Fred. Fred and Barney. Somehow Beverly had remembered that Lilly's favorite cartoon as a child had been *The Flintstones*.

It had, indeed, been a very merry Christmas.

RECIPES

CHRISTMAS JAM

2 cups fresh or frozen cranberries
2 cups fresh or frozen raspberries, thawed
1 large pear, ripe, peeled, seeded, and coarsely chopped
4 cups sugar
1.75-ounce box Sure-Jell fruit pectin
½ cup orange juice
½ cup water
1/8 teaspoon ground cinnamon
1/8 teaspoon ground nutmeg
1/8 teaspoon ground cloves (optional)

Crush raspberries in a small bowl until pulpy. Place approximately half of pulp in a sieve and press to remove as many seeds as possible. Discard seeds and return remaining pulp to bowl. Mix contents.

Combine sugar and pectin in a medium saucepan; add orange juice and water. Bring mixture to a boil over medium-high heat. Once mixture boils, add cranberries and cook, stirring often, until cranberries burst and mixture begins to thicken.

Remove cranberry mixture from heat. Add raspberry pulp, pear, and last three ingredients. Stir until combined well.

Pour mixture into clean glass jars. Cover immediately with lids. Allow to sit at room temperature for 24 hours before chilling or freezing.

Jam should last in the refrigerator up to 3 weeks; jam should last in freezer for up to 1 year.

Yield: approximately 7 cups jam

ORANGE-KISSED BISCUITS

3 cups flour
1 teaspoon salt
1 tablespoon baking powder
2 tablespoons sugar
6 tablespoons butter, softened
Grated zest from one orange
1 cup whole milk (may need a tiny bit more)

Position oven rack in top third of oven; preheat oven to 425°. Line a baking sheet with parchment paper.

In a large mixing bowl, combine flour, salt, baking powder, and sugar. Using your fingers, add butter to mixture and mix well until mixture resembles coarse crumbs. Add orange zest when you're almost done mixing.

Drizzle 1 cup milk over the mixture and combine for about 15 seconds. The dough should start to come together. If it doesn't, add a small amount of milk until you can form a rough ball with the dough.

Place dough on a lightly-floured work surface; pat dough into a rectangle about ¾ of an inch thick. Fold dough into thirds and roll gently with a floured rolling pin until dough is about ¾ of an inch thick again.

Using a biscuit cutter, cut dough into biscuits. *Gently* reroll scraps and repeat.

Place biscuits on baking sheet and brush tops lightly with milk. Bake 15-20 minutes, or until lightly browned.

FRUIT SALAD WITH HONEY-LIME DRESSING

1 cantaloupe, cut into bite-sized pieces
1 small papaya, cut into bite-sized pieces
2 mangoes, cut into bite-sized pieces
2 kiwi, sliced and halved
1 small can crushed pineapple, well drained
2 tablespoons lime juice
1 tablespoon honey
¼ teaspoon salt
Grated coconut, optional

In a medium bowl, combine first 5 ingredients. In a small bowl, whisk together remaining ingredients. Gently toss fruit with dressing. Sprinkle with grated coconut to serve, if desired.

NEWSLETTER SIGN-UP

Please visit https://www.amymreade.com/newsletter to sign up to receive monthly news, updates, promotions, contests, and recipes.

ABOUT THE AUTHOR

Amy M. Reade is a cook, chauffeur, household CEO, doctor, laundress, maid, psychiatrist, warden, seer, teacher, and pet whisperer. In other words, a wife, mother, and recovering attorney. But she is also the author of The Malice Series (*The House on Candlewick Lane, Highland Peril,* and *Murder in Thistlecross*) and three standalone books, *Secrets of Hallstead House, The Ghosts of Peppernell Manor,* and *House of the Hanging Jade.* She lives in southern New Jersey and loves to read, cook, and travel. You can find out more about her books at https://www.amymreade.com.

CPSIA information can be obtained
at www.ICGtesting.com
Printed in the USA
BVHW08s0032190918
527890BV00003B/20/P